2/13

PA

every day

Also by David Levithan

Boy Meets Boy

The Realm of Possibility

Are We There Yet?

Marly's Ghost (illustrated by Brian Selznick)

Nick & Norah's Infinite Playlist (written with Rachel Cohn)

Wide Awake

Naomi and Ely's No Kiss List (written with Rachel Cohn)

How They Met, and Other Stories

The Likely Story series (written as David Van Etten,
with David Ozanich and Chris Van Etten)

Love Is the Higher Law

Will Grayson, Will Grayson (written with John Green)

Dash & Lily's Book of Dares (written with Rachel Cohn)

The Lover's Dictionary

Every You, Every Me (with photographs by Jonathan Farmer)

every day

david levithan

alfred a. knopf
new york

THIS IS A BORZOI BOOK PUBLISHED BY ALFRED A. KNOPF

Visit us on the Web! randomhouse.com/teens

Educators and librarians, for a variety of teaching tools, visit us at
RHTeachersLibrarians.com

Library of Congress Cataloging-in-Publication Data
Levithan, David.
Every day / by David Levithan.
p. cm.
Summary: Every morning A wakes in a different person's body, a different person's life, learning over the years to never get too attached, until he wakes up in the body of Justin and falls in love with Justin's girlfriend, Rhiannon.
ISBN 978-0-307-93188-7 (trade) — ISBN 978-0-375-97111-2 (lib. bdg.) —
ISBN 978-0-307-93189-4 (tr. pbk.) — ISBN 978-0-307-97563-8 (ebook) —
ISBN 978-0-449-81553-3 (intl. tr. pbk.)
[1. Love—Fiction. 2. Interpersonal relations—Fiction.] I. Title.
PZ7.L5798Es 2012
[Fic]—dc23
2012004173

The text of this book is set in 11.5-point Goudy.

Printed in the United States of America

August 2012

10 9 8 7 6 5 4 3 2 1

First Edition

For Paige
(May you find happiness every day)

Day 5994

I wake up.

Immediately I have to figure out who I am. It's not just the body—opening my eyes and discovering whether the skin on my arm is light or dark, whether my hair is long or short, whether I'm fat or thin, boy or girl, scarred or smooth. The body is the easiest thing to adjust to, if you're used to waking up in a new one each morning. It's the life, the context of the body, that can be hard to grasp.

Every day I am someone else. I am myself—I know I am myself—but I am also someone else.

It has always been like this.

The information is there. I wake up, open my eyes, understand that it is a new morning, a new place. The biography kicks in, a welcome gift from the not-me part of the mind. Today I am Justin. Somehow I know this—my name is Justin—and at the same time I know that I'm not really Justin, I'm only borrowing his life for a day. I look around and know that this is his room. This is his home. The alarm will go off in seven minutes.

I'm never the same person twice, but I've certainly been this type before. Clothes everywhere. Far more video games than books. Sleeps in his boxers. From the taste of his mouth, a smoker. But not so addicted that he needs one as soon as he wakes up.

"Good morning, Justin," I say. Checking out his voice. Low. The voice in my head is always different.

Justin doesn't take care of himself. His scalp itches. His eyes don't want to open. He hasn't gotten much sleep.

Already I know I'm not going to like today.

It's hard being in the body of someone you don't like, because you still have to respect it. I've harmed people's lives in the past, and I've found that every time I slip up, it haunts me. So I try to be careful.

From what I can tell, every person I inhabit is the same age as me. I don't hop from being sixteen to being sixty. Right now, it's only sixteen. I don't know how this works. Or why. I stopped trying to figure it out a long time ago. I'm never going to figure it out, any more than a normal person will figure out his or her own existence. After a while, you have to be at peace with the fact that you simply *are*. There is no way to know why. You can have theories, but there will never be proof.

I can access facts, not feelings. I know this is Justin's room, but I have no idea if he likes it or not. Does he want to kill his parents in the next room? Or would he be lost without his mother coming in to make sure he's awake? It's impossible to tell. It's as if that part of me replaces the same part of whatever person I'm in. And while I'm glad to be thinking like myself, a hint every now and then of how the other person thinks would be helpful. We all contain mysteries, especially when seen from the inside.

The alarm goes off. I reach for a shirt and some jeans, but something lets me see that it's the same shirt he wore yesterday. I pick a different shirt. I take the clothes with me to the bathroom, dress after showering. His parents are in the kitchen now. They have no idea that anything is different.

Sixteen years is a lot of time to practice. I don't usually make mistakes. Not anymore.

I read his parents easily: Justin doesn't talk to them much in the morning, so I don't have to talk to them. I have grown accustomed to sensing expectation in others, or the lack of it. I shovel down some cereal, leave the bowl in the sink without washing it, grab Justin's keys and go.

Yesterday I was a girl in a town I'd guess to be two hours away. The day before, I was a boy in a town three hours farther than that. I am already forgetting their details. I have to, or else I will never remember who I really am.

Justin listens to loud and obnoxious music on a loud and obnoxious station where loud and obnoxious DJs make loud and obnoxious jokes as a way of getting through the morning. This is all I need to know about Justin, really. I access his memory to show me the way to school, which parking space to take, which locker to go to. The combination. The names of the people he knows in the halls.

Sometimes I can't go through these motions. I can't bring myself to go to school, maneuver through the day. I'll say I'm

3

sick, stay in bed and read a few books. But even that gets tiresome after a while, and I find myself up for the challenge of a new school, new friends. For a day.

As I take Justin's books out of his locker, I can feel someone hovering on the periphery. I turn, and the girl standing there is transparent in her emotions—tentative and expectant, nervous and adoring. I don't have to access Justin to know that this is his girlfriend. No one else would have this reaction to him, so unsteady in his presence. She's pretty, but she doesn't see it. She's hiding behind her hair, happy to see me and unhappy to see me at the same time.

Her name is Rhiannon. And for a moment—just the slightest beat—I think that, yes, this is the right name for her. I don't know why. I don't know her. But it feels right.

This is not Justin's thought. It's mine. I try to ignore it. I'm not the person she wants to talk to.

"Hey," I say, keeping it casual.

"Hey," she murmurs back.

She's looking at the floor, at her inked-in Converse. She's drawn cities there, skylines around the soles. Something's happened between her and Justin, and I don't know what it is. It's probably not something that Justin even recognized at the time.

"Are you okay?" I ask.

I see the surprise on her face, even as she tries to cover it. This is not something that Justin normally asks.

And the strange thing is: I want to know the answer. The fact that he wouldn't care makes me want it more.

"Sure," she says, not sounding sure at all.

I find it hard to look at her. I know from experience that

4

beneath every peripheral girl is a central truth. She's hiding hers away, but at the same time she wants me to see it. That is, she wants *Justin* to see it. And it's there, just out of my reach. A sound waiting to be a word.

She is so lost in her sadness that she has no idea how visible it is. I think I understand her—for a moment, I presume to understand her—but then, from within this sadness, she surprises me with a brief flash of determination. Bravery, even.

Shifting her gaze away from the floor, her eyes matching mine, she asks, "Are you mad at me?"

I can't think of any reason to be mad at her. If anything, I am mad at Justin, for making her feel so diminished. It's there in her body language. When she is around him, she makes herself small.

"No," I say. "I'm not mad at you at all."

I tell her what she wants to hear, but she doesn't trust it. I feed her the right words, but she suspects they're threaded with hooks.

This is not my problem; I know that. I am here for one day. I cannot solve anyone's boyfriend problems. I should not change anyone's life.

I turn away from her, get my books out, close the locker. She stays in the same spot, anchored by the profound, desperate loneliness of a bad relationship.

"Do you still want to get lunch today?" she asks.

The easy thing would be to say no. I often do this: sense the other person's life drawing me in, and run in the other direction.

But there's something about her—the cities on her shoes,

5

the flash of bravery, the unnecessary sadness—that makes me want to know what the word will be when it stops being a sound. I have spent years meeting people without ever knowing them, and on this morning, in this place, with this girl, I feel the faintest pull of wanting to know. And in a moment of either weakness or bravery on my own part, I decide to follow it. I decide to find out more.

"Absolutely," I say. "Lunch would be great."

Again, I read her: What I've said is too enthusiastic. Justin is never enthusiastic.

"No big deal," I add.

She's relieved. Or, at least, as relieved as she'll allow herself to be, which is a very guarded form of relief. By accessing, I know she and Justin have been together for over a year. That's as specific as it gets. Justin doesn't remember the exact date.

She reaches out and takes my hand. I am surprised by how good this feels.

"I'm glad you're not mad at me," she says. "I just want everything to be okay."

I nod. If there's one thing I've learned, it's this: We all want everything to be okay. We don't even wish so much for fantastic or marvelous or outstanding. We will happily settle for okay, because most of the time, okay is enough.

The first bell rings.

"I'll see you later," I say.

Such a basic promise. But to Rhiannon, it means the world.

● ● ●

At first it was hard to go through each day without making any lasting connections, leaving any life-changing effects. When I was younger, I craved friendship and closeness. I would make bonds without acknowledging how quickly and permanently they would break. I took other people's lives personally. I felt their friends could be my friends, their parents could be my parents. But after a while, I had to stop. It was too heartbreaking to live with so many separations.

I am a drifter, and as lonely as that can be, it is also remarkably freeing. I will never define myself in terms of anyone else. I will never feel the pressure of peers or the burden of parental expectation. I can view everyone as pieces of a whole, and focus on the whole, not the pieces. I have learned how to observe, far better than most people observe. I am not blinded by the past or motivated by the future. I focus on the present, because that is where I am destined to live.

I learn. Sometimes I am taught something I have already been taught in dozens of other classrooms. Sometimes I am taught something completely new. I have to access the body, access the mind and see what information it's retained. And when I do, I learn. Knowledge is the only thing I take with me when I go.

I know so many things that Justin doesn't know, that he will never know. I sit there in his math class, open his notebook, and write down phrases he has never heard. Shakespeare and Kerouac and Dickinson. Tomorrow, or some day after tomorrow, or never, he will see these words in his own handwriting and he won't have any idea where they came from, or even what they are.

That is as much interference as I allow myself.

Everything else must be done cleanly.

Rhiannon stays with me. Her details. Flickers from Justin's memories. Small things, like the way her hair falls, the way she bites her fingernails, the determination and resignation in her voice. Random things. I see her dancing with Justin's grandfather, because he's said he wants a dance with a pretty girl. I see her covering her eyes during a scary movie, peering between her fingers, enjoying her fright. These are the good memories. I don't look at any others.

I only see her once in the morning, a brief passing in the halls between first and second period. I find myself smiling when she comes near, and she smiles back. It's as simple as that. Simple and complicated, as most true things are. I find myself looking for her after second period, and then again after third and fourth. I don't even feel in control of this. I want to see her. Simple. Complicated.

By the time we get to lunch, I am exhausted. Justin's body is worn down from too little sleep and I, inside of it, am worn down from restlessness and too much thought.

I wait for her at Justin's locker. The first bell rings. The second bell rings. No Rhiannon. Maybe I was supposed to meet her somewhere else. Maybe Justin's forgotten where they always meet.

If that's the case, she's used to Justin forgetting. She finds me right when I'm about to give up. The halls are nearly empty, the cattle call has passed. She comes closer than she did before.

"Hey," I say.

"Hey," she says.

She is looking to me. Justin is the one who makes the first move. Justin is the one who figures things out. Justin is the one who says what they're going to do.

It depresses me.

I have seen this too many times before. The unwarranted devotion. Putting up with the fear of being with the wrong person because you can't deal with the fear of being alone. The hope tinged with doubt, and the doubt tinged with hope. Every time I see these feelings in someone else's face, it weighs me down. And there's something in Rhiannon's face that's more than just the disappointments. There is a gentleness there. A gentleness that Justin will never, ever appreciate. I see it right away, but nobody else does.

I take all my books and put them in the locker. I walk over to her and put my hand lightly on her arm.

I have no idea what I'm doing. I only know that I'm doing it.

"Let's go somewhere," I say. "Where do you want to go?"

I am close enough now to see that her eyes are blue. I am close enough now to see that nobody ever gets close enough to see how blue her eyes are.

"I don't know," she replies.

I take her hand.

"Come on," I tell her.

This is no longer restlessness—it's recklessness. At first we're walking hand in hand. Then we're running hand in hand. That giddy rush of keeping up with one another, of zooming through the school, reducing everything that's not us into an inconsequential blur. We are laughing, we are playful. We leave her books in her locker and move out of the building, into the air, the real air, the sunshine and the trees and the less burdensome world. I am breaking the rules as I leave the school. I am breaking the rules as we get into Justin's car. I am breaking the rules as I turn the key in the ignition.

"Where do you want to go?" I ask again. "Tell me, truly, where you'd love to go."

I don't initially realize how much hinges on her answer. If she says, *Let's go to the mall,* I will disconnect. If she says, *Take me back to your house,* I will disconnect. If she says, *Actually, I don't want to miss sixth period,* I will disconnect. And I should disconnect. I should not be doing this.

But she says, "I want to go to the ocean. I want you to take me to the ocean."

And I feel myself connecting.

It takes us an hour to get there. It's late September in Maryland. The leaves haven't begun to change, but you can tell they're starting to think about it. The greens are muted, faded. Color is right around the corner.

. I give Rhiannon control of the radio. She's surprised by this, but I don't care. I've had enough of the loud and the obnoxious, and I sense that she's had enough of it, too. She brings melody to the car. A song comes on that I know, and I sing along.

And if I only could, I'd make a deal with God. . . .

Now Rhiannon goes from surprised to suspicious. Justin never sings along.

"What's gotten into you?" she asks.

"Music," I tell her.

"Ha."

"No, really."

She looks at me for a long time. Then smiles.

"In that case," she says, flipping the dial to find the next song.

Soon we are singing at the top of our lungs. A pop song that's as substantial as a balloon, but lifts us in the same way when we sing it.

It's as if time itself relaxes around us. She stops thinking about how unusual it is. She lets herself be a part of it.

I want to give her a good day. Just one good day. I have wandered for so long without any sense of purpose, and now this ephemeral purpose has been given to me—it feels like it has been given to me. I only have a day to give—so why can't it be a good one? Why can't it be a shared one? Why can't I take the music of the moment and see how long it can last? The rules are erasable. I can take this. I can give this.

When the song is over, she rolls down her window and trails her hand in the air, introducing a new music into the car. I roll down all the other windows and drive faster, so the wind takes over, blows our hair all around, makes it seem like the car has disappeared and we are the velocity, we are the speed. Then another good song comes on and I enclose us again, this time taking her hand. I drive like that for miles, and ask her questions. Like how her parents are doing. What it's like now that her sister's off at college. If she thinks school is different at all this year.

It's hard for her. Every single answer starts with the phrase

I don't know. But most of the time she does know, if I give her the time and the space in which to answer. Her mother means well; her father less so. Her sister isn't calling home, but Rhiannon can understand that. School is school—she wants it to be over, but she's afraid of it being over, because then she'll have to figure out what comes next.

She asks me what I think, and I tell her, "Honestly, I'm just trying to live day to day."

It isn't enough, but it's something. We watch the trees, the sky, the signs, the road. We sense each other. The world, right now, is only us. We continue to sing along. And we sing with the same abandon, not worrying too much if our voices hit the right notes or the right words. We look at each other while we're singing; these aren't two solos, this is a duet that isn't taking itself at all seriously. It is its own form of conversation— you can learn a lot about people from the stories they tell, but you can also know them from the way they sing along, whether they like the windows up or down, if they live by the map or by the world, if they feel the pull of the ocean.

She tells me where to drive. Off the highway. The empty back roads. This isn't summer; this isn't a weekend. It's the middle of a Monday, and nobody but us is going to the beach.

"I should be in English class," Rhiannon says.

"I should be in bio," I say, accessing Justin's schedule.

We keep going. When I first saw her, she seemed to be balancing on edges and points. Now the ground is more even, welcoming.

I know this is dangerous. Justin is not good to her. I recognize that. If I access the bad memories, I see tears, fights, and remnants of passable togetherness. She is always there for him, and he must like that. His friends like her, and he must like that, too. But that's not the same as love. She has been hanging on to the hope of him for so long that she doesn't realize there isn't anything left to hope for. They don't have silences together; they have noise. Mostly his. If I tried, I could go deep into their arguments. I could track down whatever shards he's collected from all the times he's destroyed her. If I were really Justin, I would find something wrong with her. Right now. Tell her. Yell. Bring her down. Put her in her place.

But I can't. I'm not Justin. Even if she doesn't know it.

"Let's just enjoy ourselves," I say.

"Okay," she replies. "I like that. I spend so much time thinking about running away—it's nice to actually do it. For a day. It's good to be on the other side of the window. I don't do this enough."

There are so many things inside of her that I want to know. And at the same time, with every word we speak, I feel there may be something inside of her that I already know. When I get there, we will recognize each other. We will have that.

I park the car and we head to the ocean. We take off our shoes and leave them under our seats. When we get to the sand, I lean over to roll up my jeans. While I do, Rhiannon runs ahead. When I look back up, she is spinning around the beach, kicking up sand, calling my name. Everything, at that moment, is lightness. She is so joyful, I can't help but stop for a second and watch. Witness. Tell myself to remember.

"C'mon!" she cries. "Get over here!"

I'm not who you think I am, I want to tell her. But there's no way. Of course there's no way.

We have the beach to ourselves, the ocean to ourselves. I have her to myself. She has me to herself.

There is a part of childhood that is childish, and a part that is sacred. Suddenly we are touching the sacred part—running to the shoreline, feeling the first cold burst of water on our ankles, reaching into the tide to catch at shells before they ebb away from our fingers. We have returned to a world that is capable of glistening, and we are wading deeper within it. We stretch our arms wide, as if we are embracing the wind. She splashes me mischievously and I mount a counterattack. Our pants, our shirts get wet, but we don't care.

She asks me to help her build a sand castle, and as I do, she tells me about how she and her sister would never work on sand castles together—it was always a competition, with her sister going for the highest possible mountains while Rhiannon paid attention to detail, wanting each castle to be the dollhouse she was never allowed to have. I see echoes of this detail now as she makes turrets bloom from her cupped hands. I myself have no memories of sand castles, but there must be some sense memory attached, because I feel I know how to do this, how to shape this.

When we are done, we walk back down to the water to wash off our hands. I look back and see the way our footsteps intermingle to form a single path.

"What is it?" she asks, seeing me glance backward, seeing something in my expression.

How can I explain this? The only way I know is to say "Thank you."

She looks at me as if she's never heard the phrase before.

"For what?" she asks.

"For this," I say. "For all of it."

This escape. The water. The waves. Her. It feels like we've stepped outside of time. Even though there is no such place.

There's still a part of her that's waiting for the twist, the moment when all of this pleasure will jackknife into pain.

"It's okay," I tell her. "It's okay to be happy."

The tears come to her eyes. I take her in my arms. It's the wrong thing to do. But it's the right thing to do. I have to listen to my own words. Happiness is so rarely a part of my vocabulary, because for me it's so fleeting.

"I'm happy," she says. "Really, I am."

Justin would be laughing at her. Justin would be pushing her down into the sand, to do whatever he wanted to do. Justin would never have come here.

I am tired of not feeling. I am tired of not connecting. I want to be here with her. I want to be the one who lives up to her hopes, if only for the time I'm given.

The ocean makes its music; the wind does its dance. We hold on. At first we hold on to one another, but then it starts to feel like we are holding on to something even bigger than that. Greater.

"What's happening?" Rhiannon asks.

"Shhh," I say. "Don't question it."

She kisses me. I have not kissed anyone in years. I have not allowed myself to kiss anyone for years. Her lips are soft as flower petals, but with an intensity behind them. I take it slow, let each moment pour into the next. Feel her skin, her breath. Taste the condensation of our contact, linger in the heat of it. Her eyes are closed and mine are open. I want to remember this as more than a single sensation. I want to remember this whole.

We do nothing more than kiss. We do nothing less than kiss. At times, she moves to take it further, but I don't need that. I trace her shoulders as she traces my back. I kiss her neck. She kisses beneath my ear. The times we stop, we smile at each other. Giddy disbelief, giddy belief. She should be in English class. I should be in bio. We weren't supposed to come anywhere near the ocean today. We have defied the day as it was set out for us.

We walk hand in hand down the beach as the sun dips in the sky. I am not thinking about the past. I am not thinking about the future. I am full of such gratitude for the sun, the water, the way my feet sink into the sand, the way my hand feels holding hers.

"We should do this every Monday," she says. "And Tuesday. And Wednesday. And Thursday. And Friday."

"We'd only get tired of it," I tell her. "It's best to have it just once."

"Never again?" She doesn't like the sound of that.

"Well, never say never."

"I'd never say never," she tells me.

There are a few more people on the beach now, mostly older men and women taking an afternoon walk. They nod to us as we pass, and sometimes they say hello. We nod back, return their hellos. Nobody questions why we're here. Nobody questions anything. We're just a part of the moment, like everything else.

The sun falls farther. The temperature drops alongside it. Rhiannon shivers, so I stop holding her hand and put my arm around her. She suggests we go back to the car and get the "make-out blanket" from the trunk. We find it there, buried under empty beer bottles, twisted jumper cables, and other guy crap. I wonder how often Rhiannon and Justin have used the make-out blanket for that purpose, but I don't try to access the memories. Instead, I bring the blanket back out onto the beach and put it down for both of us. I lie down and face the sky, and Rhiannon lies down next to me and does the same. We stare at the clouds, breathing distance from one another, taking it all in.

"This has to be one of the best days ever," Rhiannon says.

Without turning my head, I find her hand with my hand.

"Tell me about some of the other days like this," I ask.

"I don't know. . . ."

"Just one. The first one that comes to mind."

Rhiannon thinks about it for a second. Then she shakes her head. "It's stupid."

"Tell me."

She turns to me and moves her hand to my chest. Makes lazy circles there. "For some reason, the first thing that comes to mind is this mother-daughter fashion show. Do you promise you won't laugh?"

I promise.

She studies me. Makes sure I'm sincere. Continues.

"It was in fourth grade or something. Renwick's was doing a fund-raiser for hurricane victims, and they asked for volunteers from our class. I didn't ask my mother or anything—I just signed up. And when I brought the information home—well, you know how my mom is. She was terrified. It's hard enough to get her out to the supermarket. But a fashion show? In front of strangers? I might as well have asked her to pose for *Playboy*. God, now there's a scary thought."

Her hand is now resting on my chest. She's looking off to the sky.

"But here's the thing: she didn't say no. I guess it's only now that I realize what I put her through. She didn't make me go to the teacher and take it back. No, when the day came, we drove over to Renwick's and went where they told us to go. I had thought they would put us in matching outfits, but it wasn't like that. Instead, they basically told us we could wear whatever we wanted from the store. So there we were, trying all these things on. I went for the gowns, of course—I was so much more of a girl then. I ended up with this light blue dress—ruffles all over the place. I thought it was so sophisticated."

"I'm sure it was classy," I say.

She hits me. "Shut up. Let me tell my story."

I hold her hand on my chest. Lean over and kiss her quickly.

"Go ahead," I say. I am loving this. I never have people tell me their stories. I usually have to figure them out myself. Because I know that if people tell me stories, they will expect them to be remembered. And I cannot guarantee that. There is no way to know if the stories stay after I'm gone. And how devastating would it be to confide in someone and have the confidence disappear? I don't want to be responsible for that.

But with Rhiannon I can't resist.

She continues. "So I had my wannabe prom dress. And then it was Mom's turn. She surprised me, because she went for the dresses, too. I'd never really seen her all dressed up before. And I think that was the most amazing thing to me: It wasn't me who was Cinderella. It was her.

"After we picked out our clothes, they put makeup on us and everything. I thought Mom was going to flip, but she was actually enjoying it. They didn't really do much with her—just a little more color. And that was all it took. She was pretty. I know it's hard to believe, knowing her now. But that day, she was like a movie star. All the other moms were complimenting her. And when it was time for the actual show, we paraded out there and people applauded. Mom and I were both smiling, and it was real, you know?

"We didn't get to keep the dresses or anything. But I remember on the ride home, Mom kept saying how great I was. When we got back to our house, Dad looked at us like we were aliens, but the cool thing is, he decided to play along. Instead of getting all weird, he kept calling us his supermodels, and asked us to do the show for him in our living room, which we did. We were laughing so much. And that was it. The day ended. I'm not sure Mom's worn makeup since. And it's not like I turned out to be a supermodel. But that day reminds me of this one. Because it was a break from everything, wasn't it?"

"It sounds like it," I tell her.

"I can't believe I just told you that."

"Why?"

"Because. I don't know. It just sounds so silly."

"No, it sounds like a good day."

"How about you?" she asks.

"I was never in a mother-daughter fashion show," I joke. Even though, as a matter of fact, I've been in a few.

She hits me lightly on the shoulder. "No. Tell me about another day like this one."

I access Justin and find out he moved to town when he was twelve. So anything before that is fair game, because Rhiannon won't have been there. I could try to find one of Justin's memories to share, but I don't want to do that. I want to give Rhiannon something of my own.

"There was this one day when I was eleven." I try to remember the name of the boy whose body I was in, but it's lost to me. "I was playing hide-and-seek with my friends. I mean, the brutal, tackle kind of hide-and-seek. We were in the woods, and for some reason I decided that what I had to do was climb a tree. I don't think I'd ever climbed a tree before. But I found one with some low branches and just started moving. Up and up. It was as natural as walking. In my memory, that tree was hundreds of feet tall. Thousands. At some point, I crossed the tree line. I was still climbing, but there weren't any other trees around. I was all by myself, clinging to the trunk of this tree, a long way from the ground."

I can see shimmers of it now. The height. The town below me.

"It was magical," I say. "There's no other word to describe it. I could hear my friends yelling as they were caught, as the game played out. But I was in a completely different place. I was seeing the world from above, which is an extraordinary thing when it happens for the first time. I'd never flown in a plane. I'm not even sure I'd been in a tall building. So there I was, hovering above everything I knew. I had made it somewhere special, and I'd gotten there all on my own. Nobody had given it to me. Nobody had told me to do it. I'd climbed and climbed and climbed, and this was my reward. To watch over the world, and to be alone with myself. That, I found, was what I needed."

Rhiannon leans into me. "That's amazing," she whispers.

"Yeah, it was."

"And it was in Minnesota?"

In truth, it was in North Carolina. But I access Justin and find that, yes, for him it would've been Minnesota. So I nod.

"You want to know another day like this one?" Rhiannon asks, curling closer.

I adjust my arm, make us both comfortable. "Sure."

"Our second date."

But this is only our first, I think. Ridiculously.

"Really?" I ask.

"Remember?"

I check to see if Justin remembers their second date. He doesn't.

"Dack's party?" she prompts.

Still nothing.

"Yeah . . . ," I hedge.

"I don't know—maybe it doesn't count as a date. But it was the second time we hooked up. And, I don't know, you were just so . . . sweet about it. Don't get mad, alright?"

I wonder where this is going.

21

"I promise, nothing could make me mad right now," I tell her. I even cross my heart to prove it.

She smiles. "Okay. Well, lately—it's like you're always in a rush. Like, we have sex but we're not really . . . intimate. And I don't mind. I mean, it's fun. But every now and then, it's good to have it be like this. And at Dack's party—it was like this. Like you had all the time in the world, and you wanted us to have it together. I loved that. It was back when you were really looking at me. It was like—well, it was like you'd climbed up that tree and found me there at the top. And we had that together. Even though we were in someone's backyard. At one point—do you remember?—you made me move over a little so I'd be in the moonlight. 'It makes your skin glow,' you said. And I felt like that. Glowing. Because you were watching me, along with the moon."

Does she realize that right now she's lit by the warm orange spreading from the horizon, as not-quite-day becomes not-quite-night? I lean over and become that shadow. I kiss her once, then we drift into each other, close our eyes, drift into sleep. And as we drift into sleep, I feel something I've never felt before. A closeness that isn't merely physical. A connection that defies the fact that we've only just met. A sensation that can only come from the most euphoric of feelings: belonging.

What is it about the moment you fall in love? How can such a small measure of time contain such enormity? I suddenly realize why people believe in déjà vu, why people believe they've lived past lives, because there is no way the years I've spent on this earth could possibly encapsulate what I'm feeling. The moment you fall in love feels like it has centuries behind it, generations—all of them rearranging themselves so that this precise, remarkable intersection could happen. In your heart, in your bones, no matter how silly you know it is, you feel that everything has been leading to this, all the secret arrows were pointing here, the universe and time itself crafted this long ago, and you are just now realizing it, you are just now arriving at the place you were always meant to be.

We wake an hour later to the sound of her phone.

I keep my eyes closed. Hear her groan. Hear her tell her mother she'll be home soon.

The water has gone deep black and the sky has gone ink blue. The chill in the air presses harder against us as we pick up the blanket, provide a new set of footprints.

She navigates, I drive. She talks, I listen. We sing some more. Then she leans into my shoulder and I let her stay there and sleep for a little longer, dream for a little longer.

I am trying not to think of what will happen next.

I am trying not to think of endings.

I never get to see people while they're asleep. Not like this. She is the opposite of when I first met her. Her vulnerability is open, but she's safe within it. I watch the rise and fall of her, the stir and rest of her. I only wake her when I need her to tell me where to go.

The last ten minutes, she talks about what we're going to do tomorrow. I find it hard to respond.

"Even if we can't do this, I'll see you at lunch?" she asks.

I nod.

"And maybe we can do something after school?"

"I think so. I mean, I'm not sure what else is going on. My mind isn't really there right now."

This makes sense to her. "Fair enough. Tomorrow is tomorrow. Let's end today on a nice note."

Once we get to town, I can access the directions to her house without having to ask her. But I want to get lost anyway. To prolong this. To escape this.

"Here we are," Rhiannon says as we approach her driveway.

I pull the car to a stop. I unlock the doors.

She leans over and kisses me. My senses are alive with the taste of her, the smell of her, the feel of her, the sound of her breathing, the sight of her as she pulls her body away from mine.

"That's the nice note," she says. And before I can say anything else, she's out the door and gone.

I don't get a chance to say goodbye.

I guess, correctly, that Justin's parents are used to him being out of touch and missing dinner. They try to yell at him, but you can tell that everyone's going through the motions, and when Justin storms off to his room, it's just the latest rerun of an old show.

I should be doing Justin's homework—I'm always pretty conscientious about that kind of thing, if I'm able to do it—but my mind keeps drifting to Rhiannon. Imagining her at home. Imagining her floating from the grace of the day. Imagining her believing that things are different, that Justin has somehow changed.

I shouldn't have done it. I know I shouldn't have done it. Even if it felt like the universe was telling me to do it.

I agonize over it for hours. I can't take it back. I can't make it go away.

I fell in love once, or at least until today I thought I had. His name was Brennan, and it felt so real, even if it was mostly words. Intense, heartfelt words. I stupidly let myself think of a possible future with him. But there was no future. I tried to navigate it, but I couldn't.

That was easy compared to this. It's one thing to fall in love. It's another to feel someone else falling in love with you, and to feel a responsibility toward that love.

There is no way for me to stay in this body. If I don't go to sleep, the shift will happen anyway. I used to think that if I stayed up all night, I'd get to remain where I was. But instead, I was ripped from the body I was in. And the ripping felt exactly like what you would imagine being ripped from a body would feel like, with every single nerve experiencing the pain of the break, and then the pain of being fused into someone new. From then on, I went to sleep every night. There was no use fighting it.

I realize I have to call her. Her number's right there in his phone. I can't let her think tomorrow is going to be like today.

"Hey!" she answers.

"Hey," I say.

"Thank you again for today."

"Yeah."

I don't want to do this. I don't want to ruin it. But I have to, don't I?

I continue, "But about today?"

"Are you going to tell me that we can't cut class every day? That's not like you."

Not like me.

"Yeah," I say, "but, you know, I don't want you to think every day is going to be like today. Because they're not going to be, alright? They can't be."

There's a silence. She knows something's wrong.

"I know that," she says carefully. "But maybe things can still be better. I know they can be."

"I don't know," I tell her. "That's all I wanted to say. I don't know. Today was something, but it's not, like, everything."

"I know that."

"Okay."

"Okay."

I sigh.

There's always a chance that, in some way, I will have brushed off on Justin. There's always a chance that his life will in fact change—that he will change. But I have no way of knowing. It's rare that I get to see a body after I've left it. And even then, it's usually months or years later. If I recognize it at all.

I want Justin to be better to her. But I can't have her expecting it.

"That's all," I tell her. It feels like a Justin thing to say.

"Well, I'll see you tomorrow."

"Yeah, you will."

"Thanks again for today. No matter what trouble we get into tomorrow for it, it was worth it."

"Yeah."

"I love you," she says.

And I want to say it. I want to say *I love you, too*. Right now, right at this moment, every part of me would mean it. But that will only last for a couple more hours.

"Sleep well," I tell her. Then I hang up.

There's a notebook on his desk.

Remember that you love Rhiannon, I write in his handwriting.

I doubt he'll remember writing it.

I go onto his computer. I open up my own email account, then type out her name, her phone number, her email address, as well as Justin's email and password. I write about the day. And I send it to myself.

As soon as I'm through, I clear Justin's history.

This is hard for me.

I have gotten so used to what I am, and how my life works.

I never want to stay. I'm always ready to leave.

But not tonight.

Tonight I'm haunted by the fact that tomorrow he'll be here and I won't be.

I want to stay.

I pray to stay.

I close my eyes and wish to stay.

Day 5995

I wake up thinking of yesterday. The joy is in remembering; the pain is in knowing it was yesterday.

I am not there. I am not in Justin's bed, not in Justin's body.

Today I am Leslie Wong. I have slept through the alarm, and her mother is mad.

"Get up!" she yells, shaking my new body. "You have twenty minutes, and then Owen leaves!"

"Okay, Mom," I groan.

"Mom! If your mother was here, I can't imagine what she'd say!"

I quickly access Leslie's mind. Grandmother, then. Mom's already left for work.

As I stand in the shower, trying to remind myself I have to make it a quick one, I lose myself for a minute in thoughts of Rhiannon. I'm sure I dreamt of her. I wonder: If I started dreaming when I was in Justin's body, did he continue the dream? Will he wake up thinking sweetly of her?

Or is that just another kind of dream on my part?

"Leslie! Come on!"

29

I get out of the shower, dry off, and get dressed quickly. Leslie is not, I can tell, a particularly popular girl. The few photos of friends she has around seem halfhearted, and her clothing choices are more like a thirteen-year-old's than a sixteen-year-old's.

I head into the kitchen and the grandmother glares at me.

"Don't forget your clarinet," she warns.

"I won't," I mumble.

There's a boy at the table giving me an evil look. Leslie's brother, I assume—and then confirm it. Owen. A senior. My ride to school.

I have gotten very used to the fact that most mornings in most homes are exactly the same. Stumbling out of the bed. Stumbling into the shower. Mumbling over the breakfast table. Or, if the parents are still asleep, the tiptoe out of the house. The only way to keep it interesting is to look for the variations.

This morning's variation comes care of Owen, who lights up a joint the minute we get into the car. I'm assuming this is part of his morning routine, so I make sure Leslie doesn't seem as surprised as I am.

Still, Owen hazards a "Don't say a word" about three minutes into the ride. I stare out the window. Two minutes later, he says, "Look, I don't need your judgment, okay?" The joint is done by then; it doesn't make him any mellower.

I prefer to be an only child. In the long term, I can see how siblings could be helpful in life—someone to share family secrets with, someone of your own generation who knows if your memories are right or not, someone who sees you at eight and eighteen and forty-eight all at once, and doesn't mind. I understand that. But in the short term, siblings are at best a hassle and at worst a terror. Most of the abuse I have suffered in my admittedly unusual life has come from brothers and sisters, with older brothers and older sisters being, by and large, the worst offenders. At first I was naïve, and assumed that brothers and sisters were natural allies, instant companions. And sometimes the context would allow this to happen—if we were on a family trip, for example, or if it was a lazy Sunday where teaming up with me was my sibling's only form of entertainment. But on ordinary days, the rule is competition, not collaboration. There are times when I wonder whether brothers and sisters are, in fact, the ones who sense that something is off with whatever person I'm inhabiting, and move to take advantage. When I was eight, an older sister told me we were going to run away together—then abandoned the "together" part when we got to the train station, leaving me to wander there for hours, too scared to ask for help—scared that she would find out and berate me for ending our game. As a boy, I've had brothers—both older and younger—wrestle me, hit me, kick me, bite me, shove me, and call me more names than I could ever catalog.

The best I can hope for is a quiet sibling. At first I have Owen pegged as one of those. In the car, it appears I am wrong. But then, once we get out at school, it appears I am right again. With other kids around, he retreats into invisibility, keeping his head down as he makes his way inside, leaving me completely behind. No goodbye, no have-a-nice-day. Just a quick glance to see that my door is closed before he locks the car.

"What are you looking at?" a voice asks from over my left shoulder as I watch him enter school alone.

I turn around and do some serious accessing.

Carrie. Best friend since fourth grade.

"Just my brother."

"Why? He's such a waste of space."

Here's the strange thing: I am fine thinking the same words myself, but hearing them come out of Carrie's mouth makes me feel defensive.

"Come on," I say.

"Come on? Are you kidding me?"

Now I think: *She knows something I don't.* I decide to keep my mouth shut.

She seems relieved to change the subject.

"What did you do last night?" she asks.

Flashes of Rhiannon rise in my mind's eye. I try to tamp them down, but they're not that easy to contain. Once you experience enormity, it lingers everywhere you look, and wants to be every word you say.

"Not much," I push on, not bothering to access Leslie. This answer always works, no matter what the question. "You?"

"You didn't get my text?"

I mumble something about my phone dying.

"That explains why you haven't asked me yet! Guess what. Corey IM'd me! We chatted for, like, almost an hour."

"Wow."

"Yeah, isn't it?" Carrie sighs contentedly. "After all this

time. I didn't even know he knew my screen name. You didn't tell him, did you?"

More accessing. This is the kind of question that can really trip a person up. Maybe not right away. But in the future. If Leslie claims she wasn't the one who told Corey, and Carrie finds out she was, it could throw their friendship off balance. Or if Leslie claims she was, and Carrie finds out she wasn't.

Corey is Corey Handlemann, a junior who Carrie's had a crush on for at least three weeks. Leslie doesn't know him well, and I can't find a memory of giving a screen name to him. I think it's safe.

"No," I say, shaking my head. "I didn't."

"Well, I guess he really had to work hard to find it," she says. (*Or*, I think, *he just saw it on your Facebook profile*.)

I immediately feel guilty for my snarky thoughts. This is the hard part about having best friends that I feel no attachment to—I don't give them any benefit of the doubt. And being best friends is always about the benefit of the doubt.

Carrie is very excited about Corey, so I pretend to be very excited for her. It's only after we separate for homeroom that I feel an emotion kicking at me, one I thought I had under control: jealousy. Although I am not articulating it to myself in so many words, I am feeling jealous that Carrie can have Corey while I can never have Rhiannon.

Ridiculous, I chastise myself. *You are being ridiculous*.

When you live as I do, you cannot indulge in jealousy. If you do, it will rip you apart.

• • •

Third period is band class. I tell the teacher that I left my clarinet at home, even though it's in my locker. Leslie gets marked down and has to take the class as a study hall, but I don't care.

I don't know how to play the clarinet.

Word about Carrie and Corey travels fast. All of our friends are talking about it, and mostly they're pleased. I can't tell, though, whether they're pleased because it's a perfect match or because now Carrie will shut up about it.

When I see Corey at lunchtime, I am unsurprised by how unremarkable he is. People are rarely as attractive in reality as they are in the eyes of the people who are in love with them. Which is, I suppose, as it should be. It's almost heartening to think that the attachment you have can define your perception as much as any other influence.

Corey comes over at lunch to say hi, but he doesn't stay to eat with us, even though we make room for him at our table. Carrie doesn't seem to notice this; she's just giddy that he's come by, that she didn't dream the whole IM exchange, that chatting has escalated into speaking . . . and who knows what will happen next? As I suspected, Leslie does not move in a fast crowd. These girls are thinking of kissing, not sex. The lips are the gates of their desire.

I want to run away again, to skip the second half of the day.

But it wouldn't be right, without her.

It feels like I am wasting time. I mean, that's always the case. My life doesn't add up to anything.

Except, for an afternoon, it did.

Yesterday is another world. I want to go back there.

• • •

34

Early sixth period, right after lunch, my brother is called down to the principal's office.

At first I think I may have heard it wrong. But then I see other people in class looking at me, including Carrie, who has pity in her eyes. So I must have heard it right.

I am not alarmed. I figure if it was something really bad, they would have called us both. Nobody in my family has died. Our house hasn't burned down. It's Owen's business, not mine.

Carrie sends me a note. *What happened?*

I send a shrug in her direction. How am I supposed to know?

I just hope I haven't lost my ride home.

Sixth period ends. I gather my books and head to English class. The book is *Beowulf*, so I'm completely prepared. I've done this unit plenty of times.

I'm about ten steps away from the classroom when someone grabs me.

I turn, and there's Owen.

Owen, bleeding.

"Shh," he says. "Just come with me."

"What happened?" I ask.

"Just shh, okay?"

He's looking around like he's being chased. I decide to go along. After all, this is more exciting than *Beowulf*.

We get to a supply closet. He motions me in.

"Are you kidding me?" I say.

"Leslie."

There's no arguing. I follow him in. I find the light switch easily.

He's breathing hard. For a moment, he doesn't say anything.

"Tell me what happened," I say.

"I think I might be in trouble."

"Duh. I heard you called to the principal's office. Why aren't you down there?"

"I *was* down there. I mean, before the announcement. But then I . . . left."

"You bolted from the principal's office?"

"Yeah. Well, the waiting room. They went to check my locker. I'm sure of it."

The blood is coming from a cut above his eye.

"Who hit you?" I ask.

"It doesn't matter. Just shut up and listen to me, okay?"

"I'm listening, but you're not saying anything!"

I don't think Leslie usually talks back to her older brother. But I don't care. He isn't really paying attention to me, anyway.

"They're going to call home, okay? I need you to back me up." He hands me his keys. "Just go home after school and see what the situation is. I'll call you."

Luckily, I know how to drive.

When I don't argue, he takes it as acquiescence.

"Thanks," he tells me.

"Are you going to the principal's office now?" I ask him.

He leaves without an answer.

Carrie has the news by the end of the day. Whether it's the truth doesn't really matter. It's the news that's going around, and she's eager to report it to me.

"Your brother and Josh Wolf got into a fight out by the field, during lunch. They're saying it had to do with drugs, and that your brother is a dealer or something. I mean, I knew he was into pot and everything, but I had no idea he *dealt*. He and Josh were dragged down to the principal's office, but Owen decided to run. Can you believe it? They were paging him to come back. But I don't think he did."

"Who'd you hear it from?" I ask. She's giddy with excitement.

"From Corey! He wasn't out there, but some of the guys he hangs out with saw the fight and everything."

I see now that the fact that Corey told her is the bigger news here. She's not so selfish that she wants me to congratulate her, not with my brother in trouble. But it's clear what her priority is.

"I've got to drive home," I say.

"Do you want me to come with you?" Carrie asks. "I don't want you to have to walk in there alone."

For a second, I'm tempted. But then I imagine her giving Corey the blow-by-blow account of what went down, and even if that's not a fair assumption to make, it's enough to make me realize I don't want her there.

"It's okay," I say. "If anything, this is really going to make me look like the good daughter."

Carrie laughs, but more out of support than humor.

"Tell Corey I say hi," I say playfully as I close my locker.

She laughs again. This time, out of happiness.

• • •

"Where is he?"

I haven't even stepped through the kitchen door and the interrogation begins.

Leslie's mother, father, and grandmother are all there, and I don't need to access her mind to know this is an unusual occurrence at three in the afternoon.

"I have no idea," I say. I'm glad he didn't tell me; this way, I don't have to lie.

"What do you mean, you have no idea?" my father asks. He's the lead inquisitor in this family.

"I mean, I have no idea. He gave me the keys to the car, but he wouldn't tell me what was going on."

"And you let him walk away?"

"I didn't see any police chasing after him," I say. Then I wonder if there are, in fact, police chasing after him.

My grandmother snorts in disgust.

"You always take his side," my father intones. "But not this time. This time you are going to tell us everything."

He doesn't realize he's just helped me. Now I know that Leslie always takes Owen's side. So my instinct is correct.

"You probably know more than I do," I say.

"Why would your brother and Josh Wolf have a fight?" my mother asks, genuinely bewildered. "They're such good friends!"

My mental image of Josh Wolf is of a ten-year-old, leading me to believe that at one point, my brother probably *was* good friends with Josh Wolf. But not anymore.

"Sit down," my father commands, pointing to a kitchen chair.

I sit down.

"Now . . . where is he?"

"I genuinely don't know."

"She's telling the truth," my mother says. "I can tell when she's lying."

Even though I have way too many control issues to do drugs myself, I am starting to get a sense of why Owen likes to get stoned.

"Well, let me ask this, then," my father continues. "Is your brother a drug dealer?"

This is a very good question. My instinct is *no*. But a lot depends on what happened on the field with Josh Wolf.

So I don't answer. I just stare.

"Josh Wolf says the drugs in his jacket were sold to him by your brother," my father prods. "Are you saying they weren't?"

"Did they find any drugs on Owen?" I ask.

"No," my mother answers.

"And in his locker? Didn't they search his locker?"

My mother shakes her head.

"And in his room? Did you find any in his room?"

My mother actually looks surprised.

"I *know* you looked in his room," I say.

"We haven't found anything," my father answers. "Yet. And we also need to take a look in that car. So if you will please give me the keys . . ."

I am hoping that Owen was smart enough to clear out the car. Either way, it's not up to me. I hand over the keys.

Unbelievably, they've searched my room, too.

"I'm sorry," my mother says from the hallway, tears in her

39

eyes now. "He thought your brother might have hidden the drugs in here. Without you knowing."

"It's fine," I say, more to get her out of the room than anything else. "I'm just going to clean up now."

But I'm not quick enough. My phone rings. I hold it so my mom can't see Owen's name on the display.

"Hi, Carrie," I say.

Owen is at least smart enough to keep his voice down so it won't be overheard.

"Are they mad?" he whispers.

I want to laugh. "What do you think?"

"That bad?"

"They've ransacked his room, but they haven't found anything. They're looking in his car now!"

"Don't tell her that!" my mother says. "Get off the phone."

"Sorry—Mom's here, and not happy about me talking to you about this. Where are you? Are you at home? Can I call you back?"

"I don't know what to do."

"Yeah, he really does have to come home eventually, doesn't he?"

"Look . . . meet me in a half hour at the playground, okay?"

"I really have to go. But, yes, I'll do that."

I hang up. My mother is still looking at me.

"I'm not the one you're mad at!" I remind her.

Poor Leslie will have to clean up the mess in her room tomorrow morning—I can't be bothered to figure out where everything goes. That would take too much accessing, and the priority is finding out which playground Owen means. There's one at an elementary school about four blocks from the house. I assume that's the place.

It's not easy to sneak out of the house. I wait until the three of them return to Owen's room to tear it apart again, then skulk out the back door. I know this is a risky maneuver—the minute they realize I'm gone, there will be hell to pay. But if Owen comes back with me, that'll all be forgotten.

I know I should be focusing on the matter at hand, but I can't help but think of Rhiannon. School's now over for her, too. Is she hanging out with Justin? If so, is he treating her well? Did anything about yesterday rub off on him?

I hope, but never expect.

Owen's nowhere to be found, so I head to the swings and hang in the air for a while. Eventually he appears on the sidewalk and heads over to me.

"You always pick that swing," he says, sitting down on the swing next to mine.

"I do?" I say.

"Yeah."

I wait for him to say something else. He doesn't.

"Owen," I finally say. "What happened?"

He shakes his head. He's not going to tell me.

I stop swinging and plant my feet on the ground.

"This is stupid, Owen. You have five seconds to tell me what happened, or I'm going to head right back home, and you'll be on your own for whatever happens next."

Owen is surprised. "What do you want me to say? Josh Wolf gets me my pot. Today we got into a fight over it—he was saying I owed him, when I didn't. He started pushing me around, so I pushed him back. And we got caught. He had the drugs, so he said I'd just dealt them to him. Real smooth. I said that was totally wrong, but he's in all AP classes and everything, so who do you think they're going to believe?"

He has definitely convinced himself it's the truth. But whether it started out being the truth or not, I can't tell.

"Well," I say, "you have to come home. Dad's trashed your room, but they haven't found any drugs yet. And they didn't find any in your locker, and I'm guessing they didn't find any in the car, or I would've heard about it. So right now, it's all okay."

"I'm telling you, there aren't any drugs. I used the weed up this morning. That's why I needed more from Josh."

"Josh, your former best friend."

"What are you talking about? I haven't been friends with him since we were, like, eight."

I am sensing that this was the last time Owen had a best friend.

"Let's go," I tell him. "It's not the end of the world."

"Easy for you to say."

I am not expecting our father to hit Owen. But as soon as he sees him in the house, he decks him.

I think I am the only one who is truly stunned.

"What have you done?" my father is yelling. "What stupid, stupid thing have you done?"

Both my mother and I move to stand between them. Grandma just watches from the sidelines, looking mildly pleased.

"I haven't done anything!" Owen protests.

"Is that why you ran away? Is that why you are being expelled? Because you haven't done anything?"

"They won't expel him until they hear his side of the story," I point out, fairly sure this is true.

"Stay out of this!" my father warns.

"Why don't we all sit down and talk this over?" my mother suggests.

The anger rises off my father like heat. I feel myself receding in a way that I'm guessing is not unusual for Leslie when she's with her family.

I become nostalgic for that first waking moment of the morning, back before I had any idea what ugliness the day would bring.

We sit down this time in the den. Or, rather, Owen, our mother, and I sit down—Owen and me on the couch, our mother in a nearby chair. Our father hovers over us. Our grandmother stays in the doorway, as if she's keeping lookout.

"You are a *drug dealer*!" our father yells.

"I am *not* a drug dealer," Owen answers. "For one, if I were a drug dealer, I'd have a lot more money. And I'd have a stash of drugs that you would've found by now!"

Owen, I think, needs to shut up.

"Josh Wolf was the drug dealer," I volunteer. "Not Owen."

"So what was your brother doing—*buying from him?*"

Maybe, I think, I'm the one who needs to shut up.

"Our fight had nothing to do with drugs," Owen says. "They just found them on him afterward."

"Then what were you and Josh fighting about?" our mother asks, as if the fact that these two boyhood chums fought is the most unbelievable thing that's occurred.

"A girl," Owen says. "We were fighting about a girl."

I wonder if Owen thought this one out ahead of time, or whether it's come to him spontaneously. Whatever the case, it's probably the only thing he could have possibly said that would have made our parents momentarily . . . *happy* might be overstating it. But less angry. They don't want their son to be buying or selling drugs, being bullied or bullying anyone else. But fighting over a girl? Perfectly acceptable. Especially since, I'm guessing, it's not like Owen's ever mentioned a girl to them before.

Owen sees he's gained ground. He pushes further. "If she found out—oh God, she can't find out. I know some girls like it when you fight over them, but she definitely doesn't."

Mom nods her approval.

"What's her name?" Dad asks.

"Do I have to tell you?"

"Yes."

"Natasha. Natasha Lee."

Wow, he's even made her Chinese. Amazing.

"Do you know this girl?" Dad asks me.

"Yes," I say. "She's awesome." Then I turn to Owen and shoot him fake daggers. "But Romeo over here never told me he was into her. Although now that he says it, it's starting to make sense. He has been acting very weird lately."

Mom nods again. "He has."

44

Eyes bloodshot, I want to say. *Eating a lot of Cheetos. Staring into space. Eating more Cheetos. It must be love. What else could it possibly be?*

What was threatening to be an all-out war becomes a war council, with our parents strategizing what the principal can be told, especially about the running away. I hope for Owen's sake that Natasha Lee is, in fact, a student at the high school, whether he has a crush on her or not. I can't access any memory of her. If the name rings a bell, the bell's in a vacuum.

Now that our father can see a way of saving face, he's almost amiable. Owen's big punishment is that he has to go clean up his room before dinner.

I can't imagine I would have gotten the same reaction if I'd beaten up another girl over a boy.

I follow Owen up to his room. When we're safely inside, door closed, no parents around, I tell him, "That was kinda brilliant."

He looks at me with unconcealed annoyance and says, "I don't know what you're talking about. Get out of my room."

This is why I prefer to be an only child.

I have a sense that Leslie would let it go. So I should let it go. That's the law I've set down for myself—don't disrupt the life you're living in. Leave it as close to the same as you can.

But I'm pissed. So I diverge a little from the law. I think, perversely, that Rhiannon would want me to. Even though she has no idea who Owen and Leslie are. Or who I am.

"Look," I say, "you lying little pothead bitch. You are going to be nice to me, okay? Not only because I am covering your butt, but because I am the one person in the world right now who is being decent to you. Is that understood?"

Shocked, and maybe a little contrite, Owen mumbles his assent.

"Good," I say, knocking a few things off his shelves. "Now happy cleaning."

Nobody talks at dinner.

I don't think this is unusual.

I wait until everyone is asleep before I go on the computer. I retrieve Justin's email and password from my own email, then log in as him.

There's an email from Rhiannon, sent at 10:11 p.m.

> J –
>
> I just don't understand. was it something I did?
> yesterday was so perfect, and today you are mad at
> me again. if it's something I did, please tell me, and I'll
> fix it. I want us to be together. I want all our days to end
> on a nice note. not like tonight.
>
> with all my heart,
> r

I reel back in my seat. I want to hit reply, I want to reassure her that it will be better—but I can't. *You're not him anymore*, I have to remind myself. *You're not there.*

And then I think: *What have I done?*

46

• • •

I hear Owen moving around in his room. Hiding evidence? Or is fear keeping him awake?

I wonder if he'll be able to pull it off tomorrow.

I want to get back to her. I want to get back to yesterday.

Day 5996

All I get is tomorrow.

As I fell asleep, I had a glint of an idea. But as I wake up, I realize the glint has no light left in it.

Today I'm a boy. Skylar Smith. Soccer player, but not a star soccer player. Clean room, but not compulsively so. Video-game console in his room. Ready to wake up. Parents asleep.

He lives in a town that's about a four-hour drive from where Rhiannon lives.

This is nowhere near close enough.

It's an uneventful day, as most are. The only suspense comes from whether I can access things fast enough.

Soccer practice is the hardest part. The coach keeps calling out names, and I have to access like crazy to figure out who everyone is. It's not Skylar's best day at practice, but he doesn't embarrass himself.

I know how to play most sports, but I've also learned my limits. I found this out the hard way when I was eleven. I woke up in the body of some kid who was in the middle of a ski trip. I thought that, hey, skiing had always looked fun. So I figured I'd try. Learn it as I went. How hard could it be?

The kid had already graduated from the bunny slopes, and I didn't even know there was such a thing as a bunny slope. I thought skiing was like sledding—one hill fits all.

I broke the kid's leg in three places.

The pain was pretty bad. And I honestly wondered if, when I woke up the next morning, I would still feel the pain of the broken leg, even though I was in a new body. But instead of the pain, I felt something just as bad—the fierce, living weight of terrifying guilt. Just as if I'd rammed him with a car, I was consumed by the knowledge that a stranger was lying in a hospital bed because of me.

And if he'd died . . . I wondered if I would have died, too. There is no way for me to know. All I know is that, in a way, it doesn't matter. Whether I die or just wake up the next morning as if nothing happened, the fact of the death will destroy me.

So I'm careful. Soccer, baseball, field hockey, football, softball, basketball, swimming, track—all of those are fine. But I've also woken up in the body of an ice hockey player, a fencer, an equestrian, and once, recently, a gymnast.

I've sat all those out.

If there's one thing I'm good at, it's video games. It's a universal presence, like TV or the Internet. No matter where I am, I usually have access to these things, and video games especially help me calm my mind.

After soccer practice, Skylar's friends come over to play *World of Warcraft*. We talk about school and talk about girls (except for his friends Chris and David, who talk about boys). This, I've discovered, is the best way to waste time, because it isn't really wasted—surrounded by friends, talking crap and sometimes talking for real, with snacks around and something on a screen.

I might even be enjoying myself, if I could only unmoor myself from the place I want to be.

Day 5997

It's almost eerie how well the next day works out.

I wake up early—six in the morning.

I wake up as a girl.

A girl with a car. And a license.

In a town only an hour away from Rhiannon's.

I apologize to Amy Tran as I drive away from her house, a half hour after waking up. What I'm doing is, no doubt, a strange form of kidnapping.

I strongly suspect that Amy Tran wouldn't mind. Getting dressed this morning, the options were black, black, or . . . black. Not in a goth sense—none of the black came in the form of lace gloves—but more in a rock 'n' roll sense. The mix in her car stereo puts Janis Joplin and Brian Eno side by side, and somehow it works.

I can't rely on Amy's memory here—we're going somewhere she's never been. So I did some Google mapping right after my shower, typed in the address of Rhiannon's school and

51

watched it pop up in front of me. That simple. I printed it out, then cleared the history.

I have become very good at clearing histories.

I know I shouldn't be doing this. I know I'm poking a wound, not healing it. I know there's no way to have a future with Rhiannon.

All I'm doing is extending the past by a day.

Normal people don't have to decide what's worth remembering. You are given a hierarchy, recurring characters, the help of repetition, of anticipation, the firm hold of a long history. But I have to decide the importance of each and every memory. I only remember a handful of people, and in order to do that, I have to hold tight, because the only repetition available—the only way I am going to see them again—is if I conjure them in my mind.

I choose what to remember, and I am choosing Rhiannon. Again and again, I am choosing her, I am conjuring her, because to let go for an instant will allow her to disappear.

The same song that we heard in Justin's car comes on—*And if I only could, I'd make a deal with God.* . . .

I feel the universe is telling me something. And it doesn't even matter if it's true or not. What matters is that I feel it, and believe it.

The enormity rises within me.

The universe nods along to the songs.

• • •

I try to hold on to as few mundane, everyday memories as possible. Facts and figures, sure. Books I've read or information I need to know. The rules of soccer, for instance. The plot of *Romeo and Juliet*. The phone number to call if there's an emergency. I remember those.

But what about the thousands of everyday memories, the thousands of everyday reminders, that every person accumulates? The place you keep your house keys. Your mother's birthday. The name of your first pet. The name of your current pet. Your locker combination. The location of the silverware drawer. The channel number for MTV. Your best friend's last name.

These are the things I have no need for. And, over time, my mind has rewired itself, so all this information falls away as soon as the next morning comes.

Which is why it's remarkable—but not surprising—that I remember exactly where Rhiannon's locker is.

I have my cover story ready: If anyone asks, I am checking out the school because my parents might be moving to town.

I don't remember if there are assigned parking spaces, so just in case, I park far from the school. Then I simply walk in. I am just another random girl in the halls—the freshmen will think I'm a senior, and the seniors will think I'm a freshman. I have Amy's schoolbag with me—black with anime details, filled with books that won't really apply here. I look like I have a destination. And I do.

If the universe wants this to happen, she will be there at her locker.

I tell myself this, and there she is. Right there in front of me.

Sometimes memory tricks you. Sometimes beauty is best when it's distant. But even from here, thirty feet away, I know that the reality of her is going to match my memory.

Twenty feet away.

Even in the crowded hallway, there is something in her that radiates out to me.

Ten.

She is carrying herself through the day, and it's not an easy task.

Five.

I can stand right here and she has no idea who I am. I can stand right here and watch her. I can see that the sadness has returned. And it's not a beautiful sadness—beautiful sadness is a myth. Sadness turns our features to clay, not porcelain. She is dragging.

"Hey," I say, my voice thin, a stranger here.

At first she doesn't understand that I'm talking to her. Then it registers.

"Hey," she says back.

Most people, I've noticed, are instinctively harsh to strangers. They expect every approach to be an attack, every question to be an interruption. But not Rhiannon. She doesn't have any idea who I am, but she's not going to hold that against me. She's not going to assume the worst.

"Don't worry—you don't know me," I quickly say. "It's just—it's my first day here. I'm checking the school out. And I really like your skirt and your bag. So I thought, you know, I'd say hello. Because, to be honest, I am completely alone right now."

Again, some people would be scared by this. But not Rhiannon. She offers her hand, introduces herself as we shake, and asks me why there isn't someone showing me around.

"I don't know," I say.

"Well, why don't I take you to the office? I'm sure they can figure something out."

I panic. "No!" I blurt out. Then I try to cover for myself, and prolong my time with her. "It's just . . . I'm not here officially. Actually, my parents don't even know I'm doing this. They just told me we're moving here, and I . . . I wanted to see it and decide whether I should be freaking out or not."

Rhiannon nods. "That makes sense. So you're cutting school in order to check school out?"

"Exactly."

"What year are you?"

"A junior."

"So am I. Let's see if we can pull this off. Do you want to come around with me today?"

"I'd love that."

I know she's just being nice. Irrationally, I also want there to be some kind of recognition. I want her to be able to see behind this body, to see me inside here, to know that it's the same person she spent an afternoon with on the beach.

I follow her. Along the way, she introduces me to a few of her friends, and I am relieved to meet each one, relieved to know that she has more people in her life than Justin. The way she includes me, the way she takes this total stranger and makes her feel a part of this world, makes me care about her even more. It's one thing to be love-worthy when you are interacting with your boyfriend; it's quite another when you act the same way with a girl you don't know. I no longer think she's just being nice. She's being kind. Which is much more a sign of character than mere niceness. Kindness connects to who you are, while niceness connects to how you want to be seen.

Justin makes his first appearance between second and third period. We pass him in the hall; he barely acknowledges Rhiannon and completely ignores me. He doesn't stop walking, just nods at her. She's hurt—I can tell—but she doesn't say anything about it to me.

By the time we get to math class, fourth period, the day has turned into an exquisite form of torture. I am right there next to her, but I can't do a thing. As the teacher reduces us to theorems, I must remain silent. I write her a note, as an excuse to touch her shoulder, to pass her some words. But they are inconsequential. They are the words of a guest.

I want to know if I changed her. I want to know if that day changed her, if only for a day.

I want her to see me, even though I know she can't.

He joins us at lunch.

As strange as it is to see Rhiannon again, and to have her measure so well against my memory, it is even stranger to be sitting across from the jerk whose body I inhabited just three days ago. Mirror images do no justice to this sensation. He is more attractive than I thought, but also uglier. His features are attractive, but what he does with them is not. He wears the superior scowl of someone who can barely hide his feelings of inferiority. His eyes are full of scattershot anger, his posture one of defensive bravado.

I must have rendered him unrecognizable.

Rhiannon explains to him who I am, and where I come from. He makes it clear that he couldn't care less. He tells her he left his wallet at home, so she goes and buys him food. When she gets back to the table with it, he says thanks, and I'm almost disappointed that he does. Because I'm sure that a single thank-you will go a long way in her mind.

I want to know about three days ago, about what he remembers.

"How far is it to the ocean?" I ask Rhiannon.

"It's so funny you should say that," she tells me. "We were just there the other day. It took about an hour or so."

I am looking at him, looking again for some recognition. But he just keeps eating.

"Did you have a good time?" I ask him.

She answers. "It was amazing."

Still no response from him.

I try again. "Did you drive?"

He looks at me like I'm asking really stupid questions, which I suppose I am.

"Yes, I drove" is all he'll give me.

"We had such a great time," Rhiannon goes on. And it's making her happy—the memory is making her happy. Which only makes me sadder.

I should not have come here. I should not have tried this. I should just go.

But I can't. I am with her. I try to pretend that this is what matters.

I play along.

I don't want to love her. I don't want to be in love.

People take love's continuity for granted, just as they take their body's continuity for granted. They don't realize that the best thing about love is its regular presence. Once you can establish that, it's an added foundation to your life. But if you cannot have that regular presence, you only have the one foundation to support you, always.

She is sitting right next to me. I want to run my finger along her arm. I want to kiss her neck. I want to whisper the truth in her ear.

But instead I watch as she conjugates verbs. I listen as the air is filled with a foreign language, spoken in haphazard bursts. I try to sketch her in my notebook, but I am not an artist, and all that comes out are the wrong shapes, the wrong lines. I cannot hold on to anything that's her.

The final bell rings. She asks me where I've parked, and I know that this is it, this is the end. She is writing her email address on a piece of paper for me. This is goodbye. For all I know, Amy

Tran's parents have called the police. For all I know, there's a manhunt going on, an hour away. It is cruel of me, but I don't care. I want Rhiannon to ask me to go to a movie, to invite me over to her house, to suggest we drive to the beach. But then Justin appears. Impatient. I don't know what they are going to do, but I have a bad feeling. He wouldn't be so insistent if sex weren't involved.

"Walk me to my car?" I ask.

She looks at Justin for permission.

"I'll get my car," he says.

We have a parking lot's length of time left with each other. I know I need something from her, but I'm not sure what.

"Tell me something nobody else knows about you," I say.

She looks at me strangely. "What?"

"It's something I always ask people—tell me something about you that nobody else knows. It doesn't have to be major. Just something."

Now that she gets it, I can tell she likes the challenge of the question, and I like her even more for liking it.

"Okay," she says. "When I was ten, I tried to pierce my own ear with a sewing needle. I got it halfway through, and then I passed out. Nobody was home, so nobody found me. I just woke up, with this needle halfway in my ear, drops of blood all over my shirt. I pulled the needle out, cleaned up, and never tried it again. It wasn't until I was fourteen that I went to the mall with my mom and got my ears pierced for real. She had no idea. How about you?"

There are so many lives to choose from, although I don't remember most of them.

I also don't remember whether Amy Tran has pierced ears or not, so it won't be an ear-piercing memory.

"I stole Judy Blume's *Forever* from my sister when I was eight," I say. "I figured if it was by the author of *Superfudge*, it had to be good. Well, I soon realized why she kept it under her bed. I'm not sure I understood it all, but I thought it was unfair that the boy would name his, um, organ, and the girl wouldn't name hers. So I decided to give mine a name."

Rhiannon is laughing. "What was its name?"

"*Helena*. I introduced everyone to her at dinner that night. It went over really well."

We're at my car. Rhiannon doesn't know it's my car, but it's the farthest car, so it's not like we can keep walking.

"It was great to meet you," she says. "Hopefully, I'll see you around next year."

"Yeah," I say, "it was great to meet you, too."

I thank her about five different ways. Then Justin drives over and honks.

Our time is up.

Amy Tran's parents haven't called the police. They haven't even gotten home yet. I check the house phone's voicemail, but the school hasn't called.

It's the one lucky thing that's happened all day.

Day 5998

Something is wrong the minute I wake up the next morning. Something chemical.

It's barely even morning. This body has slept until noon. Because this body was up late, getting high. And now it wants to be high again. Right away.

I've been in the body of a pothead before. I've woken up still drunk from the night before. But this is worse. Much worse.

There will be no school for me today. There will be no parents waking me up. I am on my own, in a dirty room, sprawled on a dirty mattress with a blanket that looks like it was stolen from a child. I can hear other people yelling in other rooms of the house.

There comes a time when the body takes over the life. There comes a time when the body's urges, the body's needs, dictate the life. You have no idea you are giving the body the key. But you hand it over. And then it's in control. You mess with the wiring and the wiring takes charge.

I have only had glimpses of this before. Now I really feel it. I can feel my mind immediately combating the body. But it's not easy. I cannot sense pleasure. I have to cling to the memory of it. I have to cling to the knowledge that I am only here for one day, and I have to make it through.

I try to go back to sleep, but the body won't let me. The body is awake now, and it knows what it wants.

I know what I have to do, even though I don't really know what's going on. Even though I have not been in this situation before, I have been in situations before where it's been me against the body. I have been ill, seriously ill, and the only thing to do is to power through the day. At first I thought there was something I could do within a single day that could make everything better. But very soon I learned my own limitations. Bodies cannot be changed in a day, especially not when the real mind isn't in charge.

I don't want to leave the room. If I leave the room, anything and anyone can happen. Desperately, I look around for something to help me through. There is a decrepit bookshelf, and on it is a selection of old paperbacks. These will save me, I decide. I open up an old thriller and focus on the first line. *Darkness had descended on Manassas, Virginia. . . .*

The body does not want to read. The body is alive with electric barbed wire. The body is telling me there is only one way to fix this, only one way to end the pain, only one way to feel better. The body will kill me if I don't listen to it. The body is screaming. The body demands its own form of logic.

I read the next sentence.

I lock the door.

I read the third sentence.

The body fights back. My hand shakes. My vision blurs.

I am not sure I have the strength to resist this.

I have to convince myself that Rhiannon is on the other side. I have to convince myself that this isn't a pointless life, even though the body is telling me it is.

The body has obliterated its memories in order to hone its argument. There isn't much for me to access. I must rely on my own memories, the ones that are separate from this.

I must remain separate from this.

I read the next sentence, then the next sentence. I don't even care about the story. I am moving from word to word, fighting the body from word to word.

It's not working. The body makes me feel like it wants to defecate and vomit. First in the usual way. Then I feel I want to defecate through my mouth and vomit through the other end. Everything is being mangled. I want to claw at the walls. I want to scream. I want to punch myself repeatedly.

I have to imagine my mind as something physical, something that can control the body. I have to picture my mind holding the body down.

I read another sentence.

Then another.

There is pounding on the door. I scream that I'm reading.

They leave me alone.

I don't have what they want in this room.

They have what I want outside this room.

I must not leave this room.

I must not let the body out of this room.

I imagine her walking the hallways. I imagine her sitting next to me. I imagine her eyes meeting mine.

Then I imagine her getting in his car, and I stop.

The body is infecting me. I am getting angry. Angry that I am here. Angry that this is my life. Angry that so many things are impossible.

Angry at myself.

Don't you want it to stop? the body asks.

I must push myself as far away from the body as I can.

Even as I'm in it.

I have to go to the bathroom. I really have to go to the bathroom.

Finally, I pee in a soda bottle. It splashes all over.

But it's better than leaving this room.

If I leave the room, I will not be able to stop the body from getting what it wants.

I am ninety pages into the book. I can't remember any of it.

Word by word.

The fight is exhausting the body.

I am winning.

● ● ●

It is a mistake to think of the body as a vessel. It is as active as any mind, as any soul. And the more you give yourself to it, the harder your life will be. I have been in the bodies of starvers and purgers, gluttons and addicts. They all think their actions make their lives more desirable. But the body always defeats them in the end.

I just need to make sure the defeat doesn't take while I'm inside.

I make it to sundown. Two hundred sixty-five pages gone. I am shivering under the filthy blanket. I don't know if it's the temperature in the room or if it's me.

Almost there, I tell myself.

There is only one way out of this, the body tells me.

At this point, I don't know if it means drugs or death.

The body might not even care, at this point.

Finally, the body wants to sleep.

I let it.

Day 5999

My mind is thoroughly wrung out, but I can tell Nathan Daldry has gotten a good night's sleep.

Nathan is a good guy. Everything in his room is in order. Even though it's only Saturday morning, he's already done his homework for the weekend. He's set his alarm for eight o'clock, not wanting the day to go to waste. He was probably in bed by ten.

I go on his computer and check my email, making sure to write myself some notes about the last few days, so I can remember them. Then I log in to Justin's email and find out there's a party tonight at Steve Mason's house. Steve's address is only a Google search away. When I map out the distance between Nathan's house and Steve's, I find it's only a ninety-minute drive.

It looks like Nathan might be going to a party tonight.

First, I must convince his parents.

His mother interrupts me when I'm back on my own email,

rereading what I wrote about the day with Rhiannon. I very quickly shut the window, and oblige when she tells me that today is not a computer day, and that I am to come down for breakfast.

I very quickly discover that Nathan's parents are a very nice couple who make it very clear that their niceness shouldn't be challenged or pressed.

"Can I borrow the car?" I ask. "The school musical is tonight, and I would like to go see it."

"Have you done your homework?"

I nod.

"Your chores?"

"I will."

"And you'll be back by midnight?"

I nod. I decide not to mention to them that if I'm not back by midnight, I'll be ripped from my current body. I don't think they'd find that reassuring.

It's clear to me that they won't need the car tonight. They are the type of parents who don't believe in having a social life. They have television instead.

I spend most of the day doing chores. After I'm done with them and have had a family dinner, I'm good to go.

The party's supposed to start at seven, so I know I have to wait until nine to show up, so there will be enough people there to hide my presence. If I get there and it ends up being open to only a dozen kids, I'll have to turn back around. But that doesn't strike me as Justin's kind of party.

Nathan's kind of party, I'm guessing, involves board games and Dr Pepper. As I drive back to Rhiannon's town, I access some of his memories. I am a firm believer that every person, young or old, has at least one good story to tell. Nathan's, however, is pretty hard to find. The only tremor of emotion I can find in his life is when he was nine and his dog April died. Ever since then, nothing seems to have disturbed him too much. Most of his memories involve homework. He has friends, but they don't do very much outside of school. When Little League was over, he gave up sports. He has never, from what I can tell, sipped anything stronger than a beer, and even that was during a Father's Day barbecue, at his uncle's prodding.

Normally, I would take these as parameters. Normally, I would stay within Nathan's safe zone.

But not today. Not with a chance of seeing Rhiannon again.

I remember yesterday, and how the trail that got me through the darkness seemed to be attached in some way to her. It's as if when you love someone, they become your reason. And maybe I've gotten it backward, maybe it's just because I need a reason that I find myself falling in love with her. But I don't think that's it. I think I would have continued along, oblivious, if I hadn't happened to meet her.

Now I'm letting my life hijack these other lives for a day. I am not staying within their parameters. Even if that's dangerous.

I'm at Steve Mason's house by eight, but Justin's car is nowhere in sight. In fact, there aren't that many cars out in front. So I wait and watch. After a while, people start arriving. Even though I've just spent a day and a half at their school, I don't recognize any of them. They were all peripheral.

Finally, just after nine-thirty, Justin's car pulls up. Rhiannon is with him, as I'd hoped she'd be. As they head in, he walks a little bit in front, with her a little behind. I get out of my car and follow them inside.

I'm worried there will be someone at the door, but the party's already spiraled into its own form of chaos. The early guests are well past the point of drunkenness, and everyone else is quickly catching up. I know I look out of place—Nathan's wardrobe is more suited to a debate tournament than a Saturday-night house party. But nobody really cares; they're too caught up in each other or themselves to notice a random geek in their midst.

The lights are dim, the music is loud, and Rhiannon is hard to find. But just the fact that I am in the same place as her has me nervously exhilarated.

Justin is in the kitchen, talking with some guys. He looks at ease, in his element. He finishes one beer and immediately goes for another.

I push past him, push through the living room and find myself in the den. The instant I step in the room, I know she's here. Even though the music's blaring from a laptop connected to some speakers, she's over by the CD collection, thumbing through cases. Two girls are talking nearby, and I have a sense that at one point she was a part of their conversation, then decided to drop out.

I walk over and see that one of the CDs she's looking at has a song we listened to on our car ride.

"I really like them," I say, gesturing to the CD. "Do you?"

She startles, as if this is a quiet room and I am a sudden noise. *I notice you*, I want to say. *Even when no one else does, I do. I will.*

"Yeah," she says. "I like them, too."

I start to sing the song, the one from the car. Then I say, "I like that one in particular."

"Do I know you?" she asks.

"I'm Nathan," I say, which isn't a no or a yes.

"I'm Rhiannon," she says.

"That's a beautiful name."

"Thanks. I used to hate it, but I don't so much anymore."

"Why?"

"It's just a pain to spell." She looks at me closely. "Do you go to Octavian?"

"No. I'm just here for the weekend. Visiting my cousin."

"Who's your cousin?"

"Steve."

This is a dangerous lie, since I have no idea which of the guys is Steve, and I have no way of accessing the information.

"Oh, that explains it."

She is starting to drift away from me, just as I imagine she drifted away from the girls talking next to us.

"I hate my cousin," I say.

This gets her attention.

"I hate the way he treats girls. I hate the way he thinks he can buy all his friends by throwing parties like this. I hate the way that he only talks to you when he needs something. I hate the way he doesn't seem capable of love."

I realize I'm now talking about Justin, not Steve.

"Then why are you here?" Rhiannon asks.

"Because I want to see it fall apart. Because when this party gets busted—and if it stays this loud, it *will* get busted—I want to be a witness. From a safe distance away, of course."

"And you're saying he's incapable of loving Stephanie? They've been going out for over a year."

With a silent apology to Stephanie and Steve, I say, "That doesn't mean anything, does it? I mean, being with someone for over a year can mean that you love them . . . but it can also mean you're trapped."

At first I think I've gone too far. I can feel Rhiannon taking in my words, but I don't know what she's doing with them. The sound of words as they're said is always different from the sound they make when they're heard, because the speaker hears some of the sound from the inside.

Finally, she says, "Speaking from experience?"

It's laughable to think that Nathan—who, from what I can tell, hasn't gone on a date since eighth grade—would be speaking from experience. But she doesn't know him, which means I can be more like me. Not that I'm speaking from experience, either. Just the experience of observing.

"There are many things that can keep you in a relationship," I say. "Fear of being alone. Fear of disrupting the arrangement of your life. A decision to settle for something that's okay, because you don't know if you can get any better. Or maybe there's the irrational belief that it will get better, even if you know he won't change."

" 'He'?"

"Yeah."

71

"I see."

At first I don't understand what she sees—clearly, I was talking about her. Then I get where the pronoun has led her.

"That cool?" I ask, figuring it will make Nathan even less threatening if he's gay.

"Completely."

"How about you?" I ask. "Seeing anyone?"

"Yeah," she says. Then, deadpan, "For over a year."

"And why are you still together? Fear of being alone? A decision to settle? An irrational belief that he'll change?"

"Yes. Yes. And yes."

"So . . ."

"But he can also be incredibly sweet. And I know that, deep down, I mean the world to him."

"Deep down? That sounds like settling to me. You shouldn't have to venture deep down in order to get to love."

"Let's switch the topic, okay? This isn't a good party topic. I liked it more when you were singing to me."

I'm about to make reference to another song we heard on our car ride—hoping that maybe it'll bring her back in some way—when Justin's voice comes from over my shoulder, asking, "So who's this?" If he was relaxed when I saw him in the kitchen, now he's annoyed.

"Don't worry, Justin," Rhiannon says. "He's gay."

"Yeah, I can tell from the way he's dressed. What are you doing here?"

"Nathan, this is Justin, my boyfriend. Justin, this is Nathan."

I say hi. He doesn't respond.

"You seen Stephanie?" he asks Rhiannon. "Steve's looking for her. I think they're at it again."

"Maybe she went to the basement."

"Nah. They're dancing in the basement."

Rhiannon likes this news, I can tell.

"Want to go down there and dance?" she asks Justin.

"Hell no! I didn't come here to dance. I came here to *drink*."

"Charming," Rhiannon says, more (I think) for my benefit than his. "Do you mind if I go dance with Nathan?"

"You sure he's gay?"

"I'll sing you show tunes if you want me to prove it," I volunteer.

Justin slaps me on the back. "No, dude, don't do that, okay? Go dance."

So that's how it comes to pass that Rhiannon is leading me to Steve Mason's basement. As we hit the stairs, we can feel the bass under our feet. It's a different soundtrack here—a tide of pulse and beat. Only a few red lights are on, so all we can see are the outlines of bodies as they meld together.

"Hey, Steve!" Rhiannon calls out. "I like your cousin!"

A guy who must be Steve looks at her and nods. Whether he can't hear what she's said or whether he's trashed, I can't tell.

"Have you seen Stephanie?" he yells.

"No!" Rhiannon yells back.

Then we're in with the dancers. The sad truth is that I have about as much experience on a dance floor as Nathan does. I try to lose myself in the music, but that doesn't work. Instead, I need to lose myself in Rhiannon. I have to give myself over entirely to her—I must be her shadow, her complement, the other half of this conversation of bodies. As she moves, I move with her. I touch her back, her waist. She comes in closer.

By losing myself to her, I gain her. The conversation is working. We have found our rhythm and we are riding it. I find myself singing along, singing to her, and she loves it. She transforms once again into someone carefree, and I transform into someone whose only care is her.

"You're not bad!" she shouts over the music.

"You're amazing!" I shout back.

I know that Justin is not coming down here. She is safe with Steve Mason's gay cousin, and I am safe knowing that nobody else will interfere with this moment. The songs collide into one long song—as if one singer is taking over when the previous one stops, all of them taking turns to give us this. The sound waves push us into each other, wrap around us like colors. We are paying attention to each other and we are paying attention to the enormity. The room has no ceiling; the room has no walls. There is only the open field of our excitement, and we run across it in small movements, sometimes without our feet leaving the ground. We go for what feels like hours and also feels like no time at all. We go until the music stops, until someone turns on the lights and says the party is ending, that the neighbors have complained and the police are probably coming.

Rhiannon looks as disappointed as I feel.

"I have to find Justin," she says. "Are you going to be okay?"

No, I want to tell her. *I won't be okay until you can come with me to wherever it is that I'm going next.*

I ask her for her email address, and when she raises an eyebrow, I tell her again not to worry, that I'm still gay.

"That's too bad," she says. I want her to say more, but then she's giving me her email address, and in response I'm giving her a fake email address that I'll have to set up as soon as I get home.

People are starting to run from the house. Sirens can be heard in the distance, probably waking up as many people as the party has. Rhiannon leaves me to find Justin, promising me that she'll be the one to drive. I don't see them as I run to my car. I know it's late, but I don't know how late it is until I turn on the car and look at the clock.

11:15.

There's no way I'll get there in time.

Seventy miles an hour.

Eighty miles an hour.

Eighty-five.

I drive as fast as I can, but it's not fast enough.

At 11:50, I pull over to the side of the road. If I close my eyes, I should be able to fall asleep before midnight. That is the blessing of what I have to go through—I am able to fall asleep in minutes.

Poor Nathan Daldry. He is going to wake up on the side of an interstate, an hour away from his home. I can only imagine how terrified he'll be.

I am a monster for doing this to him.

But I have my reason.

Day 6000

It's time for Roger Wilson to go to church.

I quickly dress myself in his Sunday best, which either he or his mother conveniently left out the night before. Then I go downstairs and have breakfast with his mother and his three sisters. There's no father in sight. It doesn't take much accessing to know he left just after the youngest daughter was born, and it's been a struggle for their mom ever since.

There's only one computer in the house, and I have to wait until Roger's mother is getting the girls ready to go before I can quickly boot it up and create the email address I gave Rhiannon last night. I can only hope that she hasn't tried to get in touch with me already.

Roger's name is being called—it's church time. I sign off, clear the history, and join my sisters in the car. It takes me a few minutes to get their names straight—Pam is eleven, Lacey is ten, and Jenny is eight. Only Jenny seems excited about going to church.

When we get there, the girls head off to Sunday school while I join Roger's mother in the main congregation. I prepare myself for a Baptist service, and try to remember what makes it different from the other church services I've been to.

I have been to many religious services over the years. Each one I go to only reinforces my general impression that religions have much, much more in common than they like to admit. The beliefs are almost always the same; it's just that the histories are different. Everybody wants to believe in a higher power. Everybody wants to belong to something bigger than themselves, and everybody wants company in doing that. They want there to be a force of good on earth, and they want an incentive to be a part of that force. They want to be able to prove their belief and their belonging, through rituals and devotion. They want to touch the enormity.

It's only in the finer points that it gets complicated and contentious, the inability to realize that no matter what our religion or gender or race or geographic background, we all have about 98 percent in common with each other. Yes, the differences between male and female are biological, but if you look at the biology as a matter of percentage, there aren't a whole lot of things that are different. Race is different purely as a social construction, not as an inherent difference. And religion—whether you believe in God or Yahweh or Allah or something else, odds are that at heart you want the same things. For whatever reason, we like to focus on the 2 percent that's different, and most of the conflict in the world comes from that.

The only way I can navigate through my life is because of the 98 percent that every life has in common.

I think of this as I go through the rituals of a Sunday

morning at church. I keep looking at Roger's mother, who is so tired, so taxed. I feel as much belief in her as I do in God—I find faith in human perseverance, even as the universe throws challenge after challenge our way. This might be one of the things I saw in Rhiannon, too—her desire to persevere.

After church, we head to Roger's grandmother's house for Sunday dinner. There's no computer, and even if it weren't a three-hour drive away, there wouldn't be any way for me to get to Rhiannon. So I take it as a day of rest. I play games with my sisters and make a ring of hands with the rest of my family when it's time to say grace.

The only discord comes when we're driving home and a fight breaks out in the backseat. As sisters, they probably have closer to 99 percent in common, but they're not about to recognize that. They'd rather fight over what kind of pet they're going to get . . . even though I'm not sensing any indication from their mother that a pet is in their near future. It's an argument for its own sake.

When we get home, I bide my time before asking if I can use the computer. It's in a very public place, and I will need everyone to be in another room in order to check my email. While the three girls run around, I retire to Roger's room and do his weekend homework the best that I can. I am banking on the fact that Roger has a later bedtime than his sisters, and in this I am correct. After Sunday supper, the girls get an hour of television in the same room as the computer. Then Roger's mother tells them it's time to get ready for bed. There's much protest, but it falls on deaf ears. This is its own kind of ritual, and Mom always wins.

While Roger's mother is getting the girls into their pajamas and getting out their clothes for tomorrow, I have a few minutes on my own. I quickly check the email I set up in the morning, and there's no message from Rhiannon yet. I decide it can't hurt to be proactive here, so I type in her address and start an email before I can stop myself.

Hi Rhiannon,

I just wanted to say that it was lovely meeting you and dancing with you last night. I'm sorry the police came and separated us. Even though you're not my type, gender-wise, you're certainly my type, person-wise. Please keep in touch.

N

That seems safe enough to me. Clever, but not self-congratulatorially so. Sincere, but not overbearing. It's only a few lines, but I reread it at least a dozen times before I hit send. I let go of the words and wonder what words will come back. If any.

Bedtime seems to be taking a while—it sounds like there's some argument about which chapter their read-aloud left off on—so I load up my personal email.

Such an ordinary gesture. One click, and the instant appearance of the inbox, in all its familiar rows.

But this time it's like walking into a room and finding a bomb right in the middle of it.

There, under a bookstore newsletter, is an incoming message from none other than Nathan Daldry.

The subject line is WARNING.

I read:

> I don't know who you are or what you are or what
> you did to me yesterday, but I want you to know you
> won't get away with it. I will not let you possess me
> or destroy my life. I will not remain quiet. I know what
> happened and I know you must be in some way
> responsible. Leave me alone. I am not your host.

"Are you okay?"

I turn and find Roger's mother in the doorway.

"I'm fine," I say, positioning myself in front of the screen.

"Alright, then. You have ten minutes more, then I want you to help me unload the dishwasher and head to bed. We have a long week ahead of us."

"Okay, Mom. I'll be there in ten minutes."

I turn back to the email. I don't know how to respond, or if I should respond. I have a vague recollection of Nathan's mother interrupting me while I was on the computer—I must have closed the window without clearing the history. So when Nathan loaded up his email, it must have been my address that popped up. But he doesn't know my password, so the account itself should be safe. Just in case, though, I know I need to change my password and move all my old emails, quick.

I will not remain quiet.

I wonder what this means.

. . .

I can't forward all my old emails in the ten minutes that I have, but I start to make a dent in them.

"Roger!"

Roger's mother calls me and I know I have to go. But clearing the history and turning off the computer can't stop my thoughts. I think about Nathan waking up on the side of the road. I try to imagine what he must have felt. But the truth is, I don't know. Did he feel like it was something he had gotten himself into? Or did he immediately know that something was wrong, that someone else had been in control? Was he sure of this when he went to his computer and saw my email address?

Who does he think I am?

What does he think I am?

I head into the kitchen and Roger's mother gives me another look of concern. She and Roger are close, I can tell. She knows how to read her son. Over the years, they've been there for each other. He's helped raise his sisters. And she's raised him.

If I really were Roger, I could tell her everything. If I really were Roger, no matter how hard it was to understand, she would be on my side. Fiercely. Unconditionally.

But I am not really her son, or anyone's son. I can't disclose what's bothering Roger today, because it doesn't have much bearing on who he'll be tomorrow. So I brush off his mother's concern, tell her it's no big deal, then help her take the dishes out of the dishwasher. We work in quiet camaraderie until the task is done, and sleep calls.

For a while, though, I can't go to sleep. I lie in bed, stare at the ceiling. This is the irony: Even though I wake up in a different body every morning, I've always felt in some way that I am in control.

But now I don't feel in control at all.

Now there are other people involved.

Day 6001

The next morning, I am even farther from Rhiannon.

I'm four hours away, and in the body of Margaret Weiss. Luckily, Margaret has a laptop that I can check before we go to school.

There's an email waiting from Rhiannon.

Nathan!

I'm so glad you emailed, because I lost the slip of paper that I wrote your email on. It was wonderful talking and dancing with you, too. How dare the police break us up! You're my type, personwise, too. Even if you don't believe in relationships that last longer than a year. (I'm not saying you're wrong, btw. Jury's still out.)

I never thought I'd say this, but I hope Steve has another party soon. If only so you can bear witness to its evil.

Love,
Rhiannon

I can imagine her smiling when she wrote this, and this makes me smile, too.

Then I open my other account, and there's another email from Nathan.

> I have given the police this email address. Don't think you can get away with this.

The police?

Quickly I type Nathan's name into a search engine. A news item comes up, dated this morning.

THE DEVIL MADE HIM DO IT
Local boy, pulled over by police, claims demonic possession

When police officers found Nathan Daldry, 16, of 22 Arden Lane, sleeping in his vehicle along the side of Route 23 early Sunday morning, they had no idea the story he would tell. Most teenagers would blame their condition on alcohol use, but not Daldry. He claimed no knowledge of how he had gotten where he was. The answer, he said, was that he must have been possessed by a demon.

"It was like I was sleepwalking," Daldry tells the *Crier*. "The whole day, this thing was in charge of my body. It made me lie to my parents and drive to a party in a town I've never been to. I don't really remember the details. I only know it wasn't me."

To make matters more mysterious, Daldry says that

when he returned home, someone else's email was on his computer.

"I wasn't myself," he says.

Officer Lance Houston of the state police says that because there was no sign of alcohol use and because the car wasn't reported stolen, Daldry was not being charged with any offense.

"Look, I'm sure he has reasons for saying what he's saying. All I can tell you is that he didn't do anything illegal," says Houston.

But that's not enough for Daldry.

"If anyone else has experienced this, I want them to come forward," he says. "I can't be the only one."

It's a local paper's website, nothing to worry too much about. And the police don't seem to feel it's a particularly pressing case. But still, I'm worried. In all my years, I've never had someone do this to me before.

It's not that I can't imagine how it happened: Nathan is woken up on the side of the road by a police officer tapping on his window. Maybe there are even flashing lights bathing the darkness in red and blue. Within seconds, Nathan realizes what kind of trouble he's in—it's well past midnight, and his parents are going to kill him. His clothes smell like cigarettes and alcohol, and he has no way of remembering whether or not he was drunk or high. He is a blank—a sleepwalker waking up. Only . . . he has a sense of me. Some lone memory of not being himself. When the officer asks him what's going on, he says he doesn't know. When the officer asks him where he's been, he says he doesn't know. The officer gets him out of the car, makes him take a Breathalyzer test. Nathan proves to be stone-cold sober. But the officer still wants answers, so Nathan tells him the truth—that his body was taken over. Only, he can't imagine anyone who takes over bodies except for the devil. This is going to be his story. He is a good kid—he knows that everybody will back him up on that. They're going to believe him.

The officer just wants him to get home safely. Maybe he even escorts Nathan home, calling ahead to his parents. They're awake when Nathan gets there. They're angry and concerned. He repeats his story to them. They don't know what to believe. Meanwhile, some reporter hears the officer talking about it on the shortwave, or maybe it gets around the station. The teenager who snuck off to a party and then tried to blame it on the devil. The reporter calls the Daldry home on Sunday, and Nathan decides to talk. Because that will make it more real, won't it?

I feel both guilty and defensive. Guilty because I did this to Nathan, whatever my intentions. Defensive because I certainly didn't force him to react in this way, which will only make it worse for him, if not me.

In the one-in-a-million chance that Nathan can persuade someone to trace my emails, I realize I can't check this account from people's homes anymore. Because if he can do that, he'll be able to chart most of the houses I've been in over the past two or three years . . . which will lead to a lot of confusing conversations.

Part of me wants to write back to him, to explain. But I'm not sure any explanation will be enough. Especially because I don't have most of the answers. I gave up on figuring out why a long time ago. I am guessing Nathan won't give up as easily.

Margaret Weiss's boyfriend, Sam, likes to kiss her. A lot. Public, private—it doesn't matter. If he gets a chance to make a move, he does.

I am not in the mood.

Margaret quickly comes down with a cold. The kissing stops, and the doting begins. Sam is rather smitten, and he surrounds Margaret with the sweet quicksand of his love. From recent memories, I can tell that Margaret is usually just as willing to do the same. Everything comes second to being with Sam. It's a miracle that she still has friends.

There's a quiz in science. Judging from my accessing, it appears that I know more about the subject than Margaret does. It's her lucky day.

I am dying to get on one of the school computers, but I have to get rid of Sam first. Even though I've separated them at the lips, I can't seem to get Sam and Margaret separated at the hips. At lunch, he puts one of his hands in her back pocket while he eats, and then pouts when Margaret doesn't do the same thing. They then have study hall together, and he spends all of it stroking her and talking to her about the movie they saw last night.

Eighth period is the only class they don't have together, so I decide to run with it. As soon as Sam drops her off at the classroom door, I have her go to the teacher, say she's going to the nurse, and head straight to the library.

First, I finish forwarding all my emails from my old account.

All that remains are the two emails from Nathan; I can't bring myself to delete them, just as I can't bring myself to delete the account. For some reason, I want him to be able to contact me. I feel that much responsibility.

I load up the new email account, with the intention of writing Rhiannon back. Much to my surprise, there's already another email from her. Giddy, I open it.

> Nathan,
>
> Apparently, Steve doesn't have a cousin Nathan, and none of his cousins were at his party. Care to explain?
>
> Rhiannon

I don't deliberate. I don't weigh my options. I just type and hit send.

> Rhiannon,
>
> I can, indeed, explain. Can we meet up? It's the kind of explanation that needs to be done in person.
>
> Love,
> Nathan

It's not that I'm planning to tell the truth. I just want to give myself time to think of the best lie.

The last bell rings, and I know Sam will be looking for

Margaret soon. When I find him at his locker, he acts as if we haven't seen each other in weeks. When I kiss him, I pretend I am practicing for Rhiannon. When I kiss him, it feels almost disloyal to Rhiannon. When I kiss him, my mind is hours away, with her.

Day 6002

The universe, it seems, is on my side the next morning, because when I wake up in the body of Megan Powell, I also wake up a mere hour away from Rhiannon.

Then, when I check my email, there's a message from her.

Nathan,

This better be a good explanation. I'll meet you in the coffee shop at the Clover Bookstore at 5.

Rhiannon

To which I reply:

Rhiannon,

I'll be there. Although not in a way you might expect. Bear with me and hear me out.

A

Megan Powell is going to have to leave cheerleading practice a little early today. I go through her closet and pick the outfit that most looks like something Rhiannon would wear; I've found that people tend to trust other people who dress like them. And whatever I do, I am going to need all the trust I can get.

The whole day, I think about what I'm going to say to her, and what she's going to say. It feels entirely dangerous to tell her the truth. I have never told anyone the truth. I have never come close.

But none of the lies fit well. And the more I stumble through possible lies, I realize I am heading in the direction of telling her everything. I am learning that a life isn't real unless someone else knows its reality. And I want my life to be real.

If I've gotten used to my life, could somebody else?

If she believes in me, if she feels the enormity like I do, she will believe in this.

And if she doesn't believe in me, if she doesn't feel the enormity, then I will simply seem like one more crazy person let loose on the world.

There's not much to lose in that.

But, of course, it will feel like losing everything.

I manufacture a doctor's appointment for Megan, and at four o'clock, I'm on the road to Rhiannon's town.

There's some traffic, and I get a little lost, so I'm ten minutes late to the bookstore. I look in the café window and see her sitting there, flipping through a magazine, looking up at the door every now and then. I want to keep her like this, hold her in this moment. I know everything is about to change, and I fear that one day I will long for this minute before anything is said, that I will want to travel back in time and undo what's coming next.

Megan is not, of course, who Rhiannon's looking for. So she's a little startled when I come over to her table and sit down.

"I'm sorry—that seat's taken," she says.

"It's okay," I tell her. "Nathan sent me."

"He sent you? Where is he?" Rhiannon is looking around the room, as if he's hiding somewhere behind a bookshelf.

I look around, too. There are other people near us, but none of them seem to be within earshot. I know I should ask Rhiannon to take a walk with me, that there shouldn't be any people around when I tell her. But I don't know why she'd go with me, and it would probably scare her if I asked. I will have to tell her here.

"Rhiannon," I say. I look in her eyes, and I feel it again. That connection. That feeling of so much beyond us. That recognition.

I don't know if she feels it, too, not for sure, but she stays where she is. She returns my gaze. She holds the connection.

"Yes?" she whispers.

"I need to tell you something. It's going to sound very, very strange. What I need is for you to listen to the whole story. You will probably want to leave. You might want to laugh. But I need you to take this seriously. I know it will sound unbelievable, but it's the truth. Do you understand?"

There is fear in her eyes now. I want to reach out my hand and hold hers, but I know I can't. Not yet.

I keep my voice calm. True.

"Every morning, I wake up in a different body. It's been happening since I was born. This morning, I woke up as Megan Powell, who you see right in front of you. Three days ago, last Saturday, it was Nathan Daldry. Two days before that, it was Amy Tran, who visited your school and spent the day with you. And last Monday, it was Justin, your boyfriend. You thought you went to the ocean with him, but it was really me. That was the first time we ever met, and I haven't been able to forget you since."

I pause.

"You're kidding me, right?" Rhiannon says. "You have to be kidding."

I press on. "When we were on the beach, you told me about the mother-daughter fashion show that you and your mother were in, and how it was probably the last time you ever saw her in makeup. When Amy asked you to tell her about something you'd never told anyone else, you told her about trying to pierce your own ear when you were ten, and she told you about reading Judy Blume's *Forever*. Nathan came over to you as you were sorting through CDs, and he sang a song that you and Justin sang during the car ride to the ocean. He told you he was Steve's cousin, but he was really there to see you. He talked to you about being in a relationship for over a year, and you told him that deep down Justin cares a lot about you, and he said that deep down isn't good enough. What I'm saying is that . . . all of these people were me. For a day. And now I'm Megan Powell, and I want to tell you the truth before I switch again.

Because I think you're remarkable. Because I don't want to keep meeting you as different people. I want to meet you as myself."

I look at the disbelief on her face, searching for one small possibility of belief. I can't find it.

"Did Justin put you up to this?" she says, disgust in her voice. "Do you really think this is funny?"

"No, it's not funny," I say. "It's true. I don't expect you to understand right away. I know how crazy it sounds. But it's true. I swear, it's true."

"I don't understand why you're doing this. I don't even know you!"

"Listen to me. Please. You know it wasn't Justin with you that day. In your heart, you know. He didn't act like Justin. He didn't do things Justin does. That's because it was me. I didn't mean to do it. I didn't mean to fall in love with you. But it happened. And I can't erase it. I can't ignore it. I have lived my whole life like this, and you're the thing that has made me wish it could stop."

The fear is still there in her face, in her body. "But why me? That makes no sense."

"Because you're amazing. Because you're kind to a random girl who just shows up at your school. Because you also want to be on the other side of the window, living life instead of just thinking about it. Because you're beautiful. Because when I was dancing with you in Steve's basement on Saturday night, it felt like fireworks. And when I was lying on the beach next to you, it felt like perfect calm. I know you think that Justin loves you deep down, but I love you through and through."

"Enough!" Rhiannon's voice breaks a little as she raises it. "It's just—enough, okay? I think I understand what you're saying to me, even though it makes *no sense whatsoever*."

"You know it wasn't him that day, don't you?"

"I don't know anything!" This is loud enough that a few people look our way. Rhiannon notices, and lowers her voice again. "I don't know. I really don't know."

She's near tears. I reach out and take her hand. She doesn't like it, but she doesn't pull away.

"I know it's a lot," I tell her. "Believe me, I know."

"It's not possible," she whispers.

"It is. I'm the proof."

When I pictured this conversation in my head, I could imagine it going in two ways: revelation or revulsion. But now we're stuck somewhere in between. She doesn't think I'm telling the truth—not to the point that she can believe it. And at the same time, she hasn't stormed out, she hasn't maintained that it's just a sick joke someone is playing on her.

I realize: I am not going to convince her. Not like this. Not here.

"Look," I say, "what if we met here again tomorrow at the same time? I won't be in the same body, but I'll be the same person. Would that make it easier to understand?"

She's skeptical. "But couldn't you just tell someone else to come here?"

"Yes, but why would I? This isn't a prank. This isn't a joke. It's my life."

"You're insane."

"You're just saying that. You know I'm not. You can sense that much."

Now it's her turn to look me in the eye. Judge me. See what connection she can find.

"What's your name?" she asks.

"Today I'm Megan Powell."

"No. I mean your real name."

My breath catches. Nobody has ever asked me this before. And I've certainly never offered it.

"A," I say.

"Just A?"

"Just A. I came up with it when I was a little kid. It was a way of keeping myself whole, even as I went from body to body, life to life. I needed something pure. So I went with the letter A."

"What do you think about my name?"

"I told you the other night. I think it's beautiful, even if you once found it hard to spell."

She stands up from her chair. I stand up, too.

She holds there. I can tell there are lots of thoughts she's considering, but I have no idea what they are. Falling in love with someone doesn't mean you know any better how they feel. It only means you know how you feel.

"Rhiannon," I say.

She holds up her hand for me to stop.

"No more," she tells me. "Not now. Tomorrow. I'll give you

tomorrow. Because that's one way to know, isn't it? If what you say is happening is really happening—I mean, I need more than a day."

"Thank you," I tell her.

"Don't thank me until I show up," she says. "This is all really confusing."

"I know."

She puts on her jacket and starts heading for the door. Then she turns around to me one last time.

"The thing is," she says, "I didn't really feel it was him that day. Not completely. And ever since then, it's like he wasn't there. He has no memory of it. There are a million possible explanations for that, but there it is."

"There it is," I agree.

She shakes her head.

"Tomorrow," I say.

"Tomorrow," she says, a little less than a promise, and a little more than a chance.

Day 6003

I am not alone when I wake up the next morning.

I am sharing the room with two other boys—my brothers, Paul and Tom. Paul is a year older than me. Tom is my twin. My name is James.

James is big—a football player. Tom is about the same size. Paul is even bigger.

The room is clean, but even before I know what town I'm in, I know we're not in the nice part of it. This is a big family in a small house. There is not going to be a computer here. James is not going to have a car.

It's Paul's job—self-appointed or otherwise—to get us up and out. Our father's not home from the night shift yet, and our mother's already on the way to her job. Our two sisters are about done with the bathroom. We're next.

I access and find that I'm in the town next to Nathan's, over an hour from Rhiannon's.

This is going to be a hard day.

• • •

The bus ride to school takes forty-five minutes. When we get there, we head to the cafeteria for free breakfast. I am amazed at James's appetite—I pile on pancake after pancake, and he's still hungry. Tom matches him bite for bite.

Luckily, I have study hall first period. Unluckily, there's still homework that James needs to do. I push through that as quick as I can, and have about ten minutes of computer time left at the end.

There's a message from Rhiannon, written at one in the morning.

A,

I want to believe you, but I don't know how.

Rhiannon

I write back:

Rhiannon,

You don't need to know how. You just make up your mind and it happens.

I am in Laurel right now, over an hour away. I am in the body of a football player named James. I know how strange that sounds. But, like everything I've told you, it's the truth.

Love,
A

There's just enough time for me to check my other email address. There's another email from Nathan.

> You can't avoid my questions forever. I want to know
> who you are. I want to know why you do what you do.
>
> Tell me.

Again, I leave him unanswered. I have no idea whether I owe him an explanation or not. I probably owe him something. But I'm not sure it's an explanation.

I make it through to lunch. I want to go immediately to the library to check the computers again. But James is hungry, and Tom is with him, and I am afraid that if he doesn't get his lunch now, there won't be anything for him to eat until dinnertime. I checked, and there's only about three dollars in his wallet, including change.

I get the free lunch and eat it quickly. Then I excuse myself to the library, which inspires no shortage of taunts from Tom, who claims that "libraries are for girls." A true brother, I shoot back with, "Well, that explains why you never find any." A wrestling match ensues. All of this takes away time from what I need to do.

When I get to the library, all the computers are taken. I have to loom large over a freshman for about two minutes before he freaks out enough to give me his space. Quickly I check out public transportation, and find out I'll need to take three buses in order to make it to Rhiannon's town. I'm ready to do it, but when I check my email, there's another message from Rhiannon, dated just two minutes ago.

A,

Do you have a car? If not, I can come to you. There's a Starbucks in Laurel. I'm told that nothing bad ever happens in a Starbucks. Let me know if you want to meet there.

Rhiannon

I type:

Rhiannon,

I would appreciate it if you could come here. Thank you.

A

Two minutes later, a new email from her:

A,

I'll be there at 5. Can't wait to see what you look like today.

(Still not believing this.)

Rhiannon

My nerves are jangling with possibility. She's had time to think about it, and that hasn't turned her against me. It's more than I could ask for. I am careful not to be too grateful, lest it be taken away.

The rest of the school day is unexceptional . . . except for a moment in seventh period. Mrs. French, the bio teacher, is hectoring a kid who hasn't done his homework. It's a lab assignment, and he's come up blank.

"I don't know what got into me," the slacker says. "I must have been possessed by the devil!"

The rest of the class laughs, and even Mrs. French shakes her head.

"Yeah, I was possessed by the devil, too," another guy says. "After I drank seven beers!"

"Okay, class," Mrs. French intones. "Enough of that."

It's the way they say it—I know Nathan's story must be spreading.

"Hey," I say to Tom as we head to football practice, "did you hear about that kid in Monroeville who says he was possessed by the devil?"

"Dude," he replies, "we were just talking about that yesterday. It was all over the news."

"Yeah, I mean, did you hear anything more about it today?"

"What more is there to say? Kid got caught in a crazy lie,

and now the religious crazies want to make him a poster child. I almost feel sorry for him."

This, I think, is not good.

Our coach has to go to his wife's Lamaze class, which he bitches about to us in detail, but it forces him to end practice early. I tell Tom that I'm going to make a Starbucks run, and he looks at me like I have been totally, irredeemably girlified. I was counting on his disgust, and am relieved to get it.

She's not there when I arrive, so I get a small black coffee—pretty much the only thing I can afford—and sit and wait for her. It's crowded, and I have to look brutish in order to keep the other chair at my table unoccupied.

Finally, about twenty minutes after five, she shows up. She scans the crowd and I wave. Even though I told her I was a football player, she's still a little startled. She comes over anyway.

"Okay," she says, sitting down. "Before we say another word, I want to see your phone." I must look confused, because she adds, "I want to see every single call you've made in the past week, and every single call you received. If this isn't some big joke, then you have nothing to hide."

I hand over James's phone, which she knows how to work better than I do.

After a few minutes of searching, she appears satisfied.

"Now, I quiz you," she says, handing back the phone. "First, what was I wearing on the day that Justin took me to the beach?"

I try to picture it. I try to grab hold of those details. But they've already eluded me. I remember her, not what she was wearing.

"I don't know," I say. "Do you remember what Justin was wearing?"

She thinks about it for a second. "Good point. Did we make out?"

I shake my head. "We used the make-out blanket, but we didn't make out. We kissed. And that was enough."

"And what did I say to you before I left the car?"

"'That's the nice note.'"

"Correct. Quick, what's Steve's girlfriend's name?"

"Stephanie."

"And what time did the party end?"

"Eleven-fifteen."

"And when you were in the body of that girl who I took to all of my classes, what did the note you passed me say?"

"Something like, 'The classes here are just as boring as in the school I'm going to now.'"

"And what were the buttons on your backpack that day?"

"Anime kittens."

"Well, either you're an excellent liar, or you switch bodies every day. I have no idea which one is true."

"It's the second one."

I see, over Rhiannon's shoulder, a woman looking at us quizzically. Has she overheard what we're saying?

"Let's go outside," I whisper. "I feel we may be getting an unintended audience."

Rhiannon looks skeptical. "Maybe if you were a petite

cheerleader again. But—I'm not sure if you fully realize this—you're a big, threatening dude today. My mother's voice is very loud and clear in my head: 'No dark corners.'"

I point out the window, to a bench along the road.

"Totally public, only without people listening in."

"Fine."

As we head out, the woman who was eavesdropping seems disappointed. I realize how many people sitting around us have open laptops and open notebooks, and hope that none of them have been taking notes.

When we get to the bench, Rhiannon lets me sit down first, so she can determine the distance that we'll sit apart, which is significant.

"So you say you've been like this since the day you were born?"

"Yes. I can't remember it being any different."

"So how did that work? Weren't you confused?"

"I guess I got used to it. I'm sure that, at first, I figured it was just how everybody's lives worked. I mean, when you're a baby, you don't really care much about who's taking care of you, as long as someone's taking care of you. And as a little kid, I thought it was some kind of a game, and my mind learned how to access—you know, look at the body's memories—naturally. So I always knew what my name was, and where I was. It wasn't until I was four or five that I started to realize I was different, and it wasn't until I was nine or ten that I really wanted it to stop."

"You did?"

"Of course. Imagine being homesick, but without having a

home. That's what it was like. I wanted friends, a mom, a dad, a dog—but I couldn't hold on to any of them more than a single day. It was brutal. There are nights I remember screaming and crying, begging my parents not to make me go to bed. They could never figure out what I was afraid of. They thought it was a monster under the bed, or a ploy to get a few more bedtime stories. I could never really explain, not in a way that made sense to them. I'd tell them I didn't want to say goodbye, and they'd assure me it wasn't goodbye. It was just good night. I'd tell them it was the same thing, but they thought I was being silly.

"Eventually I came to peace with it. I had to. I realized that this was my life, and there was nothing I could do about it. I couldn't fight the tide, so I decided to float along."

"How many times have you told this story?"

"None. I swear. You're the first."

This should make her feel special—it's meant to make her feel special—but instead it seems to worry her.

"You have to have parents, don't you? I mean, we all have parents."

I shrug. "I have no idea. I would think so. But it's not like there's anyone I can ask. I've never met anyone else like me. Not that I would necessarily know."

It's clear from her expression that she thinks this is a sad story I'm telling her—a very sad story. I don't know how to convey to her that it hasn't all been sad.

"I've glimpsed things," I say. Then I stop. I don't know what's next.

"Go on," she tells me.

"It's just—I know it sounds like an awful way to live, but I've seen so many things. It's so hard when you're in one body to get a sense of what life is really like. You're so grounded in who you are. But when who you are changes every day—you get to touch the universal more. Even the most mundane details. You see how cherries taste different to different people. Blue looks different. You see all the strange rituals boys have to show affection without admitting it. You learn that if a parent reads to you at the end of the day, it's a good sign that it's a good parent, because you've seen so many other parents who don't make the time. You learn how much a day is truly worth, because they're all so different. If you ask most people what the difference was between Monday and Tuesday, they might tell you what they had for dinner each night. Not me. By seeing the world from so many angles, I get more of a sense of its dimensionality."

"But you never get to see things over time, do you?" Rhiannon asks. "I don't mean to cancel out what you just said. I think I understand that. But you've never had a friend that you've known day in and day out for ten years. You've never watched a pet grow older. You've never seen how messed up a parent's love can be over time. And you've never been in a relationship for more than a day, not to mention for more than a year."

I should have known it would come back to that.

"But I've seen things," I tell her. "I've observed. I know how it works."

"From the outside? I don't think you can know from the outside."

"I think you underestimate how predictable some things can be in a relationship."

"I love him," she says. "I know you don't understand, but I do."

"You shouldn't. I've seen him from the inside. I know."

"For a day. You saw him for a day."

"And for a day, you saw who he could be. You fell more in love with him when he was me."

I reach out again for her hand, but this time she says, "No. Don't."

I freeze.

"I have a boyfriend," she says. "I know you don't like him, and I'm sure there are moments when I don't like him, either. But that's the reality. Now, I'll admit, you have me actually thinking that you are, in fact, the same person who I've now met in five different bodies. All this means is that I'm probably as insane as you are. I know you say you love me, but you don't really know me. You've known me a week. And I need a little more than that."

"But didn't you feel it that day? On the beach? Didn't everything seem right?"

There it is again—the pull of the ocean, the song of the universe. A better liar would deny it. But some of us don't want to live our lives as liars. She bites her lip and nods.

"Yes. But I don't know who I was feeling that for. Even if I believe it was you, you have to understand that my history with Justin plays into it. I wouldn't have felt that way with a stranger. It wouldn't have been so perfect."

"How do you know?"

"That's my point. I don't."

She looks at her phone, and whether or not she truly needs to leave, I know this is the sign that she's going to.

"I have to make it back for dinner," she says.

"Thanks for driving all this way," I tell her.

It's awkward. So awkward.

"Will I see you again?" I ask.

She nods.

"I'm going to prove it to you," I tell her. "I'm going to show you what it really means."

"What?"

"Love."

Is she scared by this? Embarrassed? Hopeful?

I don't know. I'm not close enough to tell.

Tom gives me no small amount of grief when I get home— partly because I went to Starbucks, and partly because I then had to walk two miles to get back home, and was late for dinner, which our father roundly chewed me out over.

"I hope whoever she was, she was worth it," Tom taunts.

I look at him blankly.

"Dude, don't try to tell me you were just going for the coffee or the folk tunes they play on the speakers. I know you better than that."

I remain silent.

I am assigned to wash all the dishes. While doing so, I turn on the radio, and when the local news comes on, Nathan Daldry comes with it.

"So tell us, Nathan, what you experienced last Saturday," the interviewer says.

"I was possessed. There's no other word for it. I wasn't in control of my own body. I consider myself lucky to be alive. And I want to ask anyone else who's ever been possessed like this, just for a day, to contact me. Because, I'll be honest with you, Chuck, a lot of people think I'm crazy. Other kids at school are making fun of me constantly. But I know what happened. And I know I'm not the only one."

I know I'm not the only one.

This is the sentence that haunts me. I wish I felt the same certainty.

I wish I weren't the only one.

Day 6004

The next morning I wake up in the same room.

In the same body.

I can't believe it. I don't understand. After all these years.

I look at the wall. My hands. The sheets.

And then I look to my side and see James sleeping there in his bed.

James.

And I realize: I'm not in the same body. I'm not on the same side of the room.

No, this morning I'm his twin, Tom.

I have never had this chance before. I watch as James emerges from sleep, emerges from a day away from his old body. I am looking for the traces of that oblivion, the bafflement of that waking. But what I get is the familiar scene of a football player stretching himself into the day. If he feels at all strange, at all different, he's not showing it.

"Dude, what are you staring at?"

This doesn't come from James, but from our other brother, Paul.

"Just getting up," I mumble.

But really, I don't take my eyes off James. Not through the ride to school. Not at breakfast. He seems a little out of it now, but nothing that couldn't be explained by a bad night's sleep.

"How're you doing?" I ask him.

He grunts. "Fine. Thanks for caring."

I decide to play dumb. He expects me to be dumb, so it shouldn't be much of a stretch.

"What did you do after practice yesterday?" I ask.

"I went to Starbucks."

"Who with?"

He looks at me like I've just sung the question to him in falsetto.

"I just wanted coffee, okay? I wasn't *with* anyone."

I study him, to see if he's trying to cover his conversation with Rhiannon. I don't think, though, that such duplicity would be anything but obvious on him.

He really doesn't remember seeing her. Talking to her. Being with her.

"Then why'd it take so long?" I ask him.

"What, were you timing it? I'm *touched*."

"Well, who were you emailing at lunch?"

"I was just checking my email."

"Your own email?"

"Who else's email would I be checking? You're asking seriously weird questions, dude. Isn't he, Paul?"

Paul chews on some bacon. "I swear, whenever you two talk, I just tune it right out. I have no idea what you're saying."

Paradoxically, I wish I were still in James's body, so I could see exactly what his memories of yesterday are. From where I sit, it appears that he recalls the places he was, but has somehow concocted an alternate version of events, one that fits closer to his life. Has his mind done this, some kind of adaptation? Or did my mind, right before it left, leave behind this story line?

James does not feel like he was possessed by the devil.

He thinks yesterday was just another day.

Again, the morning becomes a search to find a few minutes' worth of email access.

I should have given her my phone number, I think.

Then I stop myself. I stand there right in the middle of the hallway, shocked. It's such a mundane, ordinary observation— but that's what stops me. In the context of my life, it's nonsensical. There was no way for me to give her a phone number. I know this. And yet, the ordinary thought crept in, made me trick myself for a moment into thinking that I, too, was ordinary.

I have no idea what this means, but I suspect it's dangerous.

At lunch, I tell James I'm going to the library.

"Dude," he says, "libraries are for girls."

•   •   •

There aren't any new messages from Rhiannon, so I write to her instead.

> Rhiannon,
>
> You'd actually recognize me today. I woke up as James's twin. I thought this might help me figure things out, but so far, no luck.
>
> I want to see you again.
>
> A

There isn't anything from Nathan, either. Once more I decide to type his name into a search engine, figuring there might be a few more articles about what he's saying.

I find over two thousand results. All from the past three days.

Word is spreading. Mostly from evangelical Christian sites, which have bought Nathan's devil claims wholesale. He is, for them, just another example of the world going to H-E-double-hockey-sticks.

From what I can recall, none of the many versions I heard as a child of "The Boy Who Cried Wolf" spent that much time pondering the emotional state of the boy, especially after the wolf finally showed up. I want to know what Nathan is thinking, if he really believes what he's saying. None of the articles and blogs are any help—he's saying the same thing in all of them, and people are painting him as either a freak or an oracle. Nobody's sitting him down and treating him like a sixteen-year-old boy. They are missing the real questions in order to ask the sensational ones.

I open up his last email.

> You can't avoid my questions forever. I want to know
> who you are. I want to know why you do what you do.
>
> Tell me.

But how can I respond without confirming at least part of the story he's created? I feel that he's right—in some way, I can't avoid his questions forever. They will start to dig into me. They will follow me wherever I wake up. But to give him any answer will give him a reassurance I know I shouldn't give. It will keep him on his path.

My best bet is for him to start feeling that he is, indeed, crazy. Which is an awful thing to wish upon someone. Especially when he's not crazy.

I want to ask Rhiannon what to do. But I can imagine what she'd say. Or maybe I'm just projecting my better self onto her. Because I know the answer: Self-preservation isn't worth it if you can't live with the self you're preserving.

I am responsible for his situation. So he's become my responsibility.

I know this, even as I hate it.

I'm not going to write immediately. I need to give it some thought. I need to help him without confirming anything.

Finally, by last period, I think I have it.

> I know who you are. I've seen your story on the news.
> It doesn't have anything to do with me—you must have
> made a mistake.
>
> Still, it appears to me that you're not considering all the
> possibilities. I'm sure what happened to you was very
> stressful. But blaming the devil is not the answer.

I send it off quickly before football practice.
I also check for an email from Rhiannon.
Nothing.

The rest of the day is uneventful. And I find myself wondering once again when I started to think my days would contain actual events. Up until now, I have lived for uneventfulness, and have found smaller satisfaction in the art of getting by. I resent that the hours seem boring now, emptier. Going through the motions gives you plenty of time to examine the motions. I used to find this interesting. Now it has taken on the taint of meaninglessness.

I practice football. I get a ride home. I do some homework. I eat some dinner. I watch TV with my family.

This is the trap of having something to live for:
Everything else seems lifeless.

James and I go to bed first. Paul is in the kitchen, talking to our mother about his work schedule for the weekend. James and I don't say anything as we change into our sleep clothes, as we parade to the bathroom and back.

I get in bed and he turns out the light. I expect to hear him getting into bed next, but instead he hovers in the middle of the room.

"Tom?"

"Yeah?"

"Why did you ask me about what I was up to yesterday?"

I sit up. "I don't know. You just seemed a little . . . off."

"I just thought it was strange. You asking, I mean."

He heads to his bed now. I hear his weight fall on the mattress.

"So nothing seemed off to you?" I ask, hoping that there will be something—anything—that rises to the surface.

"Not that I can think of. I thought it was pretty funny that Snyder had to end practice so he could go, like, learn how to help his babymama breathe. But I think that was the highlight. It's just . . . do I seem off today, too?"

The truth is that I haven't been paying that much attention, not since breakfast.

"Why do you ask?"

"No reason. I feel fine. I just don't, you know, want to look like there's something wrong when there's nothing wrong."

"You seem fine," I assure him.

"Good," he says, shifting his body, getting into the right position with his pillow.

I want to say more, but don't know what the words are supposed to be. I feel such a tenderness for these vulnerable night-time conversations, the way words take a different shape in the air when there's no light in the room. I think of the rare jackpot nights when I ended the day at a sleepover or sharing the room with a sibling or a friend I genuinely liked. Those conversations could trick me into believing I could say anything, even though there was so much I was holding back. Eventually the night would take its hold, but it would always feel like I was fading to sleep rather than falling.

"Good night," I say to James. But what I really feel is goodbye. I am leaving here, leaving this family. It's only been two days, but that's twice what I'm used to. It's just a hint—the smallest hint—of what it would be like to wake up in the same place every morning.

I have to let that go.

Day 6005

Some people think mental illness is a matter of mood, a matter of personality. They think depression is simply a form of being sad, that OCD is a form of being uptight. They think the soul is sick, not the body. It is, they believe, something that you have some choice over.

I know how wrong this is.

When I was a child, I didn't understand. I would wake up in a new body and wouldn't comprehend why things felt muted, dimmer. Or the opposite—I'd be supercharged, unfocused, like a radio at top volume flipping quickly from station to station. Since I didn't have access to the body's emotions, I assumed the ones I was feeling were my own. Eventually, though, I realized these inclinations, these compulsions, were as much a part of the body as its eye color or its voice. Yes, the feelings themselves were intangible, amorphous, but the cause of the feelings was a matter of chemistry, biology.

It is a hard cycle to conquer. The body is working against you. And because of this, you feel even more despair. Which only amplifies the imbalance. It takes uncommon strength to live with these things. But I have seen that strength over and over again. When I fall into the life of someone grappling, I have to mirror their strength, and sometimes surpass it, because I am less prepared.

I know the signs now. I know when to look for the pill bottles, when to let the body take its course. I have to keep reminding myself—*this is not me*. It is chemistry. It is biology. It is not who I am. It is not who any of them are.

Kelsea Cook's mind is a dark place. Even before I open my eyes, I know this. Her mind is an unquiet one, words and thoughts and impulses constantly crashing into each other. My own thoughts try to assert themselves within this noise. The body responds by breaking into a sweat. I try to remain calm, but the body conspires against that, tries to drown me in distortion.

It is not usually this bad, first thing in the morning. If it's this bad now, it must be pretty bad at all times.

Underneath the distortion is a desire for pain. I open my eyes and see the scars. Not just on the body, although those are there—the hairline fractures across the skin, the web you create to catch your own death. The scars are in the room as well, across the walls, along the floor. The person who lives here no longer cares about anything. Posters hang half-ripped. The mirror is cracked. Clothes lay abandoned. The shades are drawn. The books sit crooked on shelves, like rows of neglected teeth. At one point she must have broken open a pen and spun it around, because if you look closely, you can see small, dried drops of ink all over the walls and ceiling.

I access her history and am shocked to realize that she's

gotten this far without any notice, without any diagnosis. She has been left to her own devices, and those devices are broken.

It is five in the morning. I have woken up without any alarm. I have woken up because the thoughts are so loud, and none of them mean me well.

I struggle to get back to sleep, but the body won't let me.

Two hours later, I get out of bed.

Depression has been likened to both a black cloud and a black dog. For someone like Kelsea, the black cloud is the right metaphor. She is surrounded by it, immersed within it, and there is no obvious way out. What she needs to do is try to contain it, get it into the form of the black dog. It will still follow her around wherever she goes; it will always be there. But at least it will be separate, and will follow her lead.

I stumble into the bathroom and start the shower.

"What are you doing?" a male voice calls. "Didn't you shower last night?"

I don't care. I need the sensation of water hitting my body. I need this prompt to start my day.

When I leave the bathroom, Kelsea's father is in the hallway, glaring at me.

"Get dressed," he says with a scowl. I hold my towel tighter around me.

Once I've got my clothes on, I gather my books for school. There's a journal in Kelsea's backpack, but I don't have time to read it. I also don't have time to check my email. Even though he's in the other room, I can sense Kelsea's father waiting.

It's just the two of them. I access and find Kelsea's lied to him in order to be driven to school—she said that the route had been redrawn, but really she doesn't want to be trapped in the bus with other kids. It's not that she's bullied—she's too busy bullying herself to notice. The problem is the confinement, the inability to leave.

Her father's car isn't much better, but at least there's only one other person she has to deal with. Even when we're moving, he doesn't stop exuding impatience. I am always amazed by people who know something is wrong but still insist on ignoring it, as if that will somehow make it go away. They spare themselves the confrontation, but end up boiling in resentment anyway.

She needs your help, I want to say. But it's not my place to say it, especially because I'm not sure he'll react in the right way.

So Kelsea remains silent the whole drive. From her father's response to this silence, I can imagine this is how their mornings always go.

Kelsea has email access on her phone, but I'm still worried about anything being traced, especially after my slip-up with Nathan.

So I walk the halls and go to classes, waiting for my chance. I have to push harder to get Kelsea through the day. Any time I let it, the weight of living creeps in and starts to drag her down. It would be too easy to say that I feel invisible. Instead, I feel painfully visible, and entirely ignored. People talk to her, but it feels like they are outside a house, talking through the walls. There are friends, but they are people to spend time with, not people to share time with. There's a false beast that takes the form of instinct and harps on the pointlessness of everything that happens.

The only person who tries to engage me is Kelsea's lab partner, Lena. We're in physics class, and the assignment is to set up a pulley system. I've done this before, so it doesn't strike me as hard. Lena, however, is surprised by Kelsea's involvement. I realize I've overstepped—this is not the kind of thing Kelsea would get excited about. But Lena doesn't let me back down. When I try to mumble apologies and step away, she insists I keep going.

"You're good at this," she says. "Much better than I am."

While I arrange things, adjusting inclines and accounting for various forms of friction, Lena talks to me about a dance that's coming up, asks me if I have any weekend plans, and tells me she might be going to DC with her parents. She seems hypersensitive to my reaction, and I'm guessing the conversation usually gets shut down long before this point. But I let her talk, let her voice counter the unspoken, insistent ones that emanate from my broken mind.

Then the period is over, and we go our separate ways. I don't see her again for the rest of the day.

I spend lunchtime in the library at the computer. I don't imagine anyone at lunch will miss me—but maybe that's just what Kelsea would think. Part of growing up is making sure your sense of reality isn't entirely grounded in your own mind; I feel Kelsea's mind isn't letting her get anywhere near that point, and I wonder how much of my own thoughts are getting stuck there as well.

Logging into my own email is a nice jolt to remind me that I am in fact me, not Kelsea. Even better, there is word from Rhiannon—the sight of which cheers me up, until I read what the email says.

A,

So, who are you today?

What a strange question to ask. But I guess it makes sense. If any of this makes sense.

Yesterday was a hard day. Justin's grandmother is sick, but instead of admitting he's upset about it, he just lashes out at the world more. I'm trying to help him, but it's hard.

I don't know if you want to hear this or not. I know how you feel about Justin. If you want me to keep that part of my life hidden from you, I can. But I don't think that's what you want.

Tell me how your day is going.

Rhiannon

I reply and tell her a little about what Kelsea is up against. Then I end with this:

I want you to be honest with me. Even if it hurts.
Although I would prefer for it not to hurt.

Love,
A

Next, I switch accounts and find a reply from Nathan.

I know I haven't made a mistake. I know what you are.
And I will find out who you are. The reverend says he
is working on that.

You want me to doubt myself. But I am not the only
one. You will see.

Confess now, before we find you.

I stare at the screen for a minute, trying to reconcile the
tone of this email with the Nathan I knew for a day. It feels
like two very different people. I wonder if it's possible that
someone else has taken over Nathan's account. I wonder who
"the reverend" is.

The bell rings, marking the end of the lunch period. I return to class and the black cloud takes hold. I find it hard to
concentrate on what's being said. I find it hard to see how any
of this is important. Nothing I'm being taught here will make
life less painful. None of the people in this room will make life
less painful. I attack my cuticles with merciless precision. It is
the only sensation that feels genuine.

• • •

Kelsea's father is not going to pick her up after school; he's still at work. Instead, she walks home, in order to avoid the bus. I am tempted to break this pattern, but it's been so long since she's ridden the bus that she has no memory of which bus is hers. So I start to walk.

Again, I find myself wishing for the mundane possibility of calling Rhiannon on the phone, for filling the next empty hour with the sound of her voice.

But instead, all I am left with is Kelsea and her damaged perceptions. The walk home is a steep one, and I wonder if it's yet another way she punishes herself. After about a half hour, with another half hour in front of me, I decide to stop at a playground I'm about to pass. The parents there give me wary looks because I am not a parent or a little kid, so I steer clear of the jungle gym, the swings, and the sandbox, and end up on the outer ring, on a seesaw that looks like it's been banished from everything else for bad behavior.

There's homework I could do, but Kelsea's journal calls out to me instead. I'm a little afraid of what I'll find inside, but mostly I'm curious. If I can't access the things she's felt, I will at least be able to read a partial transcript.

It's not a journal in the traditional sense. That becomes apparent after a page or two. There are no musings about boys or girls. There are no revisited scenes of discord with her father or her teachers. There are no secrets shared or injustices vented.

Instead, there are ways to kill yourself, listed with extraordinary detail.

Knives to the heart. Knives to the arm. Belts around the neck. Plastic bags. Hard falls. Death by burning. All of them methodically researched. Examples given. Illustrations provided—rough illustrations where the test case is clearly Kelsea. Self-portraits of her own demise.

I flip to the end, past pages of dosages and special instructions. There are still blank pages at the back, but before them is a page that reads *DEADLINE*, followed by a date that's only six days away.

I look through the rest of the notebook, trying to find other, failed deadlines.

But there's only the one.

I get off the seesaw, back away from the park. Because now I feel like I am the thing the parents are afraid of, I am the reality they want to avoid. No, not just avoid—*prevent*. They don't want me anywhere near their children, and I don't blame them. It feels as if everything I touch will turn to harm.

I don't know what to do. There's no threat in the present— I am in control of the body, and as long as I am in control of the body, I will not allow it to hurt itself. But I will not be in control six days from now.

I know I am not supposed to interfere. It is Kelsea's life, not mine. It is unfair of me to do something that limits her choices, that makes up her mind for her.

My childish impulse is to wish I hadn't opened the journal.

But I have.

I try to access any memory of Kelsea giving a cry for help. But the thing about a cry for help is that someone else needs to be around to hear it. And I am not finding a moment of that in Kelsea's life. Her father sees what he wants to see, and she doesn't want to dispel this fiction with fact. Her mother left years ago. Other relatives are distant. Friends all exist far outside the black cloud. Just because Lena was nice in physics class doesn't mean she should be freighted with this, or would know what to do.

I make it back to Kelsea's empty house, sweaty and exhausted. I turn on her computer and everything I need to know is there in her history—the sites where these plans come from, where this information can be gleaned. Right there, one click away for everyone to see. Only no one is looking.

We both need to talk to someone.

I email Rhiannon.

> I really need to speak to you right now. The girl whose body I'm in wants to kill herself. This is not a joke.

I give her Kelsea's home phone number, figuring there will be no obvious record of it, and that it can always be discounted as a wrong number.

Ten minutes later, she calls.

"Hello?" I answer.

"Is that you?" she asks.

"Yeah." I've forgotten that she doesn't know the sound of my voice. "It's me."

"I got your email. Wow."

"Yeah, wow."

"How do you know?"

I tell her briefly about Kelsea's journal.

"That poor girl," Rhiannon says. "What are you going to do?"

"I have no idea."

"Don't you have to tell someone?"

"There was no training for this, Rhiannon. I really don't know."

All I know is that I need her. But I'm afraid to say it. Because saying it might scare her away.

"Where are you?" she asks.

I tell her the town.

"That's not far. I can be there in a little while. Are you alone?"

"Yeah. Her father doesn't get home until around seven."

"Give me the address."

I do.

"I'll be right there," she says.

I don't even need to ask. It means more that she knows.

I wonder what would happen if I straightened up Kelsea's room. I wonder what would happen if she woke up tomorrow morning and found everything in its right place. Would it give her some unexpected calm? Would it make her understand that her life does not have to be chaos? Or would she just take one look and destroy it again? Because that's what her chemistry, her biology would tell her to do.

The doorbell rings. I have spent the past ten minutes staring at the ink stains on the walls, hoping they will rearrange themselves into an answer, and knowing they never will.

The black cloud is so thick at this point that not even Rhiannon's presence can send it away. I am happy to see her in the doorway, but that happiness feels more like resigned gratitude than pleasure.

She blinks, takes me in. I have forgotten that she is not used to this, that she is not expecting a new person every day. It's one thing to acknowledge it theoretically, and quite another thing to have a thin, shaky girl standing on the other side of the precipice.

"Thank you for coming," I say.

It's a little after five, so we don't have much time before Kelsea's father comes home.

We head to Kelsea's room. Rhiannon sees the journal sitting on Kelsea's bed and picks it up. I watch and wait until she's done reading.

"This is serious," she says. "I've had . . . thoughts. But nothing like this."

She sits down on the bed. I sit down next to her.

"You have to stop her," she says.

"But how can I? And is that really my right? Shouldn't she decide that for herself?"

"So, what? You just let her die? Because you didn't want to get involved?"

I take her hand.

"We don't know for sure that the deadline's real. This could just be her way of getting rid of the thoughts. Putting them on paper so she doesn't do them."

She looks at me. "But you don't believe that, do you? You wouldn't have called me if you believed that."

She looks down at our hands.

"This is weird," she says.

"What?"

She squeezes once, then pulls her hand away. "This."

"What do you mean?"

"It's not like the other day. I mean, it's a different hand. You're different."

"But I'm not."

"You can't say that. Yes, you're the same person inside. But the outside matters, too."

"You look the same, no matter what eyes I'm seeing you through. I feel the same."

It's true, but it doesn't really address what she's saying.

"You never get involved in the people's lives? The ones you're inhabiting."

I shake my head.

"You try to leave the lives the way you found them."

"Yeah."

"But what about Justin? What made that so different?"

"You," I say.

Just one word, and she finally understands. Just one word, and the door to the enormity is finally unlocked.

"That makes no sense," she says.

And the only way to show her how it makes sense, the only way to make the enormity real, is for me to lean over and kiss her. Like last time, but not at all like last time. Not our first kiss, but also our first kiss. My lips feel different against hers, our bodies fit differently. And there is also something else that surrounds us, the black cloud as well as the enormity. I am not kissing her because I want to, and I am not kissing her because I need to—I am kissing her for a reason that transcends want and need, that feels elemental to our existence, a molecular component on which our universe will be built. It is not our first kiss, but it's the first kiss where she knows me, and that makes it more of a first kiss than the first kiss ever was.

I find myself wishing that Kelsea could feel this, too. Maybe she does. It's not enough. It's not a solution. But it does lessen the weight for a moment.

Rhiannon is not smiling when we pull away from each other. There is none of the giddiness of the earlier kiss.

"This is definitely weird," she says.

"Why?"

"Because you're a girl? Because I still have a boyfriend? Because we're talking about someone else's suicide?"

"In your heart, does any of that matter?" In my heart, it doesn't.

"Yes. It does."

"Which part?"

"All of it. When I kiss you, I'm not actually kissing you, you know. You're inside there somewhere. But I'm kissing the outside part. And right now, although I can feel you underneath, all I'm getting is the sadness. I'm kissing her, and I want to cry."

"That's not what I want," I tell her.

"I know. But that's what there is."

She stands up and looks around the room, searching for clues to a murder that has yet to happen.

"If she were bleeding in the street, what would you do?" she asks.

"That's not the same situation."

"If she were going to kill someone else?"

"I would turn her in."

"So how is this different?"

"It's her own life. Not anyone else's."

"But it's still killing."

"If she really wants to do it, there's nothing I can do to stop it."

Even as I say this, it feels wrong.

"Okay," I continue, before Rhiannon can correct me. "Putting up obstacles can help. Getting other people involved can help. Getting her to the proper doctors can help."

"Just like if she had cancer, or was bleeding in the street."

This is what I need. It's not enough to hear these things in my own voice. I need to hear them told to me by somebody I trust.

"So who do I tell?"

"A guidance counselor, maybe?"

I look at the clock. "School's closed. And we only have until midnight, remember."

"Who's her best friend?"

I shake my head.

"Boyfriend? Girlfriend?"

"No."

"A suicide hotline?"

"If we call one, they'd only be giving me advice, not her. We have no way of knowing if she'll remember it tomorrow, or if it will have any effect. Believe me, I've thought about these options."

"So it has to be her father. Right?"

"I think he checked out a while ago."

"Well, you need to get him to check back in."

She makes it sound so easy. But both of us know it's not easy.

"What do I say?"

"You say, 'Dad, I want to kill myself.' Just come right out and say it."

"And if he asks me why?"

"You tell him you don't know why. Don't commit to anything. She'll have to work that out starting tomorrow."

"You've thought this through, haven't you?"

"It was a busy drive over."

"What if he doesn't care? What if he doesn't believe her?"

"Then you grab his keys and drive to the nearest hospital. Bring the journal with you."

Hearing her say it, it all makes sense.

She sits back down on the bed.

"Come here," she says. But this time we don't kiss. Instead, she hugs my frail body.

"I don't know if I can do this," I whisper.

"You can," she tells me. "Of course you can."

I am alone in Kelsea's room when her father comes home. I hear him throw down his keys, take something out of the refrigerator. I hear him walk to his bedroom, then come back out. He doesn't call out a hello. I don't even know if he realizes I'm here.

Five minutes pass. Ten minutes. Finally, he calls out, "Dinner!"

I haven't heard any activity in the kitchen, so I'm not surprised to find a KFC bucket on the table. He's already started on a drumstick.

I can guess how this usually works. He takes his dinner into the den, in front of the TV. She takes hers back to her room. And that marks the rest of the night for them.

But tonight is different. Tonight she says, "I want to kill myself."

At first I don't think he's heard me.

"I know you don't want to hear this," I say. "But it's the truth."

He drops his hand to his side, still holding the drumstick.

"What are you saying?" he asks.

"I want to die," I tell him.

"C'mon now," he says. "Really?"

If I were Kelsea, I'd probably leave the room in disgust. I'd give up.

"You need to get me help," I say. "This is something I've been thinking about for a long time." I put the journal on the table, shove it over to him. This might ultimately be my biggest betrayal of Kelsea. I feel awful, but then I conjure Rhiannon's voice in my ear, telling me I am doing the right thing.

Kelsea's father puts down the drumstick, picks up the journal. Starts reading it. I try to decode his expression. He doesn't want to be seeing this. Resents that it's happening. Hates it, even. But not her. He keeps reading because even if he hates the situation, he doesn't hate her.

"Kelsea . . . ," he chokes out.

135

I wish she could see how it hits him. The look on his face, his life caving in. Because then maybe she'd realize, if only for a split second, that even though the world doesn't matter to her, she matters to the world.

"This isn't just some . . . thing?" he asks.

I shake my head. It's a stupid question, but I'm not going to call him on it.

"So what do we do?"

There. I have him.

"We need to get help," I tell him. "Tomorrow morning we need to find a counselor who's open on Saturday, and we need to see what we have to do. I probably need medication. I definitely need to talk to a doctor. I have been living this for so long."

"But why didn't you tell me?"

Why didn't you see? I want to ask back. But now's not the time for that. He'll get there on his own.

"That doesn't matter. We need to focus on now. I am asking for help. You need to get me help."

"Are you sure it can wait until morning?"

"I'm not going to do anything tonight. But tomorrow you have to watch me. You have to force me if I change my mind. I might change my mind. I might pretend that this whole conversation didn't happen. Keep that notebook. It's the truth. If I fight you, fight me back. Call an ambulance."

"An ambulance?"

"That's how serious this is, Dad."

It's the last word that really brings it home to him. I don't think Kelsea uses it that often.

He's crying now. We just stay there, looking at each other. Finally, he says, "Have some dinner."

I take some chicken from the bucket, then bring it back to my room. I've said everything I've needed to say.

Kelsea will have to tell him the rest.

I hear him pacing throughout the house. I hear him on the phone to someone, and I hope it's someone who can help him the way Rhiannon helped me. I hear him stop outside the door, afraid to open it but still listening in. I make small stirring noises, so he knows I'm awake, alive.

I fall asleep to the sound of his concern.

Day 6006

The phone rings.

I reach for it, thinking it's Rhiannon.

Even though it can't be.

I look at the name on the screen. *Austin*.

My boyfriend.

"Hello?" I answer.

"Hugo! This is your nine a.m. wake-up call. I will be there in an hour. Go make yourself purdy."

"Whatever you say," I mumble.

There's a lot I have to do in an hour.

First, there's the usual getting up, getting showered, and getting dressed. In the kitchen, I can hear my parents talking loudly in a language I don't know. It sounds like Spanish but isn't Spanish, so I'm guessing it's Portuguese. Foreign languages throw me—I have a beginner's grasp of a few of them, but I can't really access a person's memory fast enough to pretend to be fluent in any of them. I access and find that Hugo's parents are from Brazil. But that's not going to help me understand them better. So I steer clear of the kitchen.

Austin is picking Hugo up to go to a gay pride parade in Annapolis. Two of their friends, William and Nicolas, will be coming along. It's marked on Hugo's calendar as well as his mind.

Luckily, Hugo has a laptop in his room—since it's the weekend and a school computer isn't an option, I am going to risk checking in. I quickly open my email and find something that Rhiannon sent only ten minutes ago.

A,

I hope it went well yesterday. I called her house just now and no one was home—do you think they're getting help? I'm trying to take it as a good sign.

Meanwhile, here's a link you need to see. It's out of control.

Where are you today?

R

I click on the link beneath her initial and am taken to the home page of a big Baltimore tabloid website. The headline blares:

THE DEVIL AMONG US!

It's Nathan's story, but it's not only Nathan's story. This time there are five or six other people from the area claiming to have been possessed by the devil. Much to my relief, none of them besides Nathan are familiar to me. All of them are older than I am. Most claim to have been possessed for a time much longer than a single day.

I would think the reporter would have been more skeptical, but she buys the stories uncritically. She even links to other stories of demonic possession—death-row criminals who claimed they were under the influence of satanic forces, politicians and preachers who were caught in compromising positions and said that something very uncharacteristic had come over them. It all sounds very convenient.

I quickly run Nathan through a search engine and find more coverage. The story, it seems, is going wide.

In article after article, there is one person quoted. Essentially, he says the same thing every time:

> "I have no doubt that these are cases of demonic possession," says Rev. Anderson Poole, who has been counseling Daldry. "These are textbook examples. The devil is nothing if not predictable."
>
> "These possessions should come as no surprise," says Poole. "We as a society have been leaving the door wide open. Why wouldn't the devil walk right in?"

People are believing this. The articles and posts in the comments sections are legion—all from people who see the devil's work in everything.

Even though I should know better, I shoot off a quick email to Nathan.

I am not the devil.

I hit send, but I don't feel any better.

I email Rhiannon, telling her how it went with Kelsea's father. I also let her know that I'm going to be in Annapolis for the day, and tell her what T-shirt I'm wearing and what I look like.

There's a honk outside, and I see a car that must be Austin's. I race through the kitchen and say a hurried goodbye to Hugo's parents. Then I pile into the car—the boy in the passenger seat (William) moves into the back with the other boy (Nicolas) so I can sit next to my boyfriend. For his part, Austin takes one look at my outfit and tsk-tsks, "You're wearing *that* to Pride?" But he's joking. I think.

There is conversation around me the whole car ride, but I'm not really a part of it. My mind is completely elsewhere.

I shouldn't have sent Nathan that email.

One simple line, but it admits too much.

From the moment we hit Annapolis, Austin is in his element.

"Isn't this *fun?*" he keeps asking.

William, Nicolas, and I nod, agree. In truth, the Annapolis Pride events aren't that elaborate—in many ways it feels like the navy has turned gay and lesbian for the day, and a ragtag assortment of people have come along to cheer it on. The weather is sunny and cool, and that seems to cheer everyone further. Austin likes to hold my hand and swing it like we're walking down the yellow brick road. Ordinarily, I'd be charmed. He has every right to be proud, to enjoy this day. It's not his fault I'm so distracted.

I'm looking for Rhiannon in the crowd. I can't help it. Every now and then, Austin catches me.

"See someone you know?" he asks.

"No," I say truthfully.

She's not here. She hasn't made it. And I feel foolish for expecting her to. She can't just drop her life every time I'm available. Her day is no less important than mine.

We come to a corner where there are a few people protesting the festivities. I don't understand this at all. It's like protesting the fact that some people are red-haired.

In my experience, desire is desire, love is love. I have never fallen in love with a gender. I have fallen for individuals. I know this is hard for people to do, but I don't understand why it's so hard, when it's so obvious.

I remember Rhiannon's hesitation to kiss me longer when I was Kelsea. I am hoping this reason was nowhere near the heart of it. There were so many other reasons in that moment.

One of the protestor's signs catches my eye. HOMOSEXUALITY IS THE DEVIL'S WORK, it says. And once again I think about how people use the devil as an alias for the things they fear. The cause and effect is backward. The devil doesn't make anyone do anything. People just do things and blame the devil after.

Predictably, Austin stops to kiss me in front of the protestors. I try to oblige. Philosophically, I am with him. But I'm not inside the kiss. I cannot manufacture the intensity.

He notices. He doesn't say anything, but he notices.

• • •

I want to check my email on Hugo's phone, but Austin isn't letting me out of his sight. When William and Nicolas make a move to get some lunch, Austin says he and I are going to go our own way for a little while.

I assume we're going to get lunch, too, but instead he pulls me into a hip clothing store and spends the next hour trying things on, with me giving my outside-the-changing-room opinion. At one point, he pulls me into the changing room to steal some kisses, and I oblige. But at the same time, I'm thinking that if we're inside, there's no way Rhiannon is going to find me.

While Austin debates whether the skinny jeans are skinny enough, I find myself wondering what Kelsea is doing at this moment. Is she unburdening herself, going along with it, or is she defiant, denying that she ever wanted help in the first place? I picture Tom and James in their rec room, playing video games, not having any sense that their week was disrupted. I think of Roger Wilson later tonight, preparing his clothes for church tomorrow morning.

"What do you think?" Austin asks.

"They're great," I say.

"You didn't even look."

I can't argue this. He's right. I didn't.

I look at him now. I need to pay more attention.

"I like them," I tell him.

"Well, I don't," he says. Then he storms back into the changing room.

I haven't been a good guest in Hugo's life. I access his memories and discover that he and Austin first became boyfriends at this very celebration, a year ago this weekend. They'd been friends for a little while, but they'd never talked about how they felt. They were each afraid of ruining the friendship, and instead of making it better, their caution made everything awkward. So finally, as a pair of twentysomething men passed by holding hands, Austin said, "Hey, that could be us in ten years."

And Hugo said, "Or ten months."

And Austin said, "Or ten days."

And Hugo said, "Or ten minutes."

And Austin said, "Or ten seconds."

Then they each counted to ten, and held hands for the rest of the day.

The start of it.

Hugo would have remembered this.

But I didn't.

Austin senses something has changed. He comes back from the dressing room without any clothes in his arms, looks at me, and makes a decision.

"Let's get out of here," he says. "I don't want to have this particular conversation in this particular store."

He leads me down to the water, away from the celebration, away from the crowds. He finds a somewhat secluded bench and I follow him there. Once we sit down, it all comes out.

"You haven't been with me once this whole day," he says. "You aren't listening to a word I say. You keep looking around for someone else. And kissing you is like kissing a block of wood. And today, of all days. I thought you said you were going to give it a chance. I thought you said you were snapping out of whatever it is that's been afflicting you the past couple of weeks. I am *sure* I recall you saying there wasn't anyone else. But maybe I'm mistaken. I was willing to bend over backward, Hugo. But I can't bend over backward and walk around at the same time. I can't bend over backward and have a conversation. I guess when it all comes down to it, I'm just not that damn flexible."

"Austin, I'm sorry," I say.

"Do you even love me?"

I have no idea if Hugo loves him or not. If I tried, I'm sure I could access moments when he loved him and moments when he didn't. But I can't answer the question and be sure I'm being truthful. I'm caught.

"My feelings haven't changed," I say. "I'm just a little off today. It has nothing to do with you."

Austin laughs. "Our anniversary has nothing to do with me?"

"That's not what I said. I mean my mood."

Now Austin is shaking his head.

"I can't do this, Hugo. You know I can't do this."

"Are you breaking up with me?" I ask, genuine fear in my voice. I can't believe I'm doing this to both of them.

Austin hears the fear, looks at me and maybe sees something worth keeping.

"This isn't the way I want today to go," he says. "But I have to believe that it isn't the way you want it to go, either."

I can't imagine that Hugo was planning to break up with Austin today. And if he was, he can always do it to-morrow.

"Come here," I say. Austin moves in to me and I lean into his shoulder. We sit like that for a moment, looking at the ships on the bay. I take his hand. When I turn to look at him, he's blinking back tears.

This time when I kiss him, I know there's something in it. When he feels it, it may come across as love. It is my thanks to him for not ending it. It is my thanks to him for giving it at least one day more.

We stay out until late, and I am a good boyfriend the whole time. Eventually I lose myself a little in his life, dancing along with Austin, William, Nicolas, and a few hundred other gays and lesbians when the parade organizers blast the Village People's "In the Navy."

I keep looking for Rhiannon, but only when Austin is distracted. And, at a certain point, I give up.

When I get home, there's an email from her:

A,

Sorry I couldn't make it to Annapolis—there were some things I had to do.

Maybe tomorrow?

R

I wonder what the "things I had to do" were. I have to assume they involve Justin, because otherwise, wouldn't she have told me what they were?

I'm pondering this when Austin texts me to say he ended up having a great day. I text him back and say I had a great day, too. I can only hope that's the way Hugo remembers it, because now Austin has proof if he denies it.

Hugo's mother comes in and says something to me in Portuguese. I only get about half of it.

"I'm tired," I tell her in English. "I think it's time for bed."

I don't think I've addressed her questions, but she just shakes her head—I am a typical, unforthcoming teenager—and heads back to her room.

Before I go to sleep, I decide to see if Nathan has written me back.

He has.

Two words.

Prove it.

Day 6007

I wake up the next morning in Beyoncé's body.

Not the real Beyoncé. But a body remarkably like hers. All the curves in all the right places.

I open my eyes to a blur. I reach for the glasses on the nightstand, but they're not there. So I stumble into the bathroom and put in my contact lenses.

Then I look in the mirror.

I am not pretty. I am not beautiful.

I'm top-to-bottom gorgeous.

I am always happiest when I am just attractive enough. Meaning: other people won't find me unattractive. Meaning: I make a positive impression. Meaning: my life is not defined by my attractiveness, because that brings its own perils as well as its own rewards.

Ashley Ashton's life is defined by her attractiveness. Beauty can come naturally, but it's hard to be stunning by accident. A lot of work has gone into this face, this body. I'm sure there's a complete morning regimen that I'm supposed to undergo before heading into the day.

I don't want to have any part of it, though. With girls like Ashley, I just want to shake them, and tell them that no matter how hard they fight it, these teenage looks aren't going to last forever, and that there are much better foundations to build a life upon than how attractive you are. But there's no way for me to get that message across. My only course of rebellion is to leave her eyebrows unplucked for the day.

I access where I am, and discover I'm only about fifteen minutes away from Rhiannon.

A good sign.

I log on to my email and find a message from her.

A,

I'm free and have the car today. I told my mom I have errands.

Want to be one of my errands?

R

I tell her yes. A million times yes.

Ashley's parents are away for the weekend. Her older brother, Clayton, is in charge. I worry he's going to give me a hassle, but he's got his own things to do, as he tells me repeatedly. I tell him I won't stand in his way.

"You're going out in that?" he asks.

Normally, when an older brother asks this, it means a skirt is too short, or too much cleavage is showing. But in this case, I think he's saying I'm still dressed as the private Ashley, not the public one.

I don't really care, but I have to respect the fact that Ashley would care—probably very much. So I go back and change, and even put on some makeup. I'm fascinated by the life Ashley must lead, being such a knockout. Like being very short or very tall, it must change your whole perspective on the world. If other people see you differently, you'll end up seeing them differently, too.

Even her brother defers to her in a way I bet he wouldn't if she were normal-looking. He doesn't blink when I tell him I'm going out for the day with my friend Rhiannon.

If your beauty is unquestioned, so many other things can go unquestioned as well.

The minute I get into the car, Rhiannon bursts out laughing.

"You've got to be kidding me," she says.

"What?" I say. Then I get it.

"*What?*" she mocks me. I'm happy she feels comfortable enough to do it, but I'm still being mocked.

"You have to understand—you're the first person to ever know me in more than one body. I'm not used to this. I don't know how you're going to react."

This makes her a little more serious.

"I'm sorry. It's just that you're this super hot black girl. It makes it very hard for me to have a mental image of you. I keep having to change it."

"Picture me however you want to picture me. Because odds are, that'll be more true than any of the bodies you see me in."

"I think my imagination needs a little more time to catch up to the situation, okay?"

"Okay. Now, where to?"

"Since we've already been to the ocean, I figured today we'd go to a forest."

So off we go, into the woods.

It's not like last time. The radio is on, but we're not singing along. We're sharing the same space, but our thoughts are spreading outside of it.

I want to hold her hand, but I sense it wouldn't work. I know she's not going to reach for my hand, not unless I need it. This is the problem with being so beautiful—it can render you untouchable. And this is the problem with being in a new body each day—the history is there, but it's not visible. It has to be different from last time, because I am different.

We talk a little about Kelsea; Rhiannon called her house a second time yesterday, just to see what would happen. Kelsea's father answered, and when Rhiannon introduced herself as a friend, he said that Kelsea had gone away to deal with some things, and left it at that. Both Rhiannon and I decide to take this as a good sign.

We talk some more, but not about anything that matters. I want to cut through the awkwardness, have Rhiannon treat me like her boyfriend or girlfriend again. But I can't. I'm not.

We get to the park and navigate ourselves away from the other weekenders. Rhiannon finds us a secluded picnic area, and surprises me by taking a feast from the trunk.

I watch as she picks everything out of the picnic hamper. Cheeses. French bread. Hummus. Olives. Salads. Chips. Salsa.

"Are you a vegetarian?" I ask, based on the evidence in front of me.

She nods.

"Why?"

"Because I have this theory that when we die, every animal that we've eaten has a chance at eating us back. So if you're a carnivore and you add up all the animals you've eaten—well, that's a long time in purgatory, being chewed."

"Really?"

She laughs. "No. I'm just sick of the question. I mean, I'm vegetarian because I think it's wrong to eat other sentient creatures. And it sucks for the environment."

"Fair enough." I don't tell her how many times I've accidentally eaten meat while I've been in a vegetarian's body. It's just not something I remember to check for. It's usually the friends' reactions that alert me. I once made a vegan really, really sick at a McDonald's.

Over lunch, we make more small talk. It's not until we've put away the picnic and are walking through the woods that the real words come out.

"I need to know what you want," she says.

"I want us to be together." I say it before I can think it over.

She keeps walking. I keep walking alongside her.

"But we can't be together. You realize that, don't you?"

"No. I don't realize that."

Now she stops. Puts her hand on my shoulder.

"You need to realize it. I can care about you. You can care about me. But we can't be together."

It's so ridiculous, but I ask, "Why?"

"Why? Because one morning you could wake up on the other side of the country. Because I feel like I'm meeting a new person every time I see you. Because you can't be there for me. Because I don't think I can like you no matter what. Not like this."

"Why can't you like me like this?"

"It's too much. You're too perfect right now. I can't imagine being with someone like . . . you."

"But don't look at her—look at me."

"I can't see beyond her, okay? And there's also Justin. I have to think of Justin."

"No, you don't."

"You don't know, okay? How many waking hours were you in there? Fourteen? Fifteen? Did you really get to know everything about him while you were in there? Everything about me?"

"You like him because he's a lost boy. Believe me, I've seen it happen before. But do you know what happens to girls who love lost boys? They become lost themselves. Without fail."

"You don't know me—"

"But I know how this works! I know what he's like. He doesn't care about you nearly as much as you care about him. He doesn't care about you nearly as much as I care about you."

"Stop! Just stop."

153

But I can't. "What do you think would happen if he met me in this body? What if the three of us went out? How much attention do you think he'd pay you? Because he doesn't care about who you are. I happen to think you are about a thousand times more attractive than Ashley is. But do you really think he'd be able to keep his hands to himself if he had a chance?"

"He's not like that."

"Are you sure? Are you really sure?"

"Fine," Rhiannon says. "Let me call him."

Despite my immediate protests, she dials his number and, when he answers, says she has a friend in town that she wants him to meet. Maybe we could all go for dinner? He says fine, but not until Rhiannon says it'll be her treat.

Once she hangs up, we just hang there.

"Happy?" she asks.

"I have no idea," I tell her honestly.

"Me either."

"When are we meeting him?"

"Six."

"Okay," I say. "In the meantime, I want to tell you everything, and I want you to tell me everything in return."

It's so much easier when we're talking about things that are real. We don't have to remind ourselves what the point is, because we're right there in it.

She asks me when I first knew.

"I was probably four or five. Obviously, I knew before that about changing bodies, having a different mom and dad each day. Or grandmother or babysitter or whoever. There was always someone to take care of me, and I assumed that was just what living was—a new life every morning. If I got something wrong—a name, a place, a rule—people would correct me. There was never that big a disturbance. I didn't think of myself as a boy or a girl—I never have. I would just think of myself as a boy or a girl for a day. It was like a different set of clothes.

"The thing that ended up tripping me up was the concept of tomorrow. Because after a while, I started to notice—people kept talking about doing things tomorrow. Together. And if I argued, I would get strange looks. For everyone else, there always seemed to be a tomorrow together. But not for me. I'd say, 'You won't be there,' and they'd say, 'Of course I'll be there.' And then I'd wake up, and they wouldn't be. And my new parents would have no idea why I was so upset.

"There were only two options—something was wrong with everyone else, or something was wrong with me. Because either they were tricking themselves into thinking there was a tomorrow together, or I was the only person who was leaving."

Rhiannon asks, "Did you try to hold on?"

I tell her, "I'm sure I did. But I don't remember it now. I remember crying and protesting—I told you about that. But the rest? I'm not sure. I mean, do you remember a lot about when you were five?"

She shakes her head. "Not really. I remember my mom bringing me and my sister to the shoe store to get new shoes before kindergarten started. I remember learning that a green light meant go and red meant stop. I remember coloring them in, and the teacher being a little confused about how to explain yellow. I think she told us to treat it the same as red."

"I learned my letters quickly," I tell her. "I remember the teachers being surprised that I knew them. I imagine they were just as surprised the next day, when I'd forgotten them."

"A five-year-old probably wouldn't notice taking a day off."

"Probably. I don't know."

"I keep asking Justin about it, you know. The day you were him. And it's amazing how clear his fake memories are. He doesn't disagree when I say we went to the beach, but he doesn't really remember it, either."

"James, the twin, was like that, too. He didn't notice anything wrong. But when I asked him about meeting you for coffee, he didn't remember it at all. He remembered he was at Starbucks—his mind accounted for the time. But it wasn't what actually happened."

"Maybe they remember what you want them to remember."

"I've thought about that. I wish I knew for sure."

We walk farther. Circle a tree with our fingers.

"What about love?" she asks. "Have you ever been in love?"

"I don't know that you'd call it love," I say. "I've had crushes, for sure. And there have been days where I've really regretted leaving. There were even one or two people I tried to find, but that didn't work out. The closest was this guy Brennan."

"Tell me about him."

"It was about a year ago. I was working at a movie theater, and he was in town, visiting his cousins, and when he went to get some popcorn, we flirted a little, and it just became this . . . spark. It was this small, one-screen movie theater, and when the movie was running, my job was pretty slow. I think he missed the second half of the movie, because he came back out and started talking to me more. I ended up having to tell him what happened, so he could pretend he'd been in there most of the time. At the end, he asked for my email, and I made up an email address."

"Like you did for me."

"Exactly like I did for you. And he emailed me later that night, and left the next day to go back home to Maine, and that proved to be ideal, because then the rest of our relationship could be online. I'd been wearing a name tag, so I had to give him that first name, but I made up a last name, and then I made up an online profile using some of the photos from the real guy's profile. I think his name was Ian."

"Oh—so you were a boy?"

"Yeah," I say. "Does that matter?"

"No," she tells me. "I guess not." But I can tell it does. A little. Again, her mental picture needs adjustment.

"So we'd email almost every day. We'd even chat. And while I couldn't tell him what was really happening—I emailed him from some very strange places—I still felt like I had something out there in the world that was consistently mine, and that was a pretty new feeling. The only problem was, he wanted more. More photos. Then he wanted to Skype. Then, after about a month of these intense conversations, he started talking about visiting again. His aunt and uncle had already invited him back, and summer was coming."

"Uh-oh."

"Yup—uh-oh. I couldn't figure out a way around it. And

the more I tried to dodge it, the more he noticed. All of our conversations became about us. Every now and then, a tangent would get in there, but he'd always drag it back. So I had to end it. Because there wasn't going to be a tomorrow for us."

"Why didn't you tell him the truth?"

"Because I didn't think he could take it. Because I didn't trust him enough, I guess."

"So you called it off."

"I told him I'd met someone else. I borrowed photos from the body I was in at the time. I changed my fake profile's relationship status. Brennan never wanted to talk to me again."

"Poor guy."

"I know. After that, I promised myself I wouldn't get into any more virtual entanglements, as easy as they might seem to be. Because what's the point of something virtual if it doesn't end up being real? And I could never give anyone something real. I could only give them deception."

"Like impersonating their boyfriends," Rhiannon says.

"Yeah. But you have to understand—you were the exception to the rule. And I didn't want it to be based on deception. Which is why you're the first person I've ever told."

"The funny thing is, you say it like it's so unusual that you've only done it once. But I bet a whole lot of people go through their lives without ever telling the truth, not really. And they wake up in the same body and the same life every single morning."

"Why? What aren't you telling me?"

Rhiannon looks me in the eye. "If I'm not telling you something, it's for a reason. Just because you trust me, it doesn't mean I have to automatically trust you. Trust doesn't work like that."

"That's fair."

"I know it is. But enough of that. Tell me about—I don't know—third grade."

The conversation continues. She learns the reason I now have to access information about allergies before eating anything (after having been nearly killed by a strawberry when I was nine), and I learn the origin of her fear of bunny rabbits (a particularly malevolent creature named Swizzle that liked to escape its cage and sleep on people's faces). She learns about the best mom I ever had (a water park is involved), and I learn about the highs and lows of living with the same mother for your entire life, about how no one can make you angrier, but how you can't really love anyone more. She learns that I haven't always been in Maryland, but I move great distances only when the body I'm in moves great distances. I learn that she's never been on an airplane.

She still keeps a physical space between us—there will be no leaning on shoulders or holding hands right now. But if our bodies keep apart, our words do not. I don't mind that.

We return to the car and pick at the remains of the picnic. Then we walk around and talk some more. I am astonished at the number of lives I can remember to tell Rhiannon about, and she is amazed that her single life bears as many stories as my multiple one. Because her normal existence is so foreign to me, so intriguing to me, it starts to feel a little more interesting to her as well.

I could go on like this until midnight. But at five-fifteen,

Rhiannon looks at her phone and says, "We better get going. Justin will be waiting for us."

Somehow, I'd managed to forget.

It should be a foregone conclusion. I am a seriously attractive girl. Justin is a typically horny boy.

I am hoping that Rhiannon's theory is right, and that Ashley will only remember what I want her to remember, or what her mind wants her to remember. Not that I'm going to take this far—all I need is confirmation of Justin's willingness, not actual contact.

Rhiannon's picked a clam house off the highway. True to form, I confirm that Ashley doesn't have any shellfish allergies. In truth, Ashley has tricked herself into thinking she's "allergic" to a number of things, as a way of narrowing down her diet. But shellfish never hit that particular watch list.

When she walks into the room, heads actually turn. Most of them are attached to men a good thirty years older than her. I'm sure she's used to it, but it freaks me out.

Even though Rhiannon was concerned about Justin having to wait for us, he ends up coming ten minutes after we do. The look on his face when he first sees me is priceless—when Rhiannon said she had a friend in town, Ashley was *not* what he pictured. He gives Rhiannon her hello, but he's gaping at me when he does.

We take our seats. At first I'm so focused on his reaction that I don't notice Rhiannon's. She's receding into herself, suddenly quiet, suddenly timid. I can't tell whether it's Justin's presence that's making this happen, or whether it's the combination of his presence and mine.

We've been so wrapped up in our own day that we haven't really prepared for this. So when Justin starts asking the obvious questions—how do Rhiannon and I know each other, and how come he hasn't heard about me before—I have to jump into the breach. For Rhiannon, fabrication is a ruminative act, whereas lying is a part of my necessary nature.

I tell him that my mother and Rhiannon's mother were best friends in high school. I'm now living in Los Angeles (why not?), auditioning for TV shows (because I can). My mother and I are visiting the East Coast for a week, and she wanted to check in on her old friend. Rhiannon and I have seen each other off and on through the years, but this is the first time in a while.

Justin appears to be hanging on my every word, but he isn't listening at all. I brush his leg "accidentally" under the table. He pretends he doesn't notice. Rhiannon pretends, too.

I'm brazen, but careful with my brazenness. I touch Rhiannon's hand a few times when I'm making a point, so it doesn't seem so unusual when I do it to Justin. I mention a Hollywood star that I once kissed at a party, but make it clear that it was no big deal.

I want Justin to flirt back, but he appears incapable. Especially once there's food in front of him. Then the order of attention goes: food, then Ashley, then Rhiannon. I dip my crab cakes in tartar sauce, and imagine Ashley yelling at me for doing so.

When the food is finished, he focuses back on me. Rhiannon

comes alive a little and tries to mimic my movements, first by holding his hand. He doesn't move away, but he doesn't seem all that into it; he acts like she's embarrassing him. I figure this is a good sign.

Finally, Rhiannon says she has to go to the ladies' room. This is my chance to get him to do something irredeemable, get her to see who he truly is.

I start with the leg move. This time, with Rhiannon gone, he doesn't move his leg away.

"Hello there," I say.

"Hello," he says back. And smiles.

"What are you doing after this?" I ask.

"After dinner?"

"Yeah, after dinner."

"I don't know."

"Maybe we should do something," I suggest.

"Yeah. Sure."

"Maybe just the two of us."

Click. He finally gets it.

I move in. Touch his hand. Say, "I think that would be fun."

I need him to lean in to me. I need him to give in to what he wants. I need him to take it one step further. All it takes is a yes.

He looks around, to see if Rhiannon is near, and to see if the other guys in the room are seeing this happen.

"Whoa," he says.

"It's okay," I tell him. "I really like you."

He sits back. Shakes his head. "Um . . . no."

I've been too forward. He needs it to be his idea.

"Why not?" I ask.

He looks at me like I'm a complete idiot.

"Why not?" he says. "How about Rhiannon? Jeez."

I'm trying to think of a comeback for that, but there isn't one. And it doesn't even matter, because at this point, Rhiannon returns to the table.

"I don't want this," she says. "Stop."

Justin, fool that he is, thinks she's talking to him.

"I'm not doing anything!" he protests, his leg firmly back on his side of the booth. "Your friend here is a little out of control."

"I don't want this," she repeats.

"It's okay," I say. "I'm sorry."

"You should be!" Justin yells. "God, I don't know how they do things in California, but here, you don't act like that." He stands up. I steal a glance at his groin and see that despite his denials, my flirtation did have at least one effect. But I can't really point it out to Rhiannon.

"I'm gonna go," he says. Then, as if to prove something, he kisses Rhiannon right in front of me. "Thanks, baby," he says. "I'll see you tomorrow."

He doesn't bother saying goodbye to me.

Rhiannon and I sit back down.

"I'm sorry," I tell her again.

"No, it's my fault. I should've known."

I'm waiting for the *I told you so* . . . and then it comes.

"I told you that you don't understand. You can't understand us," she says.

The check comes. I try to pay, but she waves me off.

"It's not your money," she says. And that hurts just as much as anything else.

I know she wants the night to end. I know she wants to drop me off at home, just so she can call Justin and apologize, and make everything right with him again.

Day 6008

I go to the computer as soon as I wake up the next morning. But there's no email from Rhiannon. I send her another apology. I send her more thanks for the day. Sometimes when you hit send, you can imagine the message going straight into the person's heart. But other times, like this time, it feels like the words are merely falling into a well.

I head to the social-networking sites, searching for something more. I see that Austin and Hugo still list their relationship status as being together—a good sign. Kelsea's page is locked to non-friends. So there's proof of one thing I managed to save, and another where saving is possible.

I have to remind myself it's not all bad.

Then there's Nathan. The coverage of him continues. Reverend Poole is getting more testimony by the day, and the news sites are eating it up. Even the *Onion* is getting into the act, with the headline: WILLIAM CARLOS WILLIAMS TO REVEREND POOLE: 'THE DEVIL MADE ME EAT THE PLUM.' If smart people are parodying it, that's a sure sign that some less smart people are believing it.

But what can I do? Nathan wants his proof, but I'm not sure I have any to give. All I have is my word, and what kind of proof is that?

Today I'm a boy named AJ. He has diabetes, so I have a whole other layer of concerns on top of my usual ones. I've been diabetic a couple of times, and the first time was harrowing. Not because diabetes isn't controllable, but because I had to rely on the body's memories to tell me what to look out for, and how to manage it. I ended up pretending I wasn't feeling well, just so my mother would stay at home and monitor my health with me. Now I feel I can handle it, but I am very attentive to what the body is telling me, much more so than I usually am.

AJ is full of idiosyncrasies that probably don't seem all that idiosyncratic to him anymore. He's a sports fanatic—he plays soccer on the JV squad, but his real love is baseball. His head is full of statistics, facts and figures extrapolated into thousands of different combinations and comparisons. In the meantime, his room is a shrine to the Beatles, and it appears that George is by far his favorite. It isn't hard to figure out what he's going to wear, because his entire wardrobe is blue jeans and different variations of the same button-down shirt. There are also more baseball caps than I can imagine anyone needing, but I figure he's not allowed to wear those to school.

It's a relief, in many ways, to be a guy who doesn't mind riding the bus, who has friends waiting for him when he gets on, who doesn't have to deal with anything more troubling than the fact that he ate breakfast and is still hungry.

It's an ordinary day, and I try to lose myself in that.

But between third and fourth periods, I'm dragged right back. Because there, right in the hall, is Nathan Daldry.

At first I think I might be mistaken. There are plenty of kids who could look like Nathan. But then I see the way the other kids in the hall are reacting to him, as if he's this walking joke. He's trying to make it seem like he doesn't notice the laughter, the snickers, the snarky comments. But he can't hide how uncomfortable he is.

I think: *He deserves this. He didn't have to say a word. He could've just let it slide.*

And I think: *It's my fault. I'm the one who did this to him.*

I access AJ and find out that he and Nathan were good friends in elementary school, and are still friendly now. So it makes sense that when he passes by me, I say hello. And that he says hello back.

I sit with my friends at lunch. Some of the guys ask me about the game last night, and I answer vaguely, accessing the whole time.

Out of the corner of my eye, I see Nathan sit down at his own table, eating alone. I don't remember him being friendless, just dull. But it looks as if he's friendless now.

"I'm going to go talk to Nathan," I tell my friends.

One of them groans. "Really? I'm so sick of him."

"I hear he's doing talk shows now," another chimes in.

"You would think the devil would have more important things to do than take a Subaru for a joyride on a Saturday night."

"Seriously."

167

I pick up my tray before the conversation can go any further, and tell them I'll see them later.

Nathan sees me coming over, but still seems surprised when I sit down with him.

"Do you mind?" I ask.

"No," he says. "Not at all."

I don't know what I'm doing. I think of his last email—PROVE IT—and half expect those words to flash from his eyes, for there to be some challenge that I will have to meet. I am the proof. I am right in front of him. But he doesn't know that.

"So how are you doing?" I ask, picking up a fry, trying to act like this is a normal lunchtime conversation between friends.

"Okay, I guess." I get a sense that for all the attention people have been giving him, not many people have been asking him how he's doing.

"So what's new?"

He glances over my shoulder. "Your friends are looking at us."

I turn around, and everyone from my old table suddenly looks anywhere but here.

"Whatever," I say. "Don't pay attention to them. To any of them."

"I'm not. They don't understand."

"I understand. I mean, I understand that they don't understand."

"I know."

"It must be pretty overwhelming, though, having everyone so interested. And all the blogs and stuff. And this reverend."

I wonder if I've pushed too far. But Nathan seems happy to talk. AJ is a good guy.

"Yeah, he really gets it. He knew people would give me grief. But he told me I had to be stronger. I mean, having people laugh is nothing compared to surviving a possession."

Surviving a possession. I have never thought about what I do in those terms. I never thought my presence was something that anyone would have to survive.

Nathan sees me thinking. "What?" he asks.

"I'm just curious—what do you remember from that day?"

Now a wariness creeps into his expression.

"Why are you asking?"

"Curiosity, I guess. I'm not doubting you. Not at all. I just feel like, in all the things I've read and all the things people have said, I never really got to hear your side. It's all been secondhand and thirdhand and probably seventh- or eighth-hand, so I figured I'd just come and ask you firsthand."

I know I'm on dangerous ground here. I can't make AJ too much of a confidant, because tomorrow will come and he might not remember anything that's been said, and that might make Nathan suspicious. But at the same time, I want to know what he remembers.

Nathan wants to talk. I can see it. He knows he's stepped off his own map. And while he won't pull back, he also re-grets it a little. I don't think he ever meant for it to take over his life.

"It was a pretty normal day," he tells me. "Nothing unusual. I was home with my parents. I did chores, that kind of thing. And then—I don't know. Something must have happened.

Because I made up this story about a school musical and borrowed their car for the night. I don't remember the musical part—they told me that later. But there I was, driving around. And I had these . . . urges. Like I was being drawn somewhere."

He pauses.

"Where?" I ask.

He shakes his head. "I don't know. This is the weird part. There are a few hours there that are completely blank. I have this sense of not being in control of my body, but that's it. I have flashes of a party, but I have no idea where, or who else was there. Then suddenly I'm being woken up by a policeman. And I haven't drunk a sip. I haven't done any drugs. They tested for that, you know."

"What if you had a seizure?"

"Why would I borrow my parents' car to have a seizure? No, there was something else in control. The reverend says I must have wrestled with the devil. Like Jacob. I must have known my body was being used for something evil, and I fought it. And then, when I won, the devil left me by the side of the road."

He believes this. He genuinely believes this.

And I can't tell him it's not true. I can't tell him what really happened. Because if I do, AJ will be in danger. I will be in danger.

"It didn't have to be the devil," I say.

Nathan becomes defensive. "I just know, okay? And I'm not the only one. There are lots of people out there who've experienced the same thing. I've chatted with a few of them. It's scary how many things we have in common."

"Are you afraid it will happen again?"

"No. I'm prepared this time. If the devil is anywhere near me, I'll know what to do."

I sit right there across from him and listen.

He doesn't recognize me.

I am not the devil.

This thought is what echoes through my mind the rest of the day.

I am not the devil, but I could be.

Looking at it from afar, looking at it from a perspective like Nathan's, I can see how scary it could be. Because what's to stop me from doing harm? What punishment would there be if I took the pencil in my hand and gouged out the eye of the girl sitting next to me in chem class? Or worse. I could easily get away with the perfect crime. The body that committed the murder would inevitably get caught, but the murderer would go free. Why haven't I thought of this before?

I have the potential to be the devil.

But then I think, *Stop.* I think, *No.* Because, really, does that make me any different from everyone else? Yes, I could get away with it, but certainly we all have the potential to commit the crime. We choose not to. Every single day, we choose not to. I am no different.

I am not the devil.

• • •

There is still no word from Rhiannon. Whether her silence is coming from her confusion or from a desire to be rid of me, I have no way of knowing.

I write to her and say, simply:

I have to see you again.

A

Day 6009

There's still no word from her the next morning.

I get in the car and drive.

The car belongs to Adam Cassidy. He should be in school. But I call the office pretending to be his father and say he has a doctor's appointment.

It may last the entire day.

It's a two-hour drive. I know I should spend it getting to know Adam Cassidy, but he seems incidental to me right now. I used to inhabit lives like this all the time—testing the bare minimum I needed to know in order to get through the day. I got so good at it that I made it through a few days without accessing once. I'm sure these were very blank days for the bodies I was in, because they were extraordinarily blank days for me.

Most of the drive, I think about Rhiannon. How to get her back. How to keep in her good graces. How to make this work.

It's the last part that's the hardest.

When I get to her school, I park where Amy Tran parked. The school day is already in full swing, so when I open the doors, I jump right into the fray. It's between periods, and I have all of two minutes to find her.

I don't know where she is. I don't even know what period's starting. I just push through the halls, looking for her. People brush by, tell me to watch where I'm going. I don't care. There is everyone else, and there is her. I am only focused on her.

I let the universe tell me where to go. I rely purely on instinct, knowing that this kind of instinct comes from somewhere other than me, somewhere other than this body.

She is turning in to a classroom. But she stops. Looks up. Sees me.

I don't know how to explain it. I am an island in the hall as people push around me. She is another island. I see her, and she knows exactly who I am. There is no way for her to know this. But she knows.

She walks away from the classroom, walks toward me. Another bell rings and the rest of the people drain out of the hall, leaving us alone together.

"Hey," she says.

"Hey," I say.

"I thought you might come."

"Are you mad?"

"No, I'm not mad." She glances back at the classroom. "Although Lord knows you're not good for my attendance record."

"I'm not good for anybody's attendance record."

"What's your name today?"

"A," I tell her. "For you, it's always A."

She has a test next period that she can't skip, so we stay on the school grounds. When we start to encounter other kids—kids without classes this period, kids also cutting—she grows a little more cautious.

"Is Justin in class?" I ask, to give her fear a name.

"Yeah. If he decided to go."

We find an empty classroom and go inside. From all the Shakespearean paraphernalia hanging on the walls, I'm guessing we're in an English classroom. Or drama.

We sit in the back row, out of sight of the window in the door.

"How did you know it was me?" I have to ask.

"The way you looked at me," she says. "It couldn't have been anyone else."

This is what love does: It makes you want to rewrite the world. It makes you want to choose the characters, build the scenery, guide the plot. The person you love sits across from you, and you want to do everything in your power to make it possible, endlessly possible. And when it's just the two of you, alone in a room, you can pretend that this is how it is, this is how it will be.

I take her hand and she doesn't pull away. Is this because something between us has changed, or is it only because my body has changed? Is it easier for her to hold Adam Cassidy's hand?

The electricity in the air is muted. This is not going to lead to anything more than an honest conversation.

"I'm sorry about the other night," I say again.

"I deserve part of the blame. I never should have called him."

"What did he say? Afterward?"

"He kept calling you 'that black bitch.'"

"Charming."

"I think he sensed it was a trap. I don't know. He just knew something was off."

"Which is probably why he passed the test."

Rhiannon pulls away. "That's not fair."

"I'm sorry."

I wonder why it is that she's strong enough to say no to me, but not strong enough to say no to him.

"What do you want to do?" I ask her.

She matches my glance perfectly. "What do you want me to do?"

"I want you to do whatever you feel is best for you."

"That's the wrong answer," she tells me.

"Why is it the wrong answer?"

"Because it's a lie."

You are so close, I think. *You are so close, and I can't reach you.*

"Let's go back to my original question," I say. "What do you want to do?"

"I don't want to throw everything away for something uncertain."

"What about me is uncertain?"

She laughs. "Really? Do I have to explain it to you?"

"Besides that. You know you are the most important person I've ever had in my life. That's certain."

"In just two weeks. That's uncertain."

"You know more about me than anyone else does."

"But I can't say the same for you. Not yet."

"You can't deny that there's something between us."

"No. There is. When I saw you today—I didn't know I'd been waiting for you until you were there. And then all of that waiting rushed through me in a second. That's something . . . but I don't know if it's certainty."

I know what I'm asking of you, I want to say. But I stop myself. Because I realize that would be another lie. And she'd call me on it.

She looks at the clock. "I have to get ready for my test. And you have another life to get back to."

I can't help myself. I ask, "Don't you want to see me?"

She holds there for a moment. "I do. And I don't. You would think it would make things easier, but it actually makes them harder."

"So I shouldn't just show up here?"

"Let's stick to email for now. Okay?"

And just like that, the universe goes wrong. Just like that, all the enormity seems to shrink into a ball and float away from my reach.

I feel it, and she doesn't.

Or I feel it, and she won't.

Day 6010

I am four hours away from her.

I'm a girl named Chevelle, and I can't stand the idea of going to school today. So I feign sickness, get permission to stay home. I try to read, play video games, surf the Web, do all the things I used to do to fill the time.

None of them work. The time still feels empty.

I keep checking my email.

Nothing from her.

Nothing.

Nothing.

Day 6011

I am only thirty minutes away from her.

I am woken at dawn by my sister shaking me, shouting my name, Valeria.

I think I'm late for school.

But no. I'm late for work.

I am a maid. An underage, illegal maid.

Valeria doesn't speak English, so all the thoughts I have to access are in Spanish. I barely know what's happening. It takes me time to translate what's going on.

There are four of us in the apartment. We put on our uniforms and a van comes to pick us up. I am the youngest, the least respected. My sister speaks to me, and I nod. I feel like my insides are twisting, and at first I think it's just because of the shock of the situation. Then I realize they really are twisting. Cramps.

I find the words and tell my sister this. She understands, but I'm still going to have to work.

More women join us in the van. And another girl my age. Some people chat, but my sister and I don't say a word to any of them.

The van starts dropping us off at people's homes. Always at least two of us per house, sometimes three or four. I am paired with my sister.

I am in charge of bathrooms. I must scrub the toilets. Remove the hairs from the shower. Shine the mirrors until they gleam.

Each of us is in her own room. We do not talk. We don't play music. We just work.

I am sweating in my uniform. The cramps will not go away. The medicine cabinets are full, but I know that I am here to clean, not to take. Nobody would miss two Midol, but it's not worth the risk.

When I get to the master bathroom, the woman of the house is still in her bedroom, talking on the phone. She doesn't think I can understand a word she says. What a shock it would be were Valeria to stomp right in and start talking to her about the laws of thermodynamics, or the life of Thomas Jefferson, in flawless English.

After two hours, we are done with the house. I think that will be it, but there are four more houses after that. By the end, I can barely move, and my sister, seeing this, does the bathrooms with me. We are a team, and that kinship gives the day the only memory worth keeping.

By the time we get home, I can barely speak. I force myself to have dinner, but it's a silent meal. Then I head to bed, leaving room for my sister beside me.

Email is not an option.

Day 6012

I am an hour away from her.

I open Sallie Swain's eyes and search her room for a computer. Before I'm fully awake, I am loading up my email.

A,

I'm sorry I didn't get to write to you yesterday. I meant to, but then all these other things happened (none of them important, just time-consuming). Even though it was hard to see you, it was good to see you. I mean it. But taking a break and thinking things out makes sense.

How was your day? What did you do?

R

Does she really want to know, or is she just being polite? I feel as if she could be talking to anybody. And while I once thought what I wanted from her was this normal, everyday tone, now that I have it, the normalcy disappoints.

I write her back and tell her about the last two days. Then I tell her I have to go—I can't skip school today, because Sallie Swain has a big cross-country meet, and it wouldn't be fair for her to miss it.

I run. I am made for running. Because when you run, you could be anyone. You hone yourself into a body, nothing more or less than a body. You respond as a body, to the body. If you are racing to win, you have no thoughts but the body's thoughts, no goals but the body's goals. You obliterate yourself in the name of speed. You negate yourself in order to make it past the finish line.

Day 6013

I am an hour and a half away from her, and I am part of a happy family.

The Stevens family does not let Saturdays go to waste. No, Mrs. Stevens wakes Daniel up at nine o'clock on the dot and tells him to get ready for a drive. By the time he's out of the shower, Mr. Stevens has loaded the car, and Daniel's two sisters are raring to go.

First stop in Baltimore is the art museum for a Winslow Homer exhibit. Then there's lunch at Inner Harbor, followed by a long trip to the aquarium. Then an IMAX version of a Disney movie, for the girls, and dinner at a seafood restaurant that's so famous they don't feel the need to put the word *famous* in their name.

There are brief moments of tension—a sister who is bored by the dolphins, a spot where Dad gets frustrated about the lack of available parking spaces. But for the most part, everyone remains happy. They are so caught up in their happiness that they don't realize I'm not really a part of it. I am wandering along the periphery. I am like the people in the Winslow

Homer paintings, sharing the same room with them but not really there. I am like the fish in the aquarium, thinking in a different language, adapting to a life that's not my natural habitat. I am the people in the other cars, each with his or her own story, but passing too quickly to be noticed or understood.

It is a good day, and that certainly helps me more than a bad day. There are moments when I don't think about her, or even think about me. There are moments I just sit in my frame, float in my tank, ride in my car and say nothing, think nothing that connects me to anything at all.

Day 6014

I am forty minutes away from her.

It's Sunday, so I decide to see what Reverend Poole is up to.

Orlando, the boy whose body I'm in, rarely wakes before noon on Sunday, so if I keep my typing quiet, his parents will leave me alone.

Reverend Poole has set up a website for people to tell their stories of possession. Already there are hundreds of posts and videos.

Nathan's post is perfunctory, as if it's been summarized from his earlier statements. He has not made a video. I don't learn anything new.

Other stories are more elaborate. Some are clearly the work of nutjobs—clinically paranoid people who need professional help, not arenas in which to vent their hyperbolic conspiracy theories. Other testimonials, however, are almost painfully sincere. There's a woman who genuinely feels that Satan struck her at the checkout line in the supermarket, filling her with the urge to steal. And there's a man whose son killed himself, who believes that the son must have been possessed by real demons, rather than fighting the more metaphorical ones inside.

Since I only inhabit people around my age, I look for the teenagers. Poole must screen each and every thing that appears on the site, because there's no parody, no sarcasm. So teenagers are few and far between. There is one, however, from Montana, whose story makes me shiver. He says he was possessed, but only for one day. Nothing major happened, but he knows he wasn't in control of his body.

I have never been to Montana. I'm sure of it.

But what he's describing is a lot like what I do.

There is a link on Poole's site:

IF YOU BELIEVE THE DEVIL IS WITHIN YOU,
CLICK HERE OR CALL THIS NUMBER.

But if the devil is truly within you, why would he click or call?

I go on my old email and find that Nathan's tried to get in touch with me again.

No proof, then?

Get help.

He even attaches the link to Poole's page. I want to write back to him and point out that he and I talked just the other day. I want him to ask his friend AJ how his Monday was. I want him to fear that I could be there at any moment, in any person.

No, I think. *Don't feel that way.*

It was so much easier when I didn't want anything.

Not getting what you want can make you cruel.

I check my other email and find another message from Rhiannon. She tells me vaguely about her weekend and asks me vaguely about my weekend.

I try to sleep for the rest of the day.

Day 6015

I wake up, and I'm not four hours away from her, or one hour, or even fifteen minutes.

No, I wake up in her house.

In her room.

In her body.

At first I think I'm still asleep, dreaming. I open my eyes, and I could be in any girl's room—a room she's lived in for a long time, with Madame Alexander dolls sharing space with eyeliner pencils and fashion magazines. I am sure it is only a dreamworld trick when I access my identity and find it's Rhiannon who appears. Have I had this dream before? I don't think so. But in a way, it makes sense. If she's the thought, the hope, the concern underneath my every waking moment, then why wouldn't she permeate my sleeping hours as well?

But I'm not dreaming. I am feeling the pressure of the pillow against my face. I am feeling the sheets around my legs. I am breathing. In dreams, we never bother to breathe.

I instantly feel like the world has turned to glass. Every

moment is delicate. Every movement is a risk. I know she wouldn't want me here. I know the horror she would be feeling right now. The complete loss of control.

Everything I do could break something. Every word I say. Every move I make.

I look around some more. Some girls and boys obliterate their rooms as they grow older, thinking they have to banish all their younger incarnations in order to convincingly inhabit a new one. But Rhiannon is more secure with her past than that. I see pictures of her and her family when she is three, eight, ten, fourteen. A stuffed penguin still keeps watch over her bed. J. D. Salinger sits next to Dr. Seuss on her bookshelf.

I pick up one of the photographs. If I wanted to, I could try to access the day it was taken. It looks like she and her sister are at a county fair. Her sister is wearing some kind of prize ribbon. It would be so easy for me to find out what it is. But then it wouldn't be Rhiannon telling me.

I want her here next to me, giving me the tour. Now I feel like I've broken in.

The only way to get through this is to live the day as Rhiannon would want me to. If she knows I was here—and I have a feeling she will—I want her to be certain that I didn't take any advantage. I know instinctively that this is not the way I want to learn anything. This is not the way I want to gain anything.

Because of this, it feels like all I can do is lose.

This is how it feels to raise her arm.

This is how it feels to blink her eyes.

This is how it feels to turn her head.

This is how it feels to run her tongue over her lips, to put her feet on the floor.

This is the weight of her. This is the height of her. This is the angle from which she sees the world.

I could access every memory she has of me. I could access every memory she has of Justin. I could hear what she's said when I haven't been around.

"Hello."

This is what her voice sounds like from the inside.

This is what her voice sounds like when she's by herself.

Her mother shuffles past me in the hallway, awake but not by her own choice. It has been a long night for her, leading into a short morning. She says she's going to try to go back to sleep, but adds that it's not likely.

Rhiannon's father is in the kitchen, about to leave for work. His "good morning" holds less complaint. But he's in a rush, and I have a sense that those two words are all Rhiannon's going to get. I get some cereal as he searches for his keys, then say a goodbye echo to his own quick goodbye.

I decide not to take a shower, or even to change out of last night's underwear. When I go to the bathroom, I will keep my eyes closed. I feel naked enough looking in the mirror and seeing Rhiannon's face. I can't push it any further than that. Brushing her hair is already too intimate. Putting on makeup.

Even putting on shoes. To experience her body's balance within the world, the sensation of her skin from the inside, touching her face and receiving the touch from both sides—it's unavoidable and incredibly intense. I try to think only as me, but I can't stop feeling that I'm her.

I have to access to find my keys, then find my way to school. Maybe I should stay home, but I'm not sure I could bear being alone as her for that long without any distractions. The radio station is tuned to the news, which is unexpected. Her sister's graduation tassel hangs from the rearview mirror.

I look to the passenger seat, expecting Rhiannon to be there, looking at me, telling me where to go.

I am going to try to avoid Justin. I go early to my locker, get my books, then head directly to my first class. As friends trickle into the classroom, I make as much conversation as I can. Nobody notices any difference—not because they don't care, but because it's early in the morning, and nobody's expected to be fully there. I've been so hung up on Justin that I haven't realized how much Rhiannon's friends are part of her life. I realize that until now, the most I've really seen her full life has been when I was Amy Tran, visiting the school for the day. Because she doesn't spend her day alone. These friends are not what she wants to escape when she makes her escape.

"Did you get to all the bio?" her friend Rebecca asks. At first I think she's asking to copy my homework, but then I realize she's offering hers. Sure enough, Rhiannon has a few problems left to do. I thank Rebecca and start copying away.

When class begins and the teacher starts to lecture, all I need to do is listen and take notes.

Remember this, I tell Rhiannon. *Remember how ordinary it is.*

I can't help but get glimpses of things I've never seen before. Doodles in her notebook of trees and mountains. The light imprint her socks leave on her ankles. A small red birthmark at the base of her left thumb. These are probably things she never notices. But because I'm new to her, I see everything.

This is how it feels to hold a pencil in her hand.

This is how it feels to fill her lungs with air.

This is how it feels to press her back against the chair.

This is how it feels to touch her ear.

This is what the world sounds like to her. This is what she hears every day.

I allow myself one memory. I don't choose it. It just rises, and I don't cut it off.

Rebecca is sitting next to me, chewing gum. At one point in class, she's so bored that she takes it out of her mouth and starts playing with it between her fingers. And I remember a time she did this in sixth grade. The teacher caught her, and Rebecca was so surprised at being caught that she startled, and the gum went flying from her hand and into Hannah Walker's hair. Hannah didn't know what had happened at first, and all the kids started laughing at her, making the teacher more furious. I was the one who leaned over and told her there was gum in her hair. I was the one who worked it out with my fingers, careful not to get it knotted farther in. I got it all out. I remember I got it all out.

• • •

I try to avoid Justin at lunch, but I fail.

I'm in a hallway nowhere near either of our lockers or the lunchroom, and he ends up being there, too. He's not happy to see me or unhappy to see me; he regards my presence as a fact, no different than the bell between periods.

"Wanna take it outside?" he asks.

"Sure," I say, not really knowing what I'm agreeing to.

In this case, "outside" means a pizza place two blocks from the school. We get slices and Cokes. He pays for himself, but makes no offer to pay for me. Which is fine.

He's in a talkative mood, focusing on what I imagine is his favorite theme: the injustices perpetrated against him by everyone else, all the time. It's a pretty wide conspiracy, involving everything from his car's faulty ignition to his father's nagging about college to his English teacher's "gay way of talking." I'm barely following his conversation, and *following* very much feels like the right word, because this conversation is designed for me to be at least five steps behind. He doesn't want my opinion. Anytime I offer something, he just lets it sit there on the table between us, doesn't pick it up.

As he goes on about what a bitch Stephanie is being to Steve, and keeps shoving pizza into his face, and looks at the table much more than he looks at me, I must struggle against the palpable temptation to do something drastic. Although he doesn't realize it, the power is all mine. All it would take is a minute—less—to break up with him. All it would take are a few well-chosen words to cut the tether. He could counterattack with tears or rage or promises, and I could withstand every single one.

It is so much what I want, but I don't open my mouth. I don't use this power. Because I know that this kind of ending would never lead to the beginning I want. If I end things like this, Rhiannon will never forgive me. Not only might she undo it all tomorrow, she would also define me by my betrayal for as long as I remained in her life, which wouldn't be long.

I hope she realizes: The whole time, Justin never notices. She can see me in whatever body I'm in, but he can't see she's missing. He's not looking that closely.

Then he calls her Silver. Just a simple, "Let's go, Silver," when we're done. I think maybe I've heard him wrong. So I access, and there it is. A moment between them. They've been reading *The Outsiders* for English class, lying on his bed side by side with the same book open, she a little farther along. She thinks the book's a relic from when weepy gang boys bonded over *Gone with the Wind*, but she quiets herself when she sees how much it's affecting him. She stays there after she's finished, starts reading the beginning again until he's done. Then he closes the book and says, "Wow. I mean, nothing gold can stay. How true is that?" She doesn't want to break the moment, doesn't want to question what it means. And she's rewarded when he smiles and says, "I guess that means we'll have to be silver." When she leaves that night, he calls out, "So long, Silver!" And it stays.

When we head back to school, we don't hold hands, or even talk. When we part, he doesn't wish me a good afternoon or thank me for the time we just had together. He doesn't even say he'll see me soon. He just assumes it.

I am hyperaware—as he leaves me, as I am surrounded by other people—of the perilous nature of what I am attempting, of the butterfly effect that threatens to flutter its wings with every interaction. If you think about it hard enough, if you trace potential reverberations long enough, every step can be a false step, any move can lead to an unintended consequence.

Who am I ignoring that I shouldn't be ignoring? What am I not saying that I should be saying? What won't I notice that she would absolutely notice? While I'm out in the public hallways, what private languages am I not hearing?

When we look at a crowd, our eyes naturally go to certain people, whether we know them or not. But my glance right now is blank. I know what I see, but not what she'd see.

The world is still glass.

This is how it feels to read words through her eyes.

This is how it feels to turn a page with her hand.

This is how it feels when her ankles cross.

This is how it feels to lower her head so her hair hides her eyes from view.

This is what her handwriting looks like. This is how it is made. This is how she signs her name.

There's a quiz in English class. It's *Tess of the d'Urbervilles*, which I've read. I think Rhiannon does okay.

I access enough to know she doesn't have any plans after school. Justin finds her before last period and asks her if she wants to do something. It's clear to me what this something will be, and I can't see much benefit to it.

"What do you want to do?" I ask.

He looks at me like I'm an imbecile puppy.

"What do you think?"

"Homework?"

He snorts. "Yeah, we can call it that, if you want."

I need a lie. Really, what I want to do is say yes and then blow him off. But there could be repercussions for that tomorrow. So instead I tell him I have to take my mom to some doctor for her sleep problems. It's a real drag, but they'll be drugging her up and she probably won't be able to drive herself home.

"Well, as long as they give her plenty of pills," he says. "I love your mom's pills."

He leans in for a kiss and I have to do it. Amazing how it's the same two bodies as three weeks ago, but the kiss couldn't be more different. Before, when our tongues touched, when I was on the other side of it, it felt like another form of intimate conversation. Now it feels like he's shoving something alien and gross into my mouth.

"Go get some pills," he says when we break apart.

I hope my mom has some extra birth control I can slip him.

We have been to an ocean together, and a forest. So today I decide we should go to a mountain.

A quick search shows me the nearest place to climb. I have no idea if Rhiannon's ever been there, but I'm not sure that matters.

She's not really dressed for hiking—her Converse don't have a whole lot of tread left on them. I plunge forward nonetheless, taking a water bottle and a phone with me, and leaving everything else in the car.

Again it's a Monday, and the trails are largely clear. Every now and then I'll pass another hiker on his or her way down, and we'll nod or say hello, in the way that people surrounded by acres of silence do. The paths are haphazardly marked, or perhaps I'm just not attentive enough. I can feel the incline as it's measured by Rhiannon's leg muscles, can feel her breath shift into more challenging air. I keep going.

For our afternoon, I've decided to attempt to give Rhiannon the satisfaction of being fully alone. Not the lethargy of lying on the couch or the dull monotony of drifting off in math class. Not the midnight wandering in a sleeping house or the pain of being left in a room after the door has been slammed shut. This alone is not a variation of any of those. This alone is its own being. Feeling the body, but not using it to sidetrack the mind. Moving with purpose, but not in a rush. Conversing not with the person next to you, but with all of the elements.

Sweating and aching and climbing and making sure not to slip, not to fall, not to get too lost, but lost enough.

And at the end, the pause. At the top, the view. Grappling with the last steep incline, the final turns of the path, and finding yourself above it all. It's not that there's a spectacular view. It's not that we've reached the peak of Everest. But here we are, at the highest point the eye can see, not counting the clouds, the air, the lazy sun. I am eleven again; we are atop that tree. The air feels cleaner because when the world is below us, we allow ourselves to breathe fully. When no one else is around, we open ourselves to the quieter astonishments that enormity can offer.

Remember this, I implore Rhiannon as I look out over the trees, as I catch her breath. *Remember this sensation. Remember that we were here.*

I sit down on a rock and drink some water. I know I am in her body, but it feels very much like she is here with me. Like we are two separate people, together, sharing this.

I have dinner with her parents. When they ask me what I did today, I tell them. I'm sure I tell them more than Rhiannon would, more than the day usually allows.

"That sounds wonderful," her mother says.

"Just be careful out there," her father adds. Then he changes the conversation to something that happened at work, and my day, briefly registered, becomes solely my own again.

• • •

I do her homework as best I can. I don't check her email, afraid that there will be something there that she wouldn't want me to see. I don't check my own email, because she's the only person I'd want to hear from. There's a book on her night table, but I don't read it, for fear that she won't remember what I've read, and will have to read it again anyway. I thumb through some magazines.

Finally, I decide to leave her a note. It's the only way she'll know for sure that I've been here. Another palpable temptation is to pretend that none of this has happened, to deny any accusation she makes based on whatever remnant of memory remains. But I want to be truthful. The only way this will work is if we are entirely truthful.

So I tell her. At the very beginning of my letter, I ask her to try to remember the day as much as possible before she reads on, so what I write won't taint what's really left in her mind. I explain that I never would have chosen to be in her body, that it isn't something I have control over. I tell her I tried to respect her day as much as I knew how, and that I hope not to have caused any disruption in her life. Then, in her own handwriting, I map out our day for her. It is the first time I've ever written to the person whose life I've occupied, and it feels both strange and comfortable, knowing that Rhiannon will be the reader of these words. There are so many explanations I can leave unsaid. The fact that I am writing the letter at all is an expression of faith—faith both in her and in the belief that trust can lead to trust, and truth can lead to truth.

• • •

This is how it feels as her eyelids close.

This is how sleep will taste to her.

This is how night touches her skin.

This is how the house noises sing her to bed.

This is the goodbye she feels every night. This is how her day ends.

I curl up in bed, still wearing my clothes. Now that the day is almost done, the world of glass recedes, the butterfly threat diminishes. I imagine that we're both here in this bed, that my invisible body is nestled against hers. We are breathing at the same pace, our chests rising and falling in unison. We have no need to whisper, because at this distance, all we need is thought. Our eyes close at the same time. We feel the same sheets against us, the same night. Our breath slows together. We split into different versions of the same dream. Sleep takes us at the exact same time.

Day 6016

A,

I think I remember everything. Where are you today?
Instead of writing a long email, I want to talk.

R

I am roughly two hours away from her when I read this
email, in the body of a boy named Dylan Cooper. He's a hard-
core design geek, and his room is an orchard of Apple products.
I access him enough to know that when he really, really likes a
girl, he creates a font and names it after her.

I write back to Rhiannon and tell her where I am. She writes
back immediately—she must be waiting by her computer—
and asks me if I can meet her after school. We arrange to meet
at the Clover Bookstore.

Dylan is a charmer. He also, from what I can tell, has crushes
on three different girls at the same time. I spend the day trying

not to commit him any closer to any of them. He will have to figure out for himself which font he prefers.

I am a half hour early to the bookstore, but I'm too nervous to read anything but the faces of the people around me.

She walks in the door, also early. I don't need to stand or wave. She looks around the room, sees me and the way I'm looking at her, and knows.

"Hey," she says.

"Hey," I say back.

"It feels like the morning after," she tells me.

"I know," I say.

She's gotten us coffee, and we sit there at the table with the cups sheltered in our hands.

I see some of the things I noticed yesterday—the birthmark, the scattering of pimples on her forehead. But they don't matter to me nearly as much as the complete picture.

She doesn't seem freaked out. She doesn't seem angry. If anything, she seems at peace with what's happened. When the shock wears off, you always hope there's understanding underneath. And with Rhiannon, it seems as if the understanding has already surfaced. Any vestige of doubt has been swept away.

"I woke up and I knew something was different," she tells me. "Even before I saw your letter. It wasn't the usual disorientation. But I didn't feel like I'd missed a day. It was like I woke up and something had been . . . added. Then I saw your letter and started reading, and immediately I knew it was true. It had actually happened. I stopped when you told me to stop, and tried to remember everything about yesterday. It was all there. Not the things I'd usually forget, like waking up or brushing my teeth. But climbing that mountain. Having lunch with Justin. Dinner with my parents. Even writing the letter itself—I had a memory of that. It shouldn't make sense—why would I write a letter to myself for the next morning? But in my mind, it makes sense."

"Do you feel me there? In your memories."

She shakes her head. "Not in the way you'd think. I don't feel you in control of things, or in my body, or anything. I feel like you were with me. Like, I can feel your presence there, but it's outside of me."

She stops. Starts again. "It's insane that we're having this conversation."

But I want to know more.

"I wanted you to remember everything," I tell her. "And it sounds like your mind went along with that. Or maybe it wanted you to remember everything, too."

"I don't know. I'm just glad I do."

We talk more about the day, more about how strange this is. Finally, she says, "Thank you for not messing up my life. And for keeping my clothes on. Unless, of course, you didn't want me to remember that you sneaked a peek."

"No peeks were sneaked."

"I believe you. Amazingly, I believe you about everything."

I can tell there's something else she wants to say.

"What?" I ask.

"It's just—do you feel you know me more now? Because the weird thing is . . . I feel I know you more. Because of what you did, and what you didn't do. Isn't that strange? I would have thought that you would've found out more about me . . . but I'm not sure that's true."

"I got to meet your parents," I say.

"And what was your impression?"

"I think they both care about you, in their own way."

She laughs. "Well said."

"Well, it was nice to meet them."

"I'll be sure to remember that when you really meet them. 'Mom and Dad, this is A. You think you're meeting him for the first time, but actually, you've met him before, when he was in my body.'"

"I'm sure that'll go over well."

Of course, we both know it won't go over at all. There's no way for me to meet her parents. Not as myself.

I don't say it, and neither does she. I don't even know if she's thinking it in the pause that ensues. But I am.

"It can never happen again, right?" she eventually asks. "You're never the same person twice."

"Correct. It will never happen again."

"No offense, but I'm relieved I don't have to go to sleep wondering if I'm going to wake up with you in control. Once, I guess I can deal with. But don't make a habit of it."

"I promise—I want to make a habit of being with you, but not that way."

And there it is: I had to go and bring up the issue of where we go from here. We got through the past, are enjoying the present, but now I push it and we stumble on the future.

"You've seen my life," she says. "Tell me a way you think this can work."

"We'll find a way," I tell her.

"That's not an answer. It's a hope."

"Hope's gotten us this far. Not answers."

She gives me a hint of a grin. "Good point." She takes a sip of coffee, and I can tell another question's coming. "I know this is weird, but . . . I keep wondering. Are you really not a boy or a girl? I mean, when you were in my body, did you feel more . . . at home than you would in the body of a boy?"

It's interesting to me that this is the thing she's hung up on.

"I'm just me," I tell her. "I always feel at home and I never feel at home. That's just the way it is."

"And when you're kissing someone?"

"Same thing."

"And during sex?"

"Is Dylan blushing?" I ask. "Right now, is he blushing?"

"Yeah," Rhiannon says.

"Good. Because I know I am."

"You've never had—?"

"It wouldn't be fair of me to—"

"Never!"

"I am so glad you find this funny."

"Sorry."

"There was this one girl."

"Really?"

"Yeah. Yesterday. When I was in your body. Don't you remember? I think you might have gotten her pregnant."

"That's not funny!" she says. But she's laughing.

"I only have eyes for you," I say.

Just six words, and the conversation turns serious again. I can feel it like a shift in the air, like when a cloud moves over the sun. The laughter stops, and we sit there in the moment after it's faded away.

"A—" she starts. But I don't want to hear it. I don't want to hear about Justin or impossibilities or any of the other reasons why we can't be together.

"Not now," I say. "Let's stay on the nice note."

"Okay," she says. "I can do that."

She asks me about more of the things I noticed when I was in her body, and I tell her about the birthmark, about different people I noticed in her classes, about her parents' concern. I share the Rebecca memory, but don't tell her my observations about Justin, because she already knows those things, whether or not she admits them to me or herself. And I don't mention the slight wrinkles around her eyes or her pimples, because I know they would bother her, even when they add something real to her beauty.

Both of us have to be home for dinner, but the only way I'm willing to let her leave is to extract a promise that we'll share time together soon. Tomorrow. Or if not tomorrow, the next day.

"How can I say no?" she says. "I'm dying to see who you'll be next."

I know it's a joke, but I have to tell her, "I'll always be A."

She stands up and kisses me on the forehead.

"I know," she says. "That's why I want to see you."

We leave on a nice note.

Day 6017

I have gone two days without thinking about Nathan, but it's clear that Nathan hasn't gone two days without thinking about me.

7:30 p.m., MONDAY
I still want proof.

8:14 p.m., MONDAY
Why aren't you talking to me?

11:43 p.m., MONDAY
You did this to me. I deserve an explanation.

6:13 a.m., TUESDAY
I can't sleep anymore. I wonder if you're going to come back. I wonder what you'll do to me. Are you mad?

2:30 p.m., TUESDAY
You have to be the devil. Only the devil would leave me like this.

2:12 a.m., WEDNESDAY

Do you have any idea what it's like for me now?

The burden I feel is the burden of responsibility, which is a tricky one to deal with. It makes me slower, heavier. But at the same time, it prevents me from floating away into meaninglessness.

It is six in the morning; Vanessa Martinez has gotten up early. After reading Nathan's emails, I think about what Rhiannon said, what Rhiannon feared. Nathan deserves no less of a response from me.

It will never happen again. That is an absolute. I can't explain much more than that, but this much I know: It only happens once. Then you move on.

He writes me back two minutes later.

Who are you? How am I supposed to believe you?

I know that any response I give runs the risk of being posted on Reverend Poole's website within seconds. I don't want to give him my real name. But I feel if I give him a name, it will make it less likely he sees me as the devil, and more likely he will see me for what I am: just a person like him.

My name is Andrew. You need to believe me because I am the only person who truly understands what happened to you.

Not surprisingly, he replies with:

Prove it.

I tell him:

You went to a party. You didn't drink. You chatted with a girl there. Eventually she asked you if you wanted to go dance in the basement. You did. And for about an hour, you danced. You lost track of time. You lost track of yourself. And it was one of the most fantastic moments of your life. I don't know if you remember it, but there will probably come a time when you are dancing like that again, and it will feel familiar, you will know you've done it before. That will be the day you forgot. That's how you'll get that part of it back.

This isn't enough.

But why was I there?

I try to keep it simple.

You were there to talk to the girl. For just that one day, you wanted to talk to that girl.

He asks:

What is her name?

I can't get her involved. I can't explain the whole story. So I choose to evade.

> That's not important. The important thing is that for a short time, it was worth it. You were having so much fun that you lost track of time. That's why you were at the side of the road. You didn't drink. You didn't crash. You just ran out of time.

> I'm sure it was scary. I'm positive it's hard to comprehend. But it will never happen again.

> Answerless questions can destroy you. Move on.

It's the truth, but it's not enough.

> That would be easy for you, right? If I moved on.

Every chance I give him, every truth I tell him, lightens the burden of my responsibility that much more. I sympathize with his confusion, but I feel nothing toward his hostility.

> Nathan, what you do or don't do is no concern of mine. I'm just trying to help. You're a good guy. I am not your enemy. I never have been. Our paths just happened to cross. Now they've diverged.

> I'm going to go now.

I close the window, then open a new one to see if Rhiannon will appear in it. I realize I haven't yet determined how far away I am from her, and am disheartened to find she's nearly four hours away. I break the news to her in an email, and an hour later she says that it was going to be hard to meet up today, anyway. So we aim for tomorrow.

In the meantime, there's Vanessa Martinez to contend with. She runs at least two miles every morning, and I am already late for the routine. She has to make do with a single mile, and I can almost hear her chiding me for it. At breakfast, though, nobody else says anything—Vanessa's parents and sister seem genuinely afraid of her.

This is my first tipoff to something I will see evidenced again and again throughout the day: Vanessa Martinez is not a kind person.

It's there when she meets up with her friends at the start of school. They, too, are afraid of her. They're not dressed identically, but it's clear they've all dressed within the same sartorial guidelines, dictated by you-know-who.

She has a poison personality, and I feel that even I am susceptible to it. Every time there's something mean to be said, everyone looks to her for a comment. Even the teachers. And I find myself stuck in those silences, with words on the venomous tip of my tongue. I see all the girls who aren't dressed within the guidelines, and see how easy it would be to tear them all apart.

Is that a backpack that Lauren has on? I guess she's acting like she's in third grade until her chest fills in. And, oh my God, why is Felicity wearing those socks? Are those kittens? I thought only convicted child molesters were allowed to wear those. And Kendall's top? I don't think there's anything sadder than an unsexy girl trying to dress sexy. We should have a fund-raiser for her, it's so sad. Like, tornado victims would look at her and say, "No, really, we don't need the money—give it to that unfortunate girl."

I don't want these thoughts anywhere near my mind. The weird thing is that when I withhold them, when I don't let Vanessa say them out loud, I don't sense relief from any of the people around me. I sense disappointment. They're bored. And their boredom is the thing that the meanness feeds on.

Vanessa's boyfriend, a jock named Jeff, thinks it's her time of the month. Her best friend and number one acolyte, Cynthia, asks her if someone died. They know something's off, but will never guess the real reason. They certainly won't think she's been taken over by the devil. If anything, they're suspicious that the devil's taken a day off.

I know it would be foolish of me to try to change her. I could run off this afternoon and sign her up to volunteer in a soup kitchen, but I'm sure when she arrived there tomorrow, she'd only make fun of the homeless people's clothes, and the quality of the soup. The best I could probably do would be to get Vanessa into a compromising position that someone could blackmail her about. (*Did you all see the video of Vanessa Martinez walking through the hallway in her thong underwear, singing songs from Sesame Street? And then she ran into the girls' room and flushed her own head in a toilet?*) But that would be stooping to her level, and I'm sure that using her own poison against her would cause at least a little of it to fall back inside me as well.

So I don't try to change her. I simply halt her ire for a single day.

It's exhausting, trying to make a bad person act good. You can see why it's so much easier for them to be bad.

I want to tell Rhiannon all about it. Because when something happens, she's the person I want to tell. The most basic indicator of love.

I have to resort to email, and email is not enough. I am starting to get tired of relying on words. They are full of meaning, yes, but they lack sensation. Writing to her is not the same as seeing her face as she listens. Hearing back from her is not the same as hearing her voice. I have always been grateful for technology, but now it feels as if there's a little hitch of separation woven into any digital interaction. I want to be there, and this scares me. All my usual disconnected comforts are being taken away, now that I see the greater comfort of presence.

Nathan also emails me, as I knew he would.

You can't leave now. I have more questions.

I don't have the heart to tell him that's the wrong way to think about the world. There will always be more questions. Every answer leads to more questions.

The only way to survive is to let some of them go.

Day 6018

The next day I am a boy named George, and I am only forty-five minutes away from Rhiannon. She emails me and says she'll be able to leave school at lunch.

I, however, am going to have a harder time, because today I am homeschooled.

George's mother and father are stay-at-home parents, and George and his two brothers stay at home with them each and every day. The room that in most homes would be called the rec room is instead called "the schoolhouse" by George's family. The parents have even set up three desks for them, which seem to have been left over from a one-room schoolhouse at the turn of the last century.

There is no sleeping late here. We're all woken at seven, and there's a protocol about who showers when. I manage to sneak a few minutes at the computer to read Rhiannon's message and send her one of my own, saying we'll have to see how the day plays out. Then, at eight, we're promptly at our desks, and while our father works at the other end of the house, our mother teaches us.

By accessing, I learn that George has never been in a classroom besides this one, because of a fight his parents had with his older brother's kindergarten teacher about her methods. I can't imagine what kindergarten methods would be shocking enough to pull a whole family out of school forever, but there's no way to access information about this event—George has no idea. He's only dealt with the repercussions.

I have been homeschooled before, by parents who were engaged and engaging, who made sure their kids had room to explore and grow. This is not the case here. George's mother is made of stern, unyielding material, and she also happens to be the slowest speaker I've ever heard.

"Boys . . . we're going to talk . . . about . . . the events . . . leading up . . . to . . . the Civil . . . War."

The brothers are all resigned to this. They stare forward at all times, a pantomime of paying perfect attention.

"The president . . . of the . . . South . . . was . . . a man . . . named . . . Jefferson . . . Davis."

I refuse to be held hostage like this—not when Rhiannon will soon be waiting for me. So after an hour, I decide to take a page from Nathan's playbook.

I start asking questions.

What was the name of Jefferson Davis's wife?

Which states were in the Union?

How many people actually died at Gettysburg?

Did Lincoln write the Gettysburg Address all by himself?

And about three dozen more.

My brothers look at me like I'm on cocaine, and my mother gets flustered with each question, since she has to look up each answer.

"Jefferson Davis . . . was married . . . twice. His first wife . . . Sarah . . . was the daughter of . . . President . . . Zachary Taylor. But Sarah . . . died . . . of malaria . . . three months after . . . they . . . were . . . married. He remarried . . ."

This goes on for another hour. Then I ask her if I can go to the library, to get some books on the subject.

She tells me yes, and offers to drop me off herself.

It's the middle of a school day, so I'm the only kid in the library. The librarian knows me, though, and knows where I'm coming from. She is nice to me but abrupt with my mother, leading me to believe that the kindergarten teacher isn't the only person in town who my mother thinks is not doing her job right.

I find a computer and email my location to Rhiannon. Then I take a copy of *Feed* off the shelves and try to remember where I left off reading, a number of bodies ago. I sit at a carrel by a window and keep being drawn to the traffic, even though I know it's still a couple of hours until Rhiannon will show up.

I shed my borrowed life for an hour and put on the borrowed life of the book I'm reading. Rhiannon finds me like that, in the selfless reading space that the mind loans out. I don't even notice her standing there at first.

"Ahem," she says. "I figured you were the only kid in the building, so it had to be you."

It's too easy—I can't resist.

"Excuse me?" I say somewhat abruptly.

"It's you, right?"

I make George look as confused as possible. "Do I know you?"

Now she starts to doubt herself. "Oh, I'm sorry. I just, uh, am supposed to meet somebody."

"What does he look like?"

"I don't, um, know. It's, like, an online thing."

I grunt. "Shouldn't you be in school?"

"Shouldn't *you* be in school?"

"I can't. There's this really amazing girl I'm supposed to meet."

She looks at me hard. "You jerk."

"Sorry, it was just—"

"You jerky . . . jerk."

She's seriously pissed; I've seriously messed up.

I stand up from my carrel.

"Rhiannon, I'm sorry."

"You can't do that. It's not fair." She is actually backing away from me.

"I will never do it again. I promise."

"I can't believe you just did that. Look me in the eyes and say it again. That you promise."

I look her in the eyes. "I promise."

It's enough, but not really. "I believe you," she says. "But you're still a jerk until you prove otherwise."

• • •

We wait until the librarian is distracted, then sneak out the door. I'm worried there's some law about reporting homeschooled kids when they go AWOL. I know George's mother is coming back in two hours, so we don't have much time.

We head to a Chinese restaurant in town. If they think we should be in school, they keep it to themselves. Rhiannon tells me about her uneventful morning—Steve and Stephanie got into another fight, but then made up by second period—and I tell her about being in Vanessa's body.

"I know so many girls like that," Rhiannon says when I'm done. "The dangerous ones are the ones who are actually good at it."

"I suspect she's very good at it."

"Well, I'm glad I didn't have to meet her."

But you didn't get to see me, I think. I keep it to myself.

We press our knees together under the table. My hands find hers and we hold them there. We talk as if none of this is happening, as if we can't feel life pulse through all the spots where we're touching.

"I'm sorry for calling you a jerk," she says. "I just—this is hard enough as it is. And I was so sure I was right."

"I *was* a jerk. I'm taking for granted how normal this all feels."

"Justin sometimes does that. Pretends I didn't tell him something I just told him. Or makes up this whole story, then laughs when I fall for it. I hate that."

"I'm sorry—"

"No, it's okay. I mean, it's not like he was the first one.

218

I guess there's something about me that people love to fool. And I'd probably do it—fool people—if it ever occurred to me."

I take all of the chopsticks out of their holder and put them on the table.

"What are you doing?" Rhiannon asks.

I use the chopsticks to outline the biggest heart possible. Then I use the Sweet'N Low packets to fill it in. I borrow some from two other tables when I run out.

When I'm done, I point to the heart on the table.

"This," I say, "is only about one ninety-millionth of how I feel about you."

She laughs.

"I'll try not to take it personally," she says.

"Take what personally?" I say. "You should take it very personally."

"The fact that you used artificial sweetener?"

I take a Sweet'N Low packet and fling it at her.

"Not everything is a symbol!" I shout.

She picks up a chopstick and brandishes it as a sword. I pick up another chopstick in order to duel.

We are doing this when the food arrives. I'm distracted and she gets a good shot in at my chest.

"I die!" I proclaim.

"Who has the moo shu chicken?" the waiter asks.

The waiter continues to indulge us as we laugh and talk our way through lunch. He's a real pro, the kind of waiter who refills your water glass when it's half empty, without you noticing he's doing it.

He delivers us our fortune cookies at the end of the meal. Rhiannon breaks hers neatly in half, checks out the slip of paper, and frowns.

"This isn't a fortune," she says, showing it to me.

YOU HAVE A NICE SMILE.

"No. *You will have a nice smile*—that would be a fortune," I tell her.

"I'm going to send it back."

I raise an eyebrow . . . or at least try to. I'm sure I look like I'm having a stroke.

"Do you often send back fortune cookies?"

"No. This is the first time. I mean, this is a Chinese restaurant—"

"Malpractice."

"Exactly."

Rhiannon flags the waiter down, explains the predicament, and gets a nod. When he returns to our table, he has a half dozen more fortune cookies for her.

"I only need one," she tells him. "Wait one second."

The waiter and I are both paying close attention as Rhiannon cracks open her second fortune cookie. This time, it gets a nice smile.

She shows it to both of us.

ADVENTURE IS AROUND THE CORNER.

"Well done, sir," I tell the waiter.

Rhiannon prods me to open mine. I do, and find it's the exact same fortune as hers.

I don't send it back.

We return to the library with about a half hour to spare. The librarian catches us walking back in, but doesn't say a word.

"So," Rhiannon asks me, "what should I read next?"

I show her *Feed*. I tell her all about *The Book Thief*. I drag her to find *Destroy All Cars* and *First Day on Earth*. I explain to her that these have been my companions all these years, the constants from day to day, the stories I can always return to even if mine is always changing.

"What about you?" I ask her. "What do you think I should read next?"

She takes my hand and leads me to the children's section. She looks around for a second, then heads over to a display at the front. I see a certain green book sitting there and panic.

"No! Not that one!" I say.

But she isn't reaching for the green book. She's reaching for *Harold and the Purple Crayon*.

"What could you possibly have against *Harold and the Purple Crayon*?" she asks.

"I'm sorry. I thought you were heading for *The Giving Tree*."

Rhiannon looks at me like I'm an insane duck. "I absolutely HATE *The Giving Tree*."

I am so relieved. "Thank goodness. That would've been the end of us, had that been your favorite book."

"Here—take my arms! Take my legs!"

"Take my head! Take my shoulders!"

"Because that's what love's about!"

"That kid is, like, the jerk of the century," I say, relieved that Rhiannon will know what I mean.

"The biggest jerk in the history of all literature," Rhiannon ventures. Then she puts down *Harold* and moves closer to me.

"Love means never having to lose your limbs," I tell her, moving in for a kiss.

"Exactly," she murmurs, her lips soon on mine.

It's an innocent kiss. We're not about to start making out in the beanbag chairs offered by the children's room. But that doesn't stop the ice-water effect when George's mother calls out his name, shocked and angry.

"What do you *think* you're *doing?*" she demands. I assume she's talking to me, but when she gets to us, she pummels right into Rhiannon. "I don't know who your parents are, but I did not raise *my* son to hang out with *whores.*"

"Mom!" I shout. "Leave her alone."

"Get in the car, George. Right this minute."

I know I'm only making it worse for George, but I don't care. I am not leaving Rhiannon alone with her.

"Just calm down," I tell George's mother, my voice squeaking a little as I do. Then I turn to Rhiannon and tell her I will talk to her later.

"You most certainly will not!" George's mother proclaims. I take some satisfaction in the fact that I'm only under her supervision for another eight hours or so.

Rhiannon gives me a kiss goodbye and whispers that she's

going to figure out a way to run away for the weekend. George's mother actually grabs him by the ear and pulls him outside.

I laugh, and that only makes things worse.

It's like Cinderella in reverse. I've danced with the prince, and now I'm back home, cleaning the toilets. That is my punishment—every toilet, every tub, every garbage pail. This would be bad enough, but every few minutes, George's mother stops in to give me a lecture about "the sins of the flesh." I hope that George doesn't internalize her scare tactics. I want to argue with her, tell her that "sins of the flesh" is just a control mechanism—if you demonize a person's pleasure, then you can control his or her life. I can't say how many times this tool has been wielded against me, in a variety of forms. But I see no sin in a kiss. I only see sin in the condemnation.

I don't say any of this to George's mother. If she were my full-time mother, I would. If I were the one who would shoulder the aftermath, I would. But I can't do that to George. I've messed up his life already. Hopefully for the better, but maybe for the worse.

Emailing Rhiannon is out of the question. It will just have to wait until tomorrow.

After all the toil is done, after George's father has weighed in with a speech of his own, seemingly dictated by his wife, I head to bed early, take advantage of having the silence of a room all to myself. If my time as Rhiannon is any proof, I can construct the memories that I will leave George with. So as I lie there in his bed, I conjure an alternate truth. He will remember heading to the library, and he will remember meeting a girl. She will be a stranger to town, dropped off at the library while her mother visited an old colleague. She asked him what he was reading, and a conversation began. They went for Chinese food together and had a good time. He was really into her. She was really into him. They went back to the library, had the same conversation about *The Giving Tree*, and moved in to kiss. That's when his mother arrived. That's what his mother disrupted. Something unexpected, but also something wonderful.

The girl disappeared. They never told each other their names. He has no idea where she lives. It was all there for a moment, and then the moment unraveled.

I am leaving him with longing. Which may be a cruel thing to do, but I'm hoping he will use his longing to get out of this small, small house.

Day 6019

I am much luckier the next morning, when I wake up in the body of Surita, whose parents are away, and who is being watched over by her ninety-year-old grandmother, who doesn't seem to care what Surita does, as long as it doesn't interfere with her programs on the Game Show Network. I'm only about an hour away from Rhiannon, and in the interest of her not being called to the principal for repeated attendance violations, I meet her back at the Clover Bookstore after school is out.

She is full of plans.

"I told everyone I was visiting my grandmother for the weekend, and I told my parents I would be at Rebecca's, so I'm a free agent. I'm actually staying at Rebecca's tonight, but I was thinking tomorrow night we could . . . go somewhere."

I tell her I like that plan.

We head to a park, walking around and playing on the jungle gym and talking. I notice she's less affectionate with me when I'm in a girl's body, but I don't call her on it. She's still with me, and she's still happy, and that's something.

We don't talk about Justin. We don't talk about the fact that we have no idea where I'll be tomorrow. We don't talk about how to make things work.

We block all this out, and enjoy ourselves.

Day 6020

Xavier Adams could not have imagined his Saturday was going to turn in this direction. He's supposed to go to play practice at noon, but as soon as he leaves his house, he calls his director and tells him he has a bad flu bug—hopefully the twenty-four-hour kind. The director is understanding—it's *Hamlet* and Xavier is playing Laertes, so there are plenty of scenes that can be run without him there. So Xavier is free . . . and immediately heads toward Rhiannon.

She's left me directions, but she hasn't told me what the ultimate destination is. I drive for almost two hours, west into the hinterlands of Maryland. Eventually the directions lead me to a small cabin hidden in the woods. If Rhiannon's car weren't in front, I'm sure I'd think I was hopelessly lost.

She's waiting in the doorway by the time I get out of the car. She looks happy-nervous. I still have no idea where I am.

"You're really cute today," she observes as I get closer.

"French Canadian dad, Creole mom," I say. "But I don't speak a word of French."

"Your mom isn't going to show up this time, is she?"

"Nope."

"Good. Then I can do this without being killed."

She kisses me hard. I kiss her hard back. And suddenly we're letting our bodies do the talking. We are inside the doorway, inside the cabin. But I'm not looking at the room—I am feeling her, tasting her, pressing against her as she's pressing against me. She's pulling off my coat and we're kicking off our shoes and she's directing me backward. The edge of the bed kicks the backs of my legs, and then we are awkwardly, enjoyably stumbling over, me lying down, her pinning my shoulders, us kissing and kissing and kissing. Breath and heat and contact and shirts off and skin on skin and smiles and murmurs and the enormity revealing itself in the tiniest of gestures, the most delicate sensations.

I pull back from a kiss and look at her. She stops and looks at me.

"Hey," I say.

"Hey," she says.

I trace the contours of her face, her collarbone. She runs her fingers along my shoulders, my back. Kisses my neck, my ear.

For the first time, I look around. It's a one-room cabin—the bathroom must be out back. There are deer heads on the wall, staring down at us with glass eyes.

"Where are we?" I ask.

"It's a hunting cabin my uncle uses. He's in California now, so I figured it was safe to break in."

I search for broken windows, signs of forced entry. "You broke in?"

"Well, with the spare key."

Her hand moves to the patch of hair at the center of my chest, then to my heartbeat. I rest one of my hands on her side, glide lightly over the smoothness of the skin there.

"That was quite a welcome," I tell her.

"It's not over yet," she says. And, just like that, we're pressed together again.

I am letting her take the lead. I am letting her unbutton the top of my jeans. I am letting her pull the zipper down. I am letting her remove her bra. I am following along, but with each step, the pressure builds. How far is this going? How far should this go?

I know our nakedness means something. I know our nakedness is as much a form of trust as it is a form of craving. This is what we look like when we are completely open to each other. This is where we go when we no longer want to hide. I want her. I want this. But I'm afraid.

We move as if we're in a fever, then we slow down and move as if we're in a dream. There's no clothing now, just sheets. This is not my body, but it's the body she wants.

I feel like a pretender.

This is the source of the pressure. This is the cause of my hesitation. Right now I am here with her completely. But tomorrow I may not be. I can enjoy this today. It can feel right now. But tomorrow, I don't know. Tomorrow I may be gone.

I want to sleep with her. I want to sleep with her so much.

But I also want to wake up next to her the next morning.

The body is ready. The body is close to bursting with sensation. When Rhiannon asks if I want to, I know what the body would answer.

But I tell her no. I tell her we shouldn't. Not yet. Not right now.

Even though it was a genuine question, she's surprised by the answer. She pulls away to look at me.

"Are you sure? I want to. If you're worried about me, don't be. I want to. I . . . prepared."

"I don't think we should."

"Okay," she says, pulling farther away.

"It's not you," I tell her. "And it's not that I don't want to."

"So what is it?" she asks.

"It feels wrong." .

She looks hurt by this answer.

"Let me worry about Justin," she says. "This is you and me. It's different."

"But it's not just you and me," I tell her. "It's also Xavier."

"Xavier?"

I gesture to my body. "Xavier."

"Oh."

"He's never done it before," I tell her. "And it just feels wrong . . . for him to do it for the first time, and not know it. I feel like I'm taking something from him if I do that. It doesn't seem right."

I have no idea if this is true or not, and I'm not going to access to find out. Because it is an acceptable reason to stop—acceptable because it shouldn't hurt her pride.

"Oh," Rhiannon says again. Then she moves back closer and nestles in next to me. "Do you think he would mind this?"

The body relaxes. Enjoys itself in a different way.

"I set an alarm," Rhiannon says. "So we can sleep."

We drift together, naked in the bed. My heart is still racing, but as it slows, it slows in pace with hers. We have entered the safest cocoon our affections can make, and we lie there, and we luxuriate in the wealth of the moment, and gently fall into each other, fall into sleep.

It is not the alarm that wakes us. It is the sound of a flock of birds outside the window. It is the sound of the wind hitting the eaves.

I have to remind myself that normal people feel this way, too: The desire to take a moment and make it last forever. The desire to stay like this for much longer than it will really last.

"I know we don't talk about it," I say. "But why are you with him?"

"I don't know," she tells me. "I used to think I did. But I don't know anymore."

"Who was your favorite?" she asks.

"My favorite?"

"Your favorite body. Your favorite life."

"I was once in the body of a blind girl," I tell her. "When I was eleven. Maybe twelve. I don't know if she was my favorite, but I learned more from being her for a day than I'd learn from most people over a year. It showed me how arbitrary and individual it is, the way we experience the world. Not just that the other senses were sharper. But that we find ways to navigate the world as it is presented to us. For me, it was this huge challenge. But for her, it was just life."

"Close your eyes," Rhiannon whispers.

I close my eyes, and she does the same.

We experience each other's bodies in a different way.

The alarm goes off. I don't want to be reminded of time.

We have not turned on the lights, so as the sky turns to dusk, the cabin turns to dusk as well. Haze of darkness, remnant of light.

"I'm going to stay here," she says.

"I'm going to come back tomorrow," I promise.

"I would end it," I tell her. "I would end all the changing if I could. Just to stay here with you."

"But you can't end it," she says. "I know that."

Time itself becomes the alarm. I can't look at the clock without knowing it's past the hour for me to go. Play rehearsal is over. Even if Xavier goes out with friends after, he's going to have to be home soon. And definitely by midnight.

• • •

"I'll wait for you," she tells me.

I leave her in the bed. I put on my clothes, pick up my keys, and close the door behind me. I turn back. I keep turning back to see her. Even when there are walls between us. Even when there are miles between us. I keep turning back. I keep turning in her direction.

Day 6021

I wake up, and for at least a minute, I can't figure out who I am. All I can find is the body, and the body is pounding with pain. There's a hazy blur to my thoughts, a vise compressing my head. I open my eyes and the light nearly kills me.

"Dana," a voice outside of me says. "It's noon."

I don't care that it's noon. I don't care about anything at all. I just want the pounding to go away.

Or not. Because when the pounding briefly stops, the rest of my body chimes in with nausea.

"Dana, I'm not going to let you sleep all day. Being grounded does not mean you get to sleep all day."

It takes three more attempts, but I manage to open my eyes and keep them open, even if the bedroom light feels like it has the same wattage as the sun.

Dana's mother stares down at me with as much sorrow as anger.

"Dr. P is coming in a half hour," she tells me. "I think you need to see him."

I am accessing like crazy, but it's as if my synapses have been dipped in tar.

"After all we've been through, the fact that you would pull such a stunt last night . . . it's beyond words. We have done nothing but care about you. And this is what you do? Your father and I have had enough. No more."

What did I do last night? I can remember being with Rhiannon. I can remember going home as Xavier. Talking to his friends on the phone. Hearing about play practice. But I can't reach Dana's memories. She is too hungover for them to be there.

Is this what it's like for Xavier this morning? A complete blank?

I hope not, because this is awful.

"You have half an hour to shower and get dressed. Don't expect any help from me."

Dana's mother slams the door shut, and the echo of the slam spreads through my whole body. As I start to move, it feels like I am trapped twenty miles underwater. And when I start to rise, I get a bad case of the bends. I actually have to steady myself against my bedpost, and nearly miss it when I reach out.

I don't really care about Dr. P or Dana's parents. As far as I'm concerned, Dana must have done this to herself, and she deserves the grief she gets. It must have taken *a lot* of drinking to get in this state. She is not the reason I get up. I get up because somewhere near here, Rhiannon is alone in a hunting cabin, waiting for me. I have no idea how I'm going to get out of here, but I have to.

I trudge through the hallway to the shower. I turn it on, then stand there for at least a minute, forgetting entirely why I'm standing there. The water is just background music to the

235

horror of my body. Then I remember, and I step in. The water wakes me up a little more, but I stagger through the waking. I could easily collapse into the tub, and fall asleep with the water running over me, my foot over the drain.

When I get back to Dana's room, I let the towel drop and leave it there, then put on whatever clothes are nearest. There's no computer in the room, no phone. No way to get in touch with Rhiannon. I know I should search the house, but just the thought of it takes too much energy. I need to sit down. Lie down. Close my eyes.

"Wake up!"

The command is as abrupt as the earlier door slam, and twice as close. I open my eyes and find Dana's very angry father.

"Dr. P is here," Dana's mother chimes in from behind him, with a slightly more conciliatory tone. Maybe she's feeling bad for me. Or maybe she just doesn't want her husband to kill me in front of a witness.

I wonder if what I'm feeling isn't entirely a hangover if a doctor is making a house call. But when Dr. P sits down next to me, there's not a medical bag in sight. Just a notebook.

"Dana," she says gently.

I look at her. Sit up, even as my head howls.

She turns to my parents.

"It's okay. Why don't you leave us now?"

They don't need to be told twice.

• • •

236

Accessing is still hard. I know the facts are there, but they're behind a murky wall.

"Do you want to tell me what happened?" Dr. P asks.

"I don't know," I say. "I don't remember."

"It's that bad?"

"Yeah. It's that bad."

She asks me if my parents have given me any Tylenol, and I tell her no, not since I woke up. She leaves for a second and comes back with two Tylenol and a glass of water.

I don't get the Tylenol down on the first try, and I'm embarrassed by the chalky gag that results. The second time is better, and I gulp down the rest of the water. Dr. P goes out and refills the glass, giving me time to think. But the thoughts in my head are still clumsy, dull.

When she returns, she begins with, "You can understand why your parents are upset, can't you?"

I feel so stupid, but I can't pretend.

"I really don't know what happened," I say. "I'm not lying. I wish I did."

"You were at Cameron's party." She looks at me, seeing if this registers. When it doesn't, she continues. "You snuck out to go there. And when you got there, you started drinking. A lot. Your friends were concerned, for obvious reasons. But they didn't stop you. They only tried to stop you when you went to drive home."

I'm still underwater, and my memory of this is on the surface. I know it's there. I know she's telling me the truth. But I can't see it.

"I drove?"

"Yes. Even though you weren't supposed to. You stole your father's keys."

"I stole my father's keys." I say it out loud, hoping it will spark an image.

"When you went to drive home, some of your friends tried to stop you. But you insisted. They tried to stop you. You lashed out at them. Called them awful things. And when Cameron tried to take your keys away . . ."

"What did I do?"

"You bit him on the wrist. And you ran."

This must have been how Nathan felt. The morning after.

Dr. P continues. "Your friend Lisa called your parents. They rushed over. When your father got to you, you were already in the car. He went to stop you and you nearly ran him over."

I nearly ran him over?

"You didn't get far. You were too drunk to back out of the driveway. You ended up in the neighbor's yard. You crashed into a telephone pole. Luckily, no one was hurt."

I exhale. I am pushing inside Dana's mind, trying to find any of this.

"What we want to know, Dana, is why you would do such a thing. After what happened with Anthony, why would you do this?"

Anthony. That name is the fact that is too bright to hide. My body convulses in pain. Pain is all I can feel.

Anthony. My brother.

My dead brother.

My brother who died next to me.

My brother who died next to me, in the passenger seat.

Because I crashed.

Because I was drunk.

Because of me.

"Oh my God," I cry out. "Oh my God."

I am seeing him now. His bloody body. I am screaming.

"It's okay," Dr. P says. "It's okay now."

But it's not.

It's not.

Dr. P gives me something stronger than Tylenol. I try to resist, but it's no use.

"I have to tell Rhiannon," I say. I don't mean to say it. It just comes out.

"Who's Rhiannon?" Dr. P asks.

My eyelids close. I give in before she can get an answer.

It starts to come back to me while I'm asleep, and when I wake again, I remember more of it. Not the end—I genuinely can't remember getting in the car, almost running over my father, hitting the telephone pole. I must have checked out by then. But before that, I can remember being at the party. Drinking anything anyone offered. Feeling better because of it. Feeling lighter. Flirting with Cameron. Drinking some more. Not thinking. After so much thinking, blocking it all out.

I'm like Dana's parents, or Dr. P—I want to ask her why. Even from the inside, I can't figure it out. Because the body can't answer that.

My limbs are heavy, wooden. But I prop myself up. I edge myself out of bed. I need to find a computer or a phone.

When I get to the door, I find it's locked. There should be a key that lets me out, but somebody's taken it.

I'm trapped in my own room.

Now that they know I remember at least some of it, they are letting me stew in my own guilt.

And the worst part is: it's working.

I am out of water. I call out that I need more water. Within a minute, my mother is at the door with a glass. She looks like she's been crying. She is shattered. I have shattered my mother.

"Here," she says.

"Can I come out?" I ask. "There are some things I need to look up for school."

She shakes her head. "Maybe later. After dinner. For now, Dr. P would like you to write down everything you're feeling."

She leaves and locks the door behind her. I find a piece of paper and a pen.

What I feel is helplessness, I write.

But then I stop. Because I'm not writing as Dana. I'm writing as me.

The headache and nausea are subsiding. Although every time I imagine Rhiannon alone in the cabin, I feel sick again.

I promised her. Even though I knew the risk, I promised her.

And now I'm proving to her that it's too risky to accept my promises.

I am proving to her that I won't be able to come through.

Dana's mother brings me dinner on a tray, as if I'm an invalid. I thank her for it. And then I find the words I should have been using all along.

"I'm sorry," I tell her. "I'm really, really sorry."

She nods, but I can tell it's not enough.

I must have told her I was sorry too many times before. At some point—maybe last night—she must have stopped believing it.

When I ask her where my father is, she tells me he's getting the car fixed.

They decide that I will have to go to school tomorrow, and that I will have to make amends to my friends then. They say I can use the computer for my homework, but then sit there behind me as I make up things to research.

Emailing Rhiannon is out of the question.

And they show no signs of giving me back my phone.

The previous night's events never come back to me. I spend the rest of the night staring into that blank space. And I can't help but feel it staring right back.

Day 6022

My plan is to wake up early—around six—and email Rhiannon with a full explanation. I expect she gave up on me after a while.

But my plan is foiled when I'm shaken awake a little before five.

"Michael, it's time to get up."

It's my mother—Michael's mother—and unlike with Dana's mother, there's only apology in her voice.

I figure it's time for swim practice, or something else I have to do before school. But when I get out of bed, my foot hits a suitcase.

I hear my mom in the other room, waking up my sisters.

"It's time to go to Hawaii!" she says cheerily.

Hawaii.

I access and find that, yes, we are leaving for Hawaii this morning. Michael's older sister is getting married there. And Michael's family has decided to take a weeklong vacation.

Only for me it won't be a week. Because in order to get back, I'd have to wake up in the body of a sixteen-year-old who was heading home to Maryland that day. It could take weeks. Months.

It might never happen.

"The car's coming in forty-five minutes!" Michael's dad calls up.

Under no circumstances can I go.

Michael's wardrobe consists mostly of T-shirts for heavy metal bands. I throw one on, as well as jeans.

"You're just asking Homeland Security to give you a full cavity search," one of my sisters says as I pass her in the hall.

I am still trying to figure out what to do.

Michael doesn't have his license, and I don't think it would help for me to steal one of his parents' cars. His older sister's wedding isn't until Friday, so at least I'm not jeopardizing his attendance there. But who am I kidding? Even if the wedding were this evening, I wouldn't get on that plane.

I know I am going to get Michael in a huge amount of trouble. I apologize to him profusely as I write my note and leave it on the kitchen table.

I can't go today. I am so sorry. I will be back later tonight.
Go without me. I'll get there somehow by Thursday.

While everyone else is upstairs, I walk out the back door.

• • •

I could call a cab, but I'm afraid his parents will call the local cab companies to see if they've picked up any metalhead teens lately. I am at least two hours away from Rhiannon. I take the nearest bus I can find, and ask the driver the best way to get to her town. He laughs and says, "By car." I tell him that's not an option, and in return he tells me I'll probably have to head to Baltimore and then back out again.

It takes about seven hours.

School isn't out yet when I get there, having walked about a mile from the center of town. Again, nobody stops me, even though I'm a big, hairy, sweaty guy in a Metallica T-shirt storming up the steps.

I try to remember Rhiannon's schedule from when I was inside her head, and have a vague recollection that this period is gym. I check the gymnasium and find it empty. The natural next stop is the fields, which are behind the school. When I walk out, I find a softball game in action. Rhiannon is at third base.

She sees me out of the corner of her eye. I wave. It's unclear whether she recognizes me as me or not. I feel too out in the open, too much in the line of the gym teacher's sight. So I retreat back to the school, by the door. Just another slacker, taking a smokeless smoke break.

Rhiannon walks over to one of the teachers and says something. The teacher looks sympathetic, and puts another student on third base. Rhiannon starts heading toward the school. I step back inside, and wait for her in the empty gym.

"Hey," I say once she steps inside.

"Where the hell were you?" she replies.

I've never seen her this angry before. It's the kind of anger that comes when you feel betrayed by not just a single person, but the universe.

"I was locked in my room," I tell her. "It was awful. There wasn't even a computer."

"I waited for you," she tells me. "I got up. Made the bed. Had some breakfast. And then I waited. The reception on my phone went on and off, so I figured that had to be it. I started reading old issues of *Field & Stream*, because that's the only reading material up there. Then I heard footsteps. I was so excited. When I heard someone at the door, I ran to it.

"Well, it wasn't you. It was this eighty-year-old guy. And he had this dead deer with him. I don't know who was more surprised. I just screamed when I saw him. And he nearly had a heart attack. I wasn't naked, but I was close. I was so ashamed of myself. He wasn't even sweet about it. He said I was trespassing. I told him Artie was my uncle, but he wasn't believing me. I think the only thing that saved me was that Artie and I have the same last name. I was there in my underwear, showing this guy my ID. There was blood on his hands. And he said there were other guys coming. He'd just assumed my car was one of theirs.

"The problem was—I still thought you were coming. So I couldn't leave. I put on my clothes, and had to sit there as they came and gutted that poor deer. I waited there after they left. I waited there until dark. The cabin smelled like blood, A. But I stayed there. And you never came."

I tell her about Dana. Then I tell her about Michael, and running out of his house.

It's something. But it's not enough.

"How are we supposed to do this?" she asks me. "How?"

I want there to be an answer. I want to have an answer.

"Come here," I say. And I hold her close, because that's the only answer I have.

We stand like that for a minute, each not knowing what comes next. When the door to the gym opens, we pull away from each other. But we're too late. I figure it's one of the gym teachers, or another girl from class. But it's not even that door. It's the door from the school side, and it's Justin who's walked through.

"What the hell?" he says. "What. The. Hell?"

Rhiannon tries to explain. "Justin—" she begins. But he cuts her off.

"Lindsay texted me to say you weren't feeling well. So I was going to see if you were okay. Well, I guess you're real okay. Don't let me interrupt."

"Stop it," Rhiannon says.

"Stop what, you bitch?" he asks. He's on us now.

"Justin," I say.

He turns to me. "You're not even allowed to speak, bro."

I'm about to say something else, but he's already punching me. His fist crashes right against the bridge of my nose. I'm knocked down to the ground.

Rhiannon screams and moves to help me up. Justin pulls at her arm.

"I always knew you were a slut," Justin says.

"Stop it!" Rhiannon cries out.

Justin lets go of her and comes back over to me. He starts kicking my body.

"This your new boyfriend?" Justin yells. "You love him?"

"I don't love him!" Rhiannon yells back. "But I don't love you, either."

The next time he kicks, I grab his leg and pull him down. He crashes onto the gym floor. I think this will stop him, but he jabs his boot out again and gets me in the chin. My teeth rattle.

At this point, some whistle must blow outside, because within thirty seconds, girls from softball are streaming into the gym. When they see the carnage, they cluck and gasp. One girl runs over to Rhiannon to make sure she's okay.

Justin gets up and kicks me again, just so everyone can see it. It barely grazes me, and I use the momentum of dodging the blow to stand up. I want to hit him, hurt him, but I honestly don't know how.

Plus, I have to leave. It will be easy enough to discover that I don't go to this school. And even though I'm the clear loser of this fight, they can still call the police on me for trespassing and brawling in the first place.

I teeter over to Rhiannon. Her friend makes a move to shield her from me, but Rhiannon gestures her off.

"I have to go," I tell her. "Meet me at the Starbucks where we first met. When you can."

I feel a hand on my shoulder. Justin, pulling me around. He won't hit me with my back turned.

I know I should face him. Hit him if I can. But instead I

duck out of his grip and run. He's not going to follow me. He will bask instead in the victory of seeing me run.

It is not my intention to leave Rhiannon crying, but that is exactly what I do.

I make my way back to the bus stop, then use a nearby phone booth to call a cab. Nearly fifty dollars later, I am at the Starbucks. If before I was a big, hairy, sweaty guy in a Metallica T-shirt, now I am a big, hairy, sweaty guy in a Metallica T-shirt who's beaten, bruised, and bleeding. I order a venti black coffee and leave twenty dollars in the tip jar. Now they'll let me stay as long as I want, no matter how scary I look.

I clean myself up some in the bathroom. Then I sit down and wait.

And wait.

And wait.

She doesn't arrive until a little after six.

She doesn't apologize. She doesn't explain why it took her so long. She doesn't even come to my table right away. She stops at the counter and gets a coffee first.

"I really need this," she says as she sits down. I know she's talking about the coffee, not anything else.

I'm on my fourth coffee and second scone.

"Thank you for coming," I tell her. It sounds too formal.

"I thought about not coming," she says. "But I didn't seriously consider it." She looks at my face, my bruises. "You okay?"

"I'm fine."

"Remind me—what's your name today?"

"Michael."

She looks me over again. "Poor Michael."

"This is not how I imagine he thought the day would go."

"That makes two of us."

I feel we're each standing a good hundred feet from the real subject. I have to move us closer.

"Is it over now? With the two of you?"

"Yes. So I guess you got what you wanted."

"That's an awful way to put it," I say. "Don't you want it, too?"

"Yes. But not like that. Not in front of everybody like that."

I reach up to touch her face, but she flinches. I lower my hand.

"You're free of him," I tell her.

She shakes her head. I've said yet another thing wrong.

"I forget how little you know about these things," she says. "I forget how inexperienced you are. I'm not free of him, A. Just because you break up with someone, it doesn't mean you're free of him. I'm still attached to Justin in a hundred different ways. We're just not dating anymore. It's going to take me years to be free of him."

But at least you've started, I want to say. *At least you've cut that one attachment.* I remain silent, though. This might be what she knows, but it's not what she wants to hear.

"Should I have gone to Hawaii?" I ask.

She softens to me then. It's such an absurd question, but she knows what I mean.

"No, you shouldn't have. I want you here."

"With you?"

"With me. When you can be."

I want to promise more than that, but I know I can't.

We both stay there, on our tightrope. Not looking down, but not moving, either.

We use her phone to check the local flights to Hawaii, and when we're sure there's no way Michael's family can get him on a plane, Rhiannon drives me home.

"Tell me more about the girl you were yesterday," she asks. So I do. And when I'm done, and a sadness fills the car, I decide to tell her about other days, other lives. Happier. I share with her memories of being sung to sleep, memories of meeting elephants at zoos and circuses, memories of first kisses and near first kisses in rec-room closets and at Boy Scout sleepovers and scary movies. It's my way of telling her that even though I haven't experienced so many things, I have managed to have a life.

We get closer and closer to Michael's house.

"I want to see you tomorrow," I say.

"I want to see you, too," she says. "But I think we both know it's not just a matter of want."

"I'll hope it, then," I tell her.

"And I'll hope it, too."

• • •

I want to kiss her good night, not goodbye. But when we get there, she makes no move to kiss me. I don't want to push it and make the first move. And I don't want to ask her, for fear that she'll say no.

So we leave with me thanking her for the ride, and so much else going unspoken.

I don't go straight into the house. I walk around to run out the clock more. It's ten o'clock when I am at the front door. I access Michael to find out where the spare key is kept, but by the time I've found it, the door has opened and Michael's father is there.

At first he doesn't say a word. I stand there in the lamplight, and he stares.

"I want to beat the crap out of you," he says, "but it looks like someone else got there first."

My mother and sisters have been sent ahead to Hawaii. My father has stayed back for me.

In order to apologize, I have to give him some kind of explanation. I come up with one that's as pathetic as I feel— there was a concert I had to go to, and there was just no way to tell him ahead of time. I feel awful messing up Michael's life to such a degree, and this awfulness must come through as I speak, because Michael's father is much less hostile than he has every right to be. I'm in no way off the hook: the change fee for the tickets will be coming out of my allowance for the next year, and when we're in Hawaii, I may be grounded from doing anything that isn't wedding-related. I will be getting guilt for this for the rest of my life. The only saving grace is that there were tickets available for the next day.

That night I create a memory of the best concert Michael will ever go to. It is the only thing I can think to give him to make any of it worth it.

Day 6023

Even before I open my eyes, I like Vic. Biologically female, gendered male. Living within the definition of his own truth, just like me. He knows who he wants to be. Most people our age don't have to do that. They stay within the realm of the easy. If you want to live within the definition of your own truth, you have to choose to go through the initially painful and ultimately comforting process of finding it.

It's supposed to be a busy day for Vic. There's a history test and a math test. There's band practice, which is the thing he looks forward to the most in the day. There's a date with a girl named Dawn.

I get up. I get dressed. I get my keys and get in my car.

But when I get to the place where I should turn off for school, I keep driving.

It's just over a three-hour drive to Rhiannon. I've emailed to let her know Vic and I are coming. I didn't give her time to reply, or to say no.

On the drive, I access pieces of Vic's history. There are few things harder than being born into the wrong body. I had to deal with it a lot when I was growing up, but only for a day. Before I became so adaptable—so acquiescent to the way my life worked—I would resist some of the transitions. I loved having long hair, and would resent it when I woke up to find my long hair was gone. There were days I felt like a girl and days I felt like a boy, and those days wouldn't always correspond with the body I was in. I still believed everyone when they said I had to be one or the other. Nobody was telling me a different story, and I was too young to think for myself. I had yet to learn that when it came to gender, I was both and neither.

It is an awful thing to be betrayed by your body. And it's lonely, because you feel you can't talk about it. You feel it's something between you and the body. You feel it's a battle you will never win . . . and yet you fight it day after day, and it wears you down. Even if you try to ignore it, the energy it takes to ignore it will exhaust you.

Vic was lucky in the parents he was given. They didn't care if he wanted to wear jeans instead of skirts, or play with trucks instead of dolls. It was only as he grew older, into his teens, that it gave them some pause. They knew that their daughter liked girls. But it took a while for him to articulate—even to himself—that he liked them as a boy. That he was meant to be a boy, or at least to live as a boy, to live in the blur between a boyish girl and a girlish boy.

His father, a quiet man, understood and supported him in a quiet way. His mother took it harder. She respected Vic's desire to be who he needed to be, but at the same time had a difficult time giving up the fact of having a daughter for the fact of having a son. Some of Vic's friends understood, even at thirteen and fourteen. Others were freaked out—the girls more than the boys. To the boys, Vic had always been the tagalong, the nonsexual friend. This didn't change that.

Dawn was always there in the background. They'd gone to school together since kindergarten, friendly without ever really becoming friends. When they got to high school, Vic was hanging out with the kids who furiously scribbled poems into their notebooks and let them lie there, while Dawn was with the kids who would submit their poems to the literary magazine the minute they were finished. The public girl, running for class treasurer and joining the debate club, and the private boy, the sidekick on 7-Eleven runs. Vic never would have noticed Dawn, never would have thought it was a possibility, if Dawn hadn't noticed him first.

But Dawn did notice him. He was the corner that her eye always strayed toward. When she closed her eyes to go to sleep, it was thoughts of him that would lead her into her dreams. She had no idea what she was attracted to—the boyish girl, the girlish boy—and eventually she decided it didn't really matter. She was attracted to Vic. And Vic had no idea she existed. Not in that way.

Finally, as Dawn would later recount to Vic, it became unbearable. They had plenty of mutual friends who could have done reconnaissance, but Dawn felt that if she was going to risk it, she was going to risk it firsthand. So one day when she saw Vic piling in with some of the other guys for a 7-Eleven run, she jumped into her car and followed them. As she'd hoped,

Vic decided to hang out in front while his friends played in the aisles. Dawn walked over and said hello. Vic didn't understand at first why Dawn was talking to him, or why she seemed so nervous, but then he slowly realized what was happening, and that he wanted it to happen, too. When the chime of the front door marked his friends' exit, he waved them off and stayed with Dawn, who didn't even remember to pretend she needed something from the store. Dawn would have talked there for hours; it was Vic who suggested they go get coffee, and it all went from there.

There had been ups and downs since, but the heart of it remained: When Dawn looked at Vic, she saw Vic exactly as he wanted to be seen. Whereas Vic's parents couldn't help seeing who he used to be, and so many friends and strangers couldn't help seeing who he didn't want to be anymore, Dawn only saw him. Call it a blur if you want, but Dawn didn't see a blur. She saw a very distinct, very clear person.

As I sift through these memories, as I put together this story, I feel such gratitude and such longing—not Vic's, but my own. This is what I want from Rhiannon. This is what I want to give Rhiannon.

But how can I make her look past the blur, if I'm a body she'll never really see, in a life she'll never really be able to hold?

I arrive the period before lunch and park in my usual spot.

By now, I know which class Rhiannon is in. So I wait outside the door for the bell to ring. When it does, she's in the middle of a crowd, talking to her friend Rebecca. She doesn't see me; she doesn't even look up. I have to follow behind her for a ways, not knowing whether I'm the ghost of her past, present, or future. Finally, she and Rebecca head in different directions, and I can talk to her alone.

"Hey," I say.

And it's there—a moment's hesitation before she turns. But then she does, and I see that recognition again.

"Hey," she says. "You're here. Why am I not surprised?"

This isn't exactly the welcome I was hoping for, but it's a welcome I understand. When we're alone together, I'm the destination. When I'm here in her life at school, I'm the disruption.

"Lunch?" I ask.

"Sure," she says. "But I really have to get back after."

I tell her that's okay.

We're silent as we walk. When I'm not focused on Rhiannon, I can sense that people are looking at her differently. Some positive, but more negative.

She sees me noticing.

"Apparently, I'm now a metalhead slut," she says. "According to some sources, I've even slept with members of Metallica. It's kind of funny, but also kind of not." She looks me over. "You, however, are something completely different. I don't even know what I'm dealing with today."

"My name's Vic. I'm a biological female, but my gender is male."

Rhiannon sighs. "I don't even know what that means."

I start to explain, but she cuts me off.

"Let's just wait until we're off school grounds, okay? Why don't you walk behind me for a while. I think it'll just make things easier."

I have no choice but to follow.

We head to a diner where the average age of the customers is ninety-four, and applesauce seems to be the most popular item on the menu. Not exactly a high school hangout.

Once we've sat down and ordered, I ask her more about the aftermath of the previous day.

"I can't say Justin seems that upset," she says. "And there's no shortage of girls who want to comfort him. It's pathetic. Rebecca's been awesome. I swear, there should be an occupation called Friendship PR—Rebecca would be ace at that. She's getting my half of the story out there."

"Which is?"

"Which is that Justin's a jerk. And that the metalhead and I weren't doing anything besides talking."

The first part is irrefutable, but even to me, the second part sounds weak.

"I'm sorry it had to all go down like that," I say.

"It could've been worse. And we have to stop apologizing to each other. Every sentence can't start with 'I'm sorry.'"

There's such resignation in her voice, but I can't tell what she's actually resigned herself to.

"So you're a girl who's a boy?" she says.

"Something like that." I sense she doesn't want to get into it.

"And how far did you drive?"

"Three hours."

"And what are you missing?"

"A couple of tests. A date with my girlfriend."

"Do you think that's fair?"

I'm stuck for a second. "What do you mean?" I ask.

"Look," Rhiannon says, "I'm happy you've come all this way. Really, I am. But I didn't get much sleep last night, and I'm cranky as hell, and this morning when I got your email, I just thought: Is all of this really fair? Not to me or to you. But to these . . . people whose lives you're kidnapping."

"Rhiannon, I'm always careful—"

"I know you are. And I know it's just a day. But what if something completely unexpected was supposed to happen today? What if her girlfriend is planning this huge surprise party for her? What if her lab partner is going to fail out of class if she's not there to help? What if—I don't know. What if there's this huge accident, and she's supposed to be nearby to pull a baby to safety?"

"I know," I tell her. "But what if *I'm* the one that something is supposed to happen to? What if I'm supposed to be here, and if I'm not, the world will go the wrong direction? In some infinitesimal but important way."

"But shouldn't her life come above yours?"

"Why?"

"Because you're just the guest."

I know this is true, but it's shocking to hear her say it. She immediately moves to soften what sounds like an accusation.

"I'm not saying you're any less important. You know I'm not. Right now, you are the person I love the most in the entire world."

"Really?"

"What do you mean, *really*?"

"Yesterday you said you didn't love me."

"I was talking about the metalhead. Not you."

Our food arrives, but Rhiannon just stabs the ketchup with her French fries.

"I love you, too, you know," I say.

"I know," she tells me. But she doesn't seem any happier.

"We're going to get through this. Every relationship has a hard part at the beginning. This is our hard part. It's not like a puzzle piece where there's an instant fit. With relationships, you have to shape the pieces on each end before they go perfectly together."

"And your piece changes shape every day."

"Only physically."

"I know." She finally eats one of the fries. "I guess I need to work on my piece more. There's too much going on. And you being here—that adds to the too much."

"I'll go," I say. "After lunch."

"It's not that I want you to. I just think I need you to."

"I understand," I say. And I do.

"Good." She smiles. "Now, tell me about this date you're going on tonight. If I don't get to be with you, I want to know who does."

I've texted Dawn to tell her I'm not in school, but the date is still on. We're meeting for dinner after she's done with field-hockey practice.

I get back to Vic's house at the usual time he'd come back home from school. Safe in my room, I feel the usual set of pre-date jitters. I see that Vic has a large selection of ties in his closet, leading me to believe that he likes wearing them. So I put together a dapper outfit—maybe a little too dapper, but if what I've accessed about Dawn is true, I know she'll appreciate it.

I whittle away the hours online. There's no new email from Rhiannon, and there are eight new emails from Nathan, none of which I open. Then I go to Vic's playlists and listen to some of the songs he's listened to the most. I often find new music this way.

Finally, it's a little before six and I'm out the door. It's almost strange how much I'm looking forward to this. I want to be a part of something that works, no matter what the challenge.

Dawn does not disappoint. She loves the way Vic looks, using the word *debonair* instead of *dapper*. She is full of news of the day, and full of questions about what I've been up to. This is a delicate area—I don't want him to be caught in a lie later on—so I tell her I simply had the impulse to take the day off. No tests, no hallways, just driving to somewhere I've never been before . . . as long as I was back in time for her. She fully supports this decision, and doesn't even ask why I didn't invite her along. This is, I hope, how Vic will remember the day.

I have to access rapid-fire in order to follow all Dawn's reference points, but even still, it's a good time. Vic's memory of her is absolutely correct—she sees him so precisely, so wonderfully, so offhandedly. She doesn't broadcast her understanding at all. It's just there.

I know their situation is different from ours. I know I am not Vic, just as Rhiannon is not Dawn. But part of me wants to make the analogy. Part of me wants us to transcend in the same way. Part of me wants love to be that strong, that powerful.

Both Vic and Dawn have their own cars, but at Dawn's request, Vic follows her home, just so he can walk her to the door and they can have a proper goodnight kiss. I think this is sweet, and go along, walking hand in hand with Dawn up the front steps. I have no idea if her parents are home, but if she doesn't care, neither do I. We get to the screen door and then hang there for a moment, like a courting couple from the 1950s. Then Dawn leans over and kisses me hard, and I kiss her back hard, and it's not the door we're propelled toward but the bushes. She's pushing me back into the darkness, and I am taking all of her in, and it's so intense that I lose my mind, or lose track of Vic's mind so that I'm in my own mind completely, and I am kissing her and feeling it and out of my mouth comes the word *Rhiannon*. At first I don't think Dawn's heard it, but she pulls back for a second and asks me what I just said, and I tell her it's like the song—doesn't she know the song?—and I've always wondered what that word meant, but this is what it is, this is what it feels like, and Dawn says she has no idea what song I'm talking about, but it doesn't matter, she's used to my quirks by now, and I tell her I'll play it for her later, but in the meantime there's this and this and this. We are covered in leaves, my tie is caught on a branch, but it's just so full of life that we don't mind. We don't mind any of it.

• • •

That night there's an email from Rhiannon.

A,

Today was awkward, but I think that's because it feels like a very awkward time. It isn't about you, and it isn't about love. It's about everything crashing together at once. I think you know what I mean.

Let's try again. But I don't think it can be at school. I think that's too much for me. Let's meet after. Somewhere with no traces of the rest of my life. Only us.

I'm having a hard time imagining how, but I want these pieces to fit.

Love,

R

Day 6024

No alarm wakes me the next day. Instead, I awake to find a mother—someone's mother, my mother—sitting at the edge of my bed, watching me. She is sorry to wake me, I can see, but that sorrow is a minor part of a much larger sadness. She touches my leg lightly.

"It's time to wake up," she says quietly, as if she wants the transition from sleep to waking to be the easiest it can be. "I've hung your clothes on the door of the closet. We'll be leaving in about forty-five minutes. Your father is . . . very upset. We all are. But he's taking this particularly hard, so just . . . give him room, okay?"

While she's talking to me, I don't really have the focus to figure out who I am or what's going on. But after she leaves and I see the dark suit hanging on the closet door, I piece it all together.

My grandfather has died, and I'm about to go to my first funeral.

• • •

I tell my mother I forgot to tell friends to cover me for homework, and get on the computer to let Rhiannon know that it's not likely I'll be able to see her today. From what I can tell, the service is at least two hours away. At least we won't be spending the night.

My father has stayed in my parents' bedroom for most of the morning, but as I'm hitting send on my message to Rhiannon, he emerges. He doesn't just look upset—he looks newly blind. There is such loss in his eyes, and it permeates every other part of his body. A tie hangs feebly from his neck, barely knotted.

"Marc," he says to me. *"Marc."* This is my name, and coming from his lips right now it sounds like both an incantation and a cry of disbelief. I have no idea how to react.

Marc's mother sweeps in.

"Oh, honey," she says, wrapping her arms around her husband for a second, then pulling back to straighten his tie. She turns to me and asks me if I'm ready to go.

I clear the history, turn off the computer, and tell her I just need to put on my shoes.

The car ride to the funeral is largely silent. The news plays on the radio, but after the third loop, I don't think any of us are listening. Instead, I imagine that Marc's mother and father are doing the same thing that I'm doing—accessing memories of Marc's grandfather.

Most of the memories I find are wordless. Silent, strong stretches of sitting together in fishing boats, waiting for a pull on the line. The sight of him sitting at the head of the

Thanksgiving table, carving the turkey like it was his birth-right to do so. When I was younger, he took me to the zoo—all I can remember is the authority in his voice as he told me about the lions and the bears. I don't remember the lions or the bears themselves, just the sense of them that he created.

There's my grandmother's death, before I really knew what death meant. She is the ghost in the background of all of these memories, but I am sure she is much more prominent in my parents' thoughts. My own thoughts now turn to the last few months, the sight of my grandfather's diminishment, the awkwardness between us as I grew taller than him and he seemed to shrink into himself, into age. His death was still a surprise—we knew it was coming, but not that particular day. My mother was the one to answer the phone. I didn't have to hear her words to know something was wrong. She drove to my father's office to tell him. I wasn't there. I didn't see it.

It is my father who looks diminished now. As if when someone close to us dies, we momentarily trade places with them, in the moment right before. And as we get over it, we're really living their life in reverse, from death to life, from sickness to health.

The fish in all the nearby lakes and rivers will be safe today, because it seems like every fisherman in the state of Maryland is here at the funeral. There are few suits to be seen, and fewer ties. My extended family is here, too—crying cousins, tearful aunts, stoic uncles. My father seems to be taking it the hardest, and he is the magnet for everyone else's condolences. My mother and I stand at his side, and get nods and pats on the shoulder.

I feel like a complete imposter. I am observing, trying to record as much as I can for Marc's memories, because I know he is going to want to have been here, is going to want to remember this.

I am not prepared for the open casket, to have Marc's grandfather right there in front of me when we walk into the chapel. We are in the front row, and I can't take my eyes off of it. This is what a body looks like with nothing inside. If I could step out of Marc for a moment—if he did not come back in—this is what he would look like. It's very different from sleeping, no matter how much the undertaker has tried to make it look like sleeping.

Marc's grandfather grew up in this town, and has been a member of this congregation for his whole life. There's a lot to be said, and a lot of emotion in the saying of it. Even the preacher seems moved—so used to saying the words, but not for someone who he's cared about. Marc's father gets up to speak, and his body seems at war with his sentences—every time he tries to release one, his breath stops, his shoulders seize. Marc's mother goes up and stands next to him. It looks like he's going to ask her to read his words for him, but then he decides against it. Instead, he puts away the speech. He talks. He unspools the memories, and sometimes they have knots in them, and sometimes they are frayed, but they are the things he thinks of when he thinks about his father. Around him, the congregation laughs and cries and nods in recognition.

Tears are welling up in my eyes, streaming down my face. At first I don't understand it, because I don't really know the man they're talking about—I don't know any of the people in this room. I am not a part of this . . . and that is why I'm crying. Because I am not a part of this, and will never be a part of something like this. I've known this for a while, but you can know something for years without it really hitting you. Now it's hitting me. I will never have a family to grieve for me. I will never have people feel about me the way they feel about Marc's grandfather. I will not leave the trail of memories that he's left. No one will ever have known me or what I've done. If I die, there will be no body to mark me, no funeral to attend, no burial. If I die, there will be nobody but Rhiannon who will ever know I've been here.

I cry because I am so jealous of Marc's grandfather, because I am jealous of anyone who can make other people care so much.

Even after my father's done speaking, I am sobbing. When my parents return to the pew, they sit on either side of me, comforting me.

I cry for a little while longer, knowing full well that Marc will remember these as tears for his grandfather, that he will never remember I've been here at all.

Such a strange ritual, to send the body into the ground. I am there as they lower him. I am there as we say our prayers. I take my place in the line as the dirt is shoveled onto the coffin.

He will never again have this many people thinking of him at a single time. Even though I never knew him, I wish he were here to see it.

• • •

We go back to his house afterward. Soon enough there will be sorting and dispersing, but now it's the museum backdrop for the exhibition of grief. Stories are told—sometimes the same exact story in different rooms. I don't know many of the people here, but that's not a failure of accessing. There were simply more people in Marc's grandfather's life than his grandson could comprehend.

After the food and the stories and the consolation, there's the drinking, and after the drinking, there's the ride home. Marc's mother has stayed sober the whole time, so she's behind the wheel as we make our way back in the darkness. I can't tell if Marc's father is asleep or lost in thought.

"It's been a long day," Marc's mother murmurs. Then we listen to the news wrap around itself, repeat at half-hour intervals until we are finally home.

I try to pretend this is my life. I try to pretend these are my parents. But it all feels hollow, because I know better.

Day 6025

The next morning it's hard to raise my head from the pillow, hard to raise my arms from my sides, hard to raise my body from the bed.

This is because I must weigh at least three hundred pounds.

I have been heavy before, but I don't think I've ever been this heavy. It's as if sacks of meat have been tied to my limbs, to my torso. It takes so much more effort to do anything. Because this is not muscular heaviness. I am not a linebacker. No, I'm fat. Flabby, unwieldy fat.

When I finally take a look around and take a look inside, I'm not very excited about what I see. Finn Taylor has retreated from most of the world; his size comes from negligence and laziness, a carelessness that would be pathological if it had any meticulousness to it. While I'm sure if I access deep enough I will find some well of humanity, all I can see on the surface is the emotional equivalent of a burp.

I trudge to the shower, pick a ball of lint the size of a cat's paw out of Finn's belly button. I have to push hard to get anything done. There must have come a time when it became too exhausting to do anything, and Finn just gave in to it.

Within five minutes of getting out of the shower, I'm sweating.

I don't want Rhiannon to see me like this. But I have to see Rhiannon—I can't cancel on her for a second day in a row, not when things feel so precarious between us.

I warn her. I say in my email that I am huge today. But I still want to see her after school. I'm close to the Clover Bookstore today, so I propose that as a meeting place.

I pray that she'll come.

There's nothing in Finn's memory that leads me to believe that he'd be upset about missing school, but I go anyway. I'll let him save his absences for when he's actually conscious of them.

Because of the size of this body, I must concentrate much harder than I usually do. Even the small things—my foot on the gas pedal, the amount of space I have to leave around me in the halls—require major adjustment.

And there are the looks I get—such undisguised disgust. Not just from other students. From teachers. From strangers. The judgment flows freely. It's possible that they're reacting to the thing that Finn has allowed himself to become. But there's also something more primal, something more defensive in their disgust. I am what they fear becoming.

I've worn black today, because I've heard so often that it's supposed to be slimming. But instead I am this sphere of darkness submarining through the halls.

The only respite is lunch, where Finn has his two best friends, Ralph and Dylan. They've been best friends since third grade. They make fun of Finn's size, but it's clear they don't really care. If he were thin, they'd make fun of him for that, too.

I feel I can relax around them.

I go home after school to take another shower and change. As I'm drying myself off, I wonder if I could plant a traumatic memory in Finn's brain, something so shocking that he'd stop eating so much. Then I'm horrified at myself for even thinking such a thing. I remind myself that it's not my business to tell Finn what to do.

I've put on Finn's best clothes—an XXXL button-down and some size 46 jeans—to meet up with Rhiannon. I even try a tie, but it looks ridiculous, ski-sloping off my stomach.

The chairs are wobbly underneath me at the bookstore's café. I decide to walk the aisles instead, but they're too narrow, and I keep knocking things off the shelves. In the end, I wait for her out front.

She spots me right away; it's not like she can miss me. The recognition's in her eyes, but it's not a particularly happy one.

"Hey," I say.

"Yeah, hey."

We just stand there.

"What's up?" I ask.

"Just taking you all in, I guess."

"Don't look at the package. Look at what's inside."

"That's easy for you to say. I never change, do I?"

Yes and no, I think. Her body's the same. But a lot of the time, I feel like I'm meeting a slightly different Rhiannon. As if each mood presents a variation.

"Let's go," I say.

"Where to?"

"Well, we've been to the ocean and to the mountain and to the woods. So I thought this time we'd try . . . dinner and a movie."

This gets a smile.

"That sounds suspiciously like a date," she says.

"I'll even buy you flowers if you'd like."

"Go ahead," she dares. "Buy me flowers."

Rhiannon is the only girl in the movie theater with a dozen roses on the seat next to her. She is also the only girl whose companion is spilling over his chair and into hers. I try to make it less awkward by draping my arm around her. But then I'm conscious of my sweat, of how my fleshy arm must feel against the back of her neck. I'm also conscious of my breathing, which wheezes a little if I exhale too much. After the previews are over, I move over a seat. But then I move my hand to the seat in between us, and she takes it. We last like that for at least ten minutes, until she pretends she has an itch, and doesn't return her hand to mine.

• • •

I've chosen a nice place for dinner, but that doesn't guarantee that it will be a nice dinner.

She keeps staring at me—staring at Finn.

"What is it?" I finally ask.

"It's just that . . . I can't see you inside. Usually I can. Some glimmer of you in the eyes. But not tonight."

In some way, this is flattering. But the way she says it, it's also disheartening.

"I promise I'm in here."

"I know. But I can't help it. I just don't feel anything. When I see you like this, I don't. I can't."

"That's okay. The reason you're not seeing it is because he's so unlike me. You're not feeling it because I'm not like this. So in a way, it's consistent."

"I guess," she says, spearing some asparagus.

She doesn't sound convinced. And I feel I've already lost if we've gotten to the convincing stage.

It doesn't feel like a date. It doesn't feel like friendship. It feels like something that fell off the tightrope but hasn't yet hit the net.

Our cars are still at the bookstore, so we head back there. Instead of cradling her roses, she dangles them at her side, as if at any moment she might need to use them as a bat.

"What's going on?" I ask her.

"Just an off night, I guess." She holds the roses up to her nose, smells them. "We're allowed to have off nights, right? Especially considering . . ."

"Yeah. Especially considering."

If I were in a different body, this would be the time I would lean down and kiss her. If I were in a different body, that kiss could transform the night from off to on. If I were in a different body, she would see me inside. She would see what she wanted to see.

But now it's awkward.

She holds the roses to my nose. I breathe in the perfume.

"Thanks for the flowers," she says.

That is our goodbye.

Day 6026

I feel guilty about how relieved I am to be a normal size the next morning. I feel guilty because I realize that while before I didn't care what other people thought, or how other people saw me, now I am conscious of it, now I am judging alongside them, now I am seeing myself through Rhiannon's eyes. I guess this is making me more like everyone else, but I feel something is being lost, too.

Lisa Marshall looks a lot like Rhiannon's friend Rebecca—dark straight hair, a scattering of freckles, blue eyes. She is not someone you'd go out of your way to notice if you saw her on the street, but you'd definitely notice her if she was sitting next to you in class.

Rhiannon won't mind me today, I think. Then I feel guilty for thinking it.

There's an email from her waiting in my inbox. It starts like this:

I really want to see you today.

And I think, *That's good.* But then it continues.

We need to talk.

And I don't know what to think anymore

The day becomes a waiting game, a countdown, even if I'm not sure what I'm counting down toward. The clock brings me closer. My fears pound louder.

Lisa's friends don't get much out of her today.

Rhiannon's told me to meet her at a park by her school. Since I'm a girl today, I'm guessing that's safe neutral ground. No one from town is going to see the two of us and assume something R-rated. They already think male metalheads are her type.

I'm early, so I sit on a bench with Lisa's copy of an Alice Hoffman novel, stopping every now and then to watch a jogger push by. I'm so lost in the pages that I don't realize Rhiannon's here until she sits down next to me.

I can't help but smile when I see that it's her.

"Hey," I say.

"Hey," she says.

Before she can tell me what she wants to tell me, I ask her about her day, ask her about school, ask her about the weather—anything to avoid the topic of her and me. But this only lasts for about ten minutes.

"A," she says. "There are things that I need to say to you."

I know that this sentence is rarely followed by good things. But still I hope.

Even though she's said *things*, even though she's implied there's more than one, it all comes down to her next sentence.

"I don't think I can do this."

I only pause for a moment. "You don't think you can do it, or you don't *want* to do it?"

"I want to. Really, I do. But how, A? I just don't see how it's possible."

"What do you mean?"

"I mean, you're a different person every day. And I just can't love every single person you are equally. I know it's you underneath. I know it's just the package. But I can't, A. I've tried. And I can't. I want to—I want to be the person who can do that—but I can't. And it's not just that. I've just broken up with Justin—I need time to process that, to put that away. And there are just so many things you and I can't do. We'll never hang out with my friends. I can't even talk about you to my friends, and that's driving me crazy. You'll never meet my parents. I will never be able to go to sleep with you at night and then wake up with you the next morning. Never. And I've been trying to argue myself into thinking these things don't matter, A. Really, I have. But I've lost the argument. And I can't keep having it, when I know what the real answer is."

This is the part where I should be able to say *I'll change*. This is the part where I should be able to assure her that things can be different, show her it's possible. But the best I can do is to give her my deepest fantasy, the one I've been too self-conscious to share.

"It's not impossible," I tell her. "Do you think I haven't been having the same arguments with myself, the same thoughts? I've been trying to imagine how we can have a future together. So what about this? I think one way for me to not travel so far would be if we lived in a city. I mean, there would be more bodies the right age nearby, and while I don't know how I get passed from one body to the next, I do feel certain that the distance I travel is related to how many possibilities there are. So if we were in New York City, I'd probably never leave. There are so many people to choose from. So we could see each other all the time. Be with each other. I know it's crazy. I know you can't just leave home on a moment's notice. But eventually we could do that. Eventually, that could be our life. I will never be able to wake up next to you, but I can be with you all the time. It won't be a normal life—I know that. But it will be a life. A life together."

I've pictured us there, having an apartment to ourselves. Me coming home each day, kicking off my shoes, us making dinner together, then crawling into bed, with me tiptoeing out when midnight approaches. Growing up together. Knowing more of the world through knowing her.

But she's shaking her head. There are tears becoming possible in her eyes. And that's all it takes for my fantasy to pop. That's all it takes for my fantasy to become another fool's dream.

"That will never happen," she says gently. "I wish I could believe it, but I can't."

"But, Rhiannon—"

"I want you to know, if you were a guy I met—if you were

the same guy every day, if the inside was the outside—there's a good chance I could love you forever. This isn't about the heart of you—I hope you know that. But the rest is too difficult. There might be girls out there who could deal with it. I hope there are. But I'm not one of them. I just can't do it."

Now my tears are coming. "So . . . what? This is it? We stop?"

"I want us to be in each other's lives. But your life can't keep derailing mine. I need to be with my friends, A. I need to go to school and go to prom and do all the things I'm supposed to do. I am grateful—truly grateful—not to be with Justin anymore. But I can't let go of the other things."

I'm surprised by my own bitterness. "You can't do that for me the way I can do that for you?"

"I can't. I'm sorry, but I can't."

We are outside, but the walls are closing in. We are on solid ground, but the bottom has just dropped out.

"Rhiannon . . . ," I say. But the words stop there. I can't think of anything else to say. I've run out of my own argument.

She leans over and kisses me on the cheek.

"I should go," she says. "Not forever. But for now. Let's talk again in a few days. If you really think about it, you'll come to the same conclusion. And then it won't be as bad. Then we'll be able to work through it together, and figure out what comes next. I want there to be something next. It just can't be . . ."

"Love?"

"A relationship. Dating. What you want."

She stands up. I am left stranded on the bench.

"We'll talk," she assures me.

"We'll talk," I echo. It sounds empty.

She doesn't want to leave it like this. She will stay until I give some indication of being alright, of surviving this moment.

"Rhiannon, I love you," I say.

"And I love you."

That isn't the question, she's saying.

But it's not the answer, either.

I wanted love to conquer all. But love can't conquer anything. It can't do anything on its own.

It relies on us to do the conquering on its behalf.

I get home and Lisa's mother is cooking dinner. It smells amazing, but I can't imagine having to sit at the table and make conversation. I can't imagine talking to a single other person. I can't imagine making it through the next few hours without screaming.

I tell her I'm not feeling well, and head upstairs.

I lock myself in Lisa's bedroom, and feel that's where I'll always be. Locked inside a room. Trapped with myself.

Day 6027

I wake up the next morning with a broken ankle. Luckily, I've had it for a while and the crutches are next to my bed. It's the one thing about me that feels newly healed.

I can't help it—I check my email. But there's no word from Rhiannon. I feel alone. Completely alone. Then I realize there's one other person in the world who vaguely knows who I am. I check to see if he's written me lately.

And indeed he has. There are now twenty unread messages from Nathan, each more desperate than the previous one, ending with:

> All I ask is for an explanation. I will leave you alone
> after that. I just need to know.

I write him back.

> Fine. Where should we meet?

• • •

With her broken ankle, Kasey can't exactly drive. And since he's still in trouble for his blanked-out joyride, Nathan's not allowed to use the car, either. So our parents have to drop us off. Even though I don't say it is, mine just assume it's a date.

The hitch is that Nathan is expecting me to be a guy named Andrew, since that's who I said I was last time. But if I'm going to tell him the truth, being Kasey will help me illustrate my point.

We're meeting at a Mexican restaurant by his house. I wanted somewhere public, but also somewhere our parents could drop us off without raising eyebrows. I see him walk in, and it's almost like he's dressed for a date, too—even if he doesn't look sporty, he's certainly trying to be his best self. I raise one of my crutches and wave to him; he knows I have crutches, just not that I'm a girl. I figured I'd save that for in-person.

He looks very confused as he's walking over.

"Nathan," I say when he gets to me. "Have a seat."

"You're . . . Andrew?"

"I can explain. Sit down."

Sensing tension, the waiter swoops in and smothers us with specials. Our water glasses are filled. We give our drink order. Then we're forced to talk to each other.

"You're a girl," he says.

I want to laugh. It freaks him out so much more to think he was possessed by a girl, not a guy. As if that really matters.

"Sometimes," I say. Which only confuses him more.

"Who are you?" he asks.

"I'll tell you," I reply. "I promise. But let's order first."

I don't really trust him, but I tell him I do, as a way of inspiring a reciprocal trust. It's still a risk I'm taking, but I can't think of any other way to give him peace of mind.

"Only one other person knows this," I begin. And then I tell him what I am. I tell him how it works. I tell him again what happened the day I was inside his body. I tell him how I know it won't happen another time.

I know that, unlike Rhiannon, he won't doubt me. Because my explanation feels right to him. It fits nicely into his own experience. It what he's always suspected. Because in some way, I primed him to remember it. I don't know why, but when my mind and his mind concocted our cover story, we left a hole in it. Now I'm filling in that hole.

When I'm done, Nathan doesn't know what to say.

"So . . . whoa . . . I guess . . . so, like, tomorrow, you're not going to be her?"

"No."

"And she'll . . . ?"

"She'll have some other memory of today. Probably that she met a boy for a date, but that it didn't work out. She won't remember it's you. It'll just be this vague idea of a person, so if her parents ask tomorrow how it went, she won't be surprised by the question. She'll never know she wasn't here."

"So why did I know?"

"Maybe because I left you so fast. Maybe I didn't lay the groundwork for a proper memory. Or maybe I wanted you to find me, in some way. I don't know."

Our food, which arrived while I was talking, remains largely untouched on the table.

"This is huge," Nathan says.

"You can't tell anyone," I remind him. "I'm trusting you."

"I know, I know." He nods absently, and starts to eat. "This is between you and me."

At the end of the meal, Nathan tells me it's really helped to talk to me and to know the truth. He also asks if we can meet again the next day, just so he can see the switch for himself. I tell him I can't make any guarantees, but I'll try.

Our parents pick us up. On the drive back home, Kasey's mom asks me how it went.

"Good . . . I think," I tell her.

It's the only truthful thing I tell her the whole ride.

Day 6028

The next day, a Sunday, I wake up as Ainsley Mills. Allergic to gluten, afraid of spiders, proud owner of three Scotties, two of which sleep in her bed.

In ordinary circumstances, I would think this was going to be an ordinary day.

Nathan emails me, saying he wants to meet up, and that if I have a car, I can come to his house. His parents are away for the day, so he doesn't have a ride.

Rhiannon doesn't email me, so I go with Nathan.

Ainsley tells her parents she'll be shopping with some friends. They don't question her. They give her the keys to her mom's car and tell her not to be back too late. They need her to baby-sit her sister starting at five.

It's only eleven. Ainsley assures them she'll be back in plenty of time.

Nathan is only fifteen minutes away. I figure I won't have to stay too long. I'll just have to prove to him that I am the same person as yesterday. Then that's it—I don't think I have anything else to offer. The rest is up to him.

He looks surprised when he opens the door and sees me. I guess he didn't really believe it would be true, and now it is. He looks nervous, and I chalk it up to the fact that I'm here in his house. I recognize it, but already it's started to blend into all the other houses I've lived in. If you put me in the main hallway and all the doors were closed, I don't think I could tell you which door led to which room.

Nathan takes me into his living room—this is where guests go, and even if I've been him for a day, I am still a guest.

"So it's really you," he says. "In a different body."

I nod and sit down on the couch.

"Do you want something to drink?" he offers.

I tell him water will be fine. I do not tell him that I plan on leaving soon, and water probably isn't necessary.

As he goes to get it, I study some of the family portraits on display. Nathan looks uncomfortable in each of them . . . just like his father. Only his mother beams.

I hear Nathan come back in and don't look up. So it's a jolt when a voice that isn't Nathan's says, "I'm so glad I have a chance to meet you."

It's a man with silver hair and a gray suit. He's wearing a tie, but it's loose at the neck; this is casual time for him. I stand up, but in Ainsley's slight body, there's no way I can meet him eye to eye.

"Please," Reverend Poole says, "there's no need for you to stand. Let's sit."

He closes the door behind him, then chooses an armchair that's between me and the door. He is probably twice Ainsley's size, so he could stop me if he wanted to. The question is whether he'd really want to. The fact that my instinct is to wonder about these things is a tip-off that there may be cause for alarm.

I decide to come on tough.

"It's Sunday," I say. "Shouldn't you be in church?"

He smiles. "More important things for me here."

This must have been what it was like when Red Riding Hood first met the big bad wolf. What she felt must have been as much intrigue as terror.

"What do you want?" I ask.

He folds his leg across his knee. "Well, Nathan told me the most interesting story, and I'm wondering if it's true."

There's no use denying it. "Nathan wasn't supposed to tell anyone!" I say loudly, hoping Nathan hears me.

"While for the past month you've left Nathan hanging, I have been attempting to give him answers. It's natural that he should confide in me when he is told such a thing."

Poole has an angle. That much is clear. I just don't know what it is yet.

"I am not the devil," I say. "I am not a demon. I am not any of the things you want me to be. I am just a person. A person who borrows other people's lives for a day."

"But can't you see the devil at work?"

I shake my head. "No. There was no devil inside of Nathan. There is no devil inside of this girl. There is only me."

"You see," Poole says, "that's where you're wrong. Yes, you are inside of these bodies. But what's inside of you, my friend? Why do you think you are the way you are? Don't you feel it could be the devil's work?"

I speak calmly. "What I do is not the devil's work."

At this, Poole actually laughs.

"Relax, Andrew. Relax. You and I are on the same side."

I stand up. "Good. Then let me go."

I make a move to leave, but as I anticipated, he blocks me. He pushes Ainsley back to the sofa.

"Not so fast," he says. "I'm not finished."

"On the same side, I see."

The grin disappears. And for a moment, I see something in his eyes. I'm not sure what it is, but it paralyzes me.

"I know you so much better than you give me credit for," Poole says. "Do you think this is an accident? Do you think I'm just some religious zealot here to exorcise your demons away? Did you ever ask yourself why I am cataloging such things, what I'm looking for? The answer is you, Andrew. And others like you."

He's fishing. He has to be.

"There are no others like me," I tell him.

His eyes flash again at me. "Of course there are, Andrew. Just because you're different, it doesn't mean you're *unique*."

I don't know what he's saying. I don't want to know what he's saying.

"Look at me," he commands.

I do. I look into those eyes, and I know. I know what he's saying.

"The amazing thing," he tells me, "is that you still haven't learned how to make it last longer than a single day. You have no idea the power that you possess."

I back away from him. "You're not Reverend Poole," I say, unable to keep the shaking out of Ainsley's voice.

"I am today. I was yesterday. Tomorrow—who knows? I have to judge what best suits me. I wasn't going to miss *this*."

He is taking me beyond another window. But right away, I know that I don't like what's there.

"There are better ways to live your life," he continues. "I can show you."

There's recognition in his eyes, yes. But there's also menace. And something else—an entreaty. Almost as if Reverend Poole is still inside somewhere, trying to warn me.

"Get off of me," I say, standing up.

He seems amused. "I'm not touching you. I am sitting here, having a conversation."

"Get off of me!" I say louder, and start ripping at my own shirt, sending the buttons flying.

"What—"

"GET OFF OF ME!" I scream, and in that scream is a sob, and in that sob is a cry for help, and just as I'd hoped, Nathan hears it, Nathan has been listening, and the door to the living room is flung open, and there he is, just in time to see me screaming and crying, my shirt ripped open, Poole standing now with murder in his eyes.

I am betting everything on the common decency I saw in Nathan, back when I was inside of him, and even though he is clearly terrified, the common decency does rise, because instead of running away or closing the door or listening to what Poole has to say, Nathan yells, "What are you doing?" and he holds the door open for me as I flee, and he blocks the reverend—or whoever he is inside—from catching me as I run out the front door and into my car. Nathan summons the strength to hold Poole back, buying me those crucial seconds, so by the time Poole is on the lawn, my key is already in the ignition.

"There's no point in running away!" Poole yells. "You're only going to want to find me later! All the others have!"

Trembling, I turn up the radio, and drown him out with the sound of the song, and the sound of me driving away.

I don't want to believe him. I want to think he's an actor, a charlatan, a fake.

But when I looked closely at him, I saw someone else inside. I recognized him in the same way that Rhiannon recognized me.

Only, I also saw danger there.

I saw someone who does not play by the same set of rules.

As soon as I'm gone, I wish I'd stayed a few minutes longer, let him talk a little bit more. I have more questions than I've ever had before, and he might have had the answers.

But if I'd stayed just a few more minutes, I don't know if I could have left. And I would have been dooming Ainsley to the same struggle as Nathan, if not worse. I don't know what Poole would have done with her—what *we* would have done with her, if I'd stayed.

He could be lying. I have to remind myself that he could be lying.

I am not the only one.

I cannot wrap my thoughts around this. The fact that there could be others. They may have been in the same school as me, the same room as me, the same family as me. But because we keep our secret so hidden, there'd be no way to know.

I remember the boy in Montana whose story was so similar to mine. Was that true? Or was it just a trap Poole set?

There are others.

It can change everything.

Or it can change nothing.

As I drive back to Ainsley's house, I realize it's my choice.

Day 6029

Darryl Drake is very distracted the next day.

I guide him through school and say the right things when I have to. But his friends keep commenting that he's lost in space. At track practice, the coach berates him repeatedly for lack of focus.

"What's on your mind?" Darryl's girlfriend, Sasha, asks him when he drives her home.

"I guess I'm not really here today," he tells her. "But I'll be back tomorrow."

I spend the afternoon and the evening on the computer. Darryl's parents are both at work and his brother is in college, so I have the whole house to myself.

My story is front and center on Poole's website—a bastardized account of what I told Nathan, with some errors that come either from Nathan hiding something or from Poole goading me on.

Going outside his own site, I find out everything I can about Reverend Poole, but it's not much. He doesn't seem to have become outspoken about demonic possession until Nathan's story hit. I look at photos from before and from after, trying to tell if there's some difference. In photographs, he looks the same. The eyes are hidden by the flatness of the image.

I read all the stories on the site, trying to find myself within them, trying to find other people like me. Again, there are a couple from Montana. And others that could be similar, if what Poole hinted at is true: that the one-day limit is only for newcomers, and can be somehow bypassed.

It's what I want, of course. To stay in a single body. To lead a single life.

But at the same time, it's not what I want. Because I can't help thinking about what would happen to the person whose body I'd stay in. Does he or she just wink out of existence? Or is the original soul then banished to bounce from body to body—basically, are the roles reversed? I can't imagine anything sadder than having once had a single body and then suddenly not being able to stay in any for longer than a day. At least I've had the comfort of never knowing anything else. I would destroy myself if I'd actually had to give something up before leading this traveler's existence.

If there were no one else involved, it would be an easy choice. But isn't that always the case? And there's always someone else involved.

There's an email from Nathan, saying how sorry he is for what happened yesterday. He says that he'd thought Reverend Poole could help me. Now he's not sure of anything.

I write back to tell him that it isn't his fault, and that he has to get away from Reverend Poole and try to get back to his normal life.

I also tell him this is the last time I will ever email him. I don't explain that it's because I can't trust him. I figure he'll make that connection for himself.

When I'm done, I forward our email chain to my new email address. And then I close my account. Just like that, a few years of my life are over. The only through-line is gone. It's silly to feel nostalgic about an email address, but I do. There aren't many pieces to my past, so I have to mourn at least a little when one falls away.

Later that night, there's an email from Rhiannon.

How are you?

R

That's it.

I want to tell her everything that's happened in the past forty-eight hours. I want to lay the past two days in front of her to see how she reacts, to see if she understands what they mean to me. I want her help. I want her advice. I want her reassurance.

But I don't think that's what she wants. And I don't want to give it to her unless it's what she wants. So I type back:

It's been a rough two days. Apparently, I may not be the only person out there like this. Which is hard to think about.

A

There are still a few hours left in the night, but she doesn't use any of them to get back to me.

Day 6030

I wake up only two towns away from her, in someone else's arms.

I am careful not to wake this girl who enfolds me. Her feather-yellow hair covers her eyes. The beat of her heart presses against my back. Her name is Amelia, and last night she snuck in my window to be with me.

My name is Zara—or at least that's the name I've chosen for myself. I was born Clementine, and I loved that name until I turned ten. Then I started to experiment, with Zara being the name that stuck. Z has always been my favorite letter, and twenty-six is my lucky number.

Amelia stirs under the sheets. "What time is it?" she asks groggily.

"Seven," I tell her.

Instead of getting up, she curls into me.

"Will you be a good scout and check the whereabouts of your mom? I'd rather not leave the way I came in. My morning coordination is so much fuzzier than my nighttime coordination, and I'm always much more inspired when I'm approaching the maiden."

"Okay," I say, and in thanks, she kisses my bare shoulder.

The tenderness between two people can turn the air tender, the room tender, time itself tender. As I step out of bed and slip on an oversize shirt, everything around me feels like it's the temperature of happiness. Nothing from the previous night has dissipated. I've woken into the comfort they've created.

I tiptoe into the hallway and listen at my mother's door. The only sound is sleep-breathing, so it appears we're safe. When I get back to my room, Amelia is still in bed, the sheet pulled back so it's just her, her T-shirt, and her underwear. I have a feeling that Zara would not let this moment pass without crawling in beside her, but I feel I can't do that in her place.

"She's asleep," I report.

"Like, safe-to-take-a-shower asleep?"

"I think so."

"You want first shower, second shower, or both shower?"

"You can go first."

She gets out of bed, and stops to kiss me on the way out. Her hands move under my oversize shirt, and I don't resist. I fall right into it, kiss her a little bit longer.

"You sure?" she asks.

"You go first," I tell her.

And then, just like Zara would, I miss her when she's left the room.

I want it to be Rhiannon.

• • •

She sneaks out of the house while I'm in my shower. Then, twenty minutes later, she's back at the door, to pick me up for school. My mother is awake now and in the kitchen, and smiles when she sees Amelia heading up the path.

I wonder how much she knows.

We spend most of the day together at school, but not in a way that limits our interactions with other people. If anything, we incorporate our friends into what we have between us. We exist as individuals. We exist as a pair. We exist as parts of trios, quartets, and so on. And it all feels right.

I can't get Rhiannon off my mind. Remembering what she said about how her friends would never know me. How no one else would ever know me. How what we have together will only be us, always.

I am starting to realize what this means, and how sad it would be.

I am already feeling some of the sadness now, and it isn't even happening.

Seventh period, Amelia has study hall in the library while I have gym. When we meet up after, she shows me the books she's taken out for me, because they look like ones I'd like.

Will I ever know Rhiannon this well?

• • •

Amelia has basketball practice after school. I usually wait around for her, doing my homework. But she is making me miss Rhiannon too much; I have to do something about it. I ask her if I can borrow her car and run some errands.

She hands over the keys, no questions asked.

It takes me twenty minutes to get over to Rhiannon's school. I park in my usual space as most of the cars head in the other direction. Then I find a place to sit and watch the door, hoping she hasn't already left.

I am not going to talk to her. I am not going to start everything again. I just want to see her.

Five minutes after I've arrived, she appears. She is talking to Rebecca and a couple of her other friends. I can't hear what they're saying, but they're all involved in the conversation.

From here, she doesn't look like someone who's recently lost something. Her life seems to be playing on all chords. There's one moment—one small moment—when she looks up and glances around. For that moment, I can believe she's looking for me. But I can't tell you what happens in the moment after, because I quickly turn away, stare at something else. I don't want her to see my eyes.

This is the after for her, and if she's in the after, then I have to be in the after, too.

I stop off at a Target on the way back to Amelia. Zara knows all her favorite foods, and most of them are of the snack variety.

I stock up, and before I go back into the school to find her, I arrange them on the dashboard, spelling her name. It is, I believe, what Zara would want me to do.

I am not fair. I wanted Rhiannon to see me there. Even as I looked away, I wanted her to come right over and treat me just like Amelia would treat Zara after spending three days apart.

I know it's never going to happen. And that knowledge is a flash of light I can't quite see through.

Amelia is delighted by the dashboard display, and insists on taking me to dinner. I call home and tell my mother, who doesn't seem to mind.

I can sense that Amelia realizes I'm only half here, but she's going to let me be half elsewhere, because that's where I need to be. Over dinner, she fills the silence with tales from her day, some real and some completely imaginary. She makes me guess which is which.

We've only been together for seven months. Still, considering the number of memories Zara's collected, it feels like a long time.

This is what I want, I think.

And then I can't help it. I add, *This is what I can't have.*

"Can I ask you something?" I say to Amelia.

"Sure. What?"

"If I woke up in a different body every day—if you never knew what I was going to look like tomorrow—would you still love me?"

She doesn't miss a beat, or even act like the question is strange. "Even if you were green and had a beard and a male appendage between your legs. Even if your eyebrows were orange and you had a mole covering your entire cheek and a nose that poked me in the eye every time I kissed you. Even if you weighed seven hundred pounds and had hair the size of a Doberman under your arms. Even then, I would love you."

"Likewise," I tell her.

It's so easy to say, because it never has to be true.

Before we say goodbye, she kisses me with everything she has. And I try to kiss her back with everything I want.

This is the nice note, I can't help thinking.

But just like a sound, as soon as the note hits the air, it begins to fade.

When I walk inside, Zara's mother says to her, "You know, you can invite Amelia in."

I tell her I know. Then I rush to my room, because it's too much. So much happiness can only make me sad. I close the door and begin to sob. Rhiannon's right. I know it. I can never have these things.

I don't even check my email. Either way, I don't want to know.

• • •

Amelia calls to say good night. I have to let it go to voicemail, have to compose myself into the most like Zara I can be, before I answer.

"I'm sorry," I tell her when I call her back. "I was talking to Mom. She says you need to come by more often."

"Is she referring to the bedroom window or the front door?"

"The front door."

"Well, it looks like a little bird called *progress* is now sitting on our shoulder."

I yawn, then apologize for it.

"No need to say you're sorry, sleepyhead. Dream a little dream of me, okay?"

"I will."

"I love you," she says.

"I love you," I say.

And then we hang up, because nothing else needs to be said after that.

I want to give Zara her life back. Even if I feel I deserve something like this, I don't deserve it at her expense.

She will remember all of it, I decide. Not my discontent. But the contentment that caused it.

Day 6031

I wake up feverish, sore, uncomfortable.

July's mother comes in to check on her. Says she seemed fine last night.

Is it sickness or is it heartbreak?

I can't tell.

The thermometer says I'm normal, but clearly I'm not.

Day 6032

An email from Rhiannon. Finally.

> I want to see you, but I'm not sure if we should do that.
> I want to hear about what's going on, but I'm afraid that
> will only start everything again. I love you—I do—but I
> am afraid of making that love too important. Because
> you're always going to leave me, A. We can't deny it.
> You're always going to leave.
>
> R

I don't know how to respond to that. Instead, I try to lose
myself in being Howie Middleton. His girlfriend picks a fight
with him at lunchtime, over the fact that he never spends
time with her anymore. Howie doesn't have much to say about
that. In fact, he stays entirely silent, which only infuriates her
further.

I have to go, I think. If there are things I will never have
here, there are also things I will never find here. Things I
might need to find.

Day 6033

I wake up the next morning as Alexander Lin. His alarm goes off, playing a song I really like. This makes waking up much easier.

I also like his room. Plenty of books on the shelves, some of their spines worn down from rereading. There are three guitars in the corner, one electric, the amp still plugged in from the night before. In another corner, there's a lime-green couch, and I know immediately this is a place where friends come to crash, this is their home away from home. He has Post-its all over the place with random quotes on them. On top of his computer is something from George Bernard Shaw: *Dance is the perpendicular expression of a horizontal desire.* Some of the Post-its are in his handwriting, but others have been written by friends. *I am the walrus. I'm nobody—who are you? Let all the dreamers wake the nation.*

Even before I've gotten to know him, Alexander Lin has made me smile.

● ● ●

His parents are happy to see him. I have a sense that they're always happy to see him.

"Are you sure you're going to be okay for the weekend?" his mother asks. Then she opens the refrigerator, which looks like it's been stocked for at least a month. "I think there's enough here, but if you need anything, just use the money in the envelope."

I feel something is missing here; there is something I should be doing. I access and discover it's the Lins' anniversary tomorrow. They are going on an anniversary trip. And Alexander's gift for them is up in his room.

"One second," I say. I run upstairs and find it in his closet— a bag festooned with Post-its, each of them filled in with something his parents have said to him over the years, from *A is for Apple* to *Always remember to check your blind spot*. And this is just the wrapping. When I bring the bag down to Mr. and Mrs. Lin, they open it to find ten hours of music for their ten-hour drive, as well as cookies Alexander has baked for them.

Alexander's father wraps him in a thankful hug, and Alexander's mother joins in.

For a moment, I forget who I really am.

Alexander's locker is also covered in Post-it quotes, in a rainbow of handwritings. His best friend, Mickey, comes by and offers him half a muffin—the bottom half, because Mickey only likes the tops.

Mickey starts telling me about Greg, a boy he's apparently had a crush on for ages—*ages* meaning at least three weeks. I feel the perverse desire to tell Mickey about Rhiannon, who is only two towns away. I access and find that Alexander doesn't have any crushes himself at the moment, but if he did, they'd be female. Mickey doesn't pry too much about this. And quickly other friends find them, and the talk turns to an upcoming Battle of the Bands. Apparently, Alexander is playing in at least three of the entrants, including Mickey's band. He's that kind of guy, always willing to chip in with some music.

As the day progresses, I can't help but feel that Alexander is the kind of person I try to be. But part of what makes his personality work is his ability to stick around, to be there day in and day out for people. His friends rely on him, and he relies on them—the simple balance on which so many lives are built.

I decide to make sure that this is true. I zone out of math class and tune in instead to Alexander's memories. The way I access him, it's like turning on a hundred televisions at the same time, I'm seeing so many parts of him at once. The good memories. The hard memories.

His friend Cara is telling him she's pregnant. He is not the father, but she trusts him more than she does the father. His father doesn't want him to spend so much time on the guitar, tells him music is a dead-end calling. He drinks his third can of Red Bull, trying to finish a paper at four in the morning because he was out with friends until one. He is climbing the ladder of a tree house. He is failing his driver's test and fighting back tears when the instructor tells him. He is alone in his room, playing the same tune over and over again on an acoustic guitar, trying to figure out what it means. Ginny Dulles is breaking up with him, saying it's just that she likes him as a friend, when the truth is that she likes Brandon Rogers more. He is on a swing set, six years old, going higher and higher until he is convinced this is it, this is the time he will fly. He is slipping money into Mickey's wallet while Mickey isn't looking, so later on Mickey will be able to pay his share of the check. He is dressed as the Tin Man on Halloween. His mother has burned her hand on the stove and he doesn't know what to do. The first morning he has his license, he drives to the ocean to watch the sunrise. He is the only one there.

I stop there. I stop at this. I lurch back into myself. I don't know if I can do this.

I can't block out the temptation that Poole offered: If I could stay in this life, would I? Every time I pose the question to myself, I get knocked back into my own life from Alexander's. I get ideas, and once they take hold, I can't stop them.

What if there really was a way to stay?

Every person is a possibility. The hopeless romantics feel it most acutely, but even for others, the only way to keep going is to see every person as a possibility. The more I see the Alexander that the world reflects back at him, the more of a possibility he seems. His possibility is grounded in the things that mean the most to me. Kindness. Creativity. Engagement in the world. Engagement in the possibilities of the people around him.

The day is nearly half over. I only have a short time to figure out what to do with Alexander's possibilities.

The clock always ticks. There are times you don't hear it, and there are times that you do.

I email Nathan and ask him for Poole's email address. I get a quick response. I email Poole a few simple questions.

I get another quick response.

I email Rhiannon and tell her I'm going to come by this afternoon.

I say it's important.

She tells me she'll be there.

Alexander has to tell Mickey that he can't make their band practice after school.

"Hot date?" Mickey asks, joking.

Alexander smiles mischievously and leaves it at that.

Rhiannon is waiting for me at the bookstore. It's become our place.

She knows me when I walk through the door. Her eyes follow me as I come closer. She doesn't smile, but I do. I am so grateful to see her.

"Hey," I say.

"Hey," she says.

She wants to be here, but she doesn't think it's a good idea. She is also grateful, but she is sure this gratitude will turn into regret.

"I have an idea," I tell her.

"What?"

"Let's pretend this is the first time we've ever met. Let's pretend you were here to get a book, and I happened to bump into you. We struck up a conversation. I like you. You like me. Now we're sitting down to coffee. It feels right. You don't know that I switch bodies every day. I don't know about your ex or anything else. We're just two people meeting for the first time."

"But why?"

"So we don't have to talk about everything else. So we can just be with each other. Enjoy it."

"I don't see the point—"

"No past. No future. Just present. Give it a chance."

She looks torn. She leans her chin on her fist and looks at me. Finally, she decides.

"It's very nice to meet you," she says. She doesn't understand it yet, but she's going to go with it.

I smile. "It's very nice to meet you, as well. Where should we go?"

"You decide," she says. "What's your favorite place?"

I access Alexander, and the answer is right there. As if he's handing it to me.

My smile grows wider.

"I know just the place," I say. "But first we'll need groceries."

• • •

Because this is the first time we've met, I don't have to tell her about Nathan or Poole or anything else that's happened or about to happen. The past and future are what's complicated. It's the present that's simple. And that simplicity is the sensation of it being just her and me.

Even though there are only a few things we need, we get a shopping cart and go down every aisle of the grocery store. It doesn't take long before Rhiannon is standing on the front of it, I'm standing on the back of it, and we are riding as fast as we can.

We set down a rule: Every aisle has to have a story. So in the pet-food aisle, I learn more about Swizzle, the malevolent bunny rabbit. In the produce aisle, I tell her about the day I went to summer camp and had to be part of a greased-watermelon pull, and how I ended up with three stitches after the watermelon shot out of everyone's arms and landed in my eye—the first case of watermelon abuse the hospital had ever seen. In the cereal aisle, we offer autobiographies in the form of the cereals we've eaten over the years, trying to pinpoint the year that the cereal turning the milk blue stopped being cool and started being gross.

Finally, we have enough food for a vegetarian feast.

"I should call my mom and tell her I'm eating at Rebecca's," Rhiannon says, taking out her phone.

"Tell her you're staying over," I suggest.

She pauses. "Really?"

"Really."

But she doesn't make a move to call.

"I'm not sure that's a good idea."

"Trust me," I say. "I know what I'm doing."

"You know how I feel."

"I do. But still, I want you to trust me. I'm not going to hurt you. I will never hurt you."

She calls her mother, tells her she's at Rebecca's. Then she calls Rebecca and makes sure the cover story will be intact. Rebecca asks her what's going on. Rhiannon says she'll tell her later.

"You'll tell her you met a boy," I say once she's hung up.

"A boy I just met?"

"Yeah," I say. "A boy you've just met."

We go back to Alexander's house. There's barely enough room in the refrigerator for the groceries we've bought.

"Why did we bother?" Rhiannon asks.

"Because I didn't notice what was in here this morning. And I wanted to make sure we had exactly what we desired."

"Do you know how to cook?"

"Not really. You?"

"Not really."

"I guess we'll figure it out. But first, there's something I want to show you."

She likes Alexander's bedroom as much as I do. I can tell. She loses herself in reading the Post-it notes, then runs her finger over the spines of the books. Her face is a picture of delight.

Then she turns to me, and the fact can't be denied: We're

in a bedroom, and there's a bed. But that's not why I brought her here.

"Time for dinner," I say. Then I take her hand and we walk away together.

We fill the air with music as we cook. We move in unison, move in tandem. We've never done this together before, but we establish our rhythm, our division of labor. I can't help but think this is the way it could always be—the easygoing sharing of space, the enjoyable silence of knowing each other. My parents are away, and my girlfriend has come over to help cook dinner. There she is, chopping vegetables, unaware of her posture, unaware of the wildness of her hair, even unaware that I am staring at her with so much love. Outside our kitchen-size bubble, the nighttime sings. I can see it through the window, and also see her reflection mapped out on top of it. Everything is in its right place, and my heart wants to believe this can always be true. My heart wants to make it true, even as something darker tugs it away.

It's past nine by the time we're finished.

"Should I set the table?" Rhiannon asks, gesturing to the dining room.

"No. I'm taking you to my favorite place, remember?"

I find two trays and arrange our meals on them. I even find a dozen candlesticks to take along. Then I lead Rhiannon out the back door.

"Where are we going?" she asks once we're in the yard.

"Look up," I tell her.

At first she doesn't see it—the only light is coming from the kitchen, drifting out to us like the afterglow from another world. Then, as our eyes adjust, it becomes visible to her.

"Nice," she says, walking over so that Alexander's tree house looms over us, the ladder at our fingertips.

"There's a pulley system," I say, "for the trays. I'll go up and drop it down."

I grab two of the candles and scurry up the ladder. The inside of the tree house matches Alexander's memories pretty well. It's as much a rehearsal space as a tree house, with another guitar in the corner, as well as notebooks full of lyrics and music. Even though there's an overhead light that could be turned on, I rely on candles. Then I send down the dumbwaiter and raise the trays one by one. As soon as the second tray is safely inside, Rhiannon joins me.

"Pretty cool, isn't it?" I ask as she looks around.

"Yeah."

"It's all his. His parents don't come up here."

"I love it."

There isn't any table and there aren't any chairs, so we sit cross-legged on the floor and eat, facing each other in the candlelight. We don't rush it—we let the taste of the moment sink in. I light more candles, and revel in the sight of her. We don't need the moon or the sun in here. She is beautiful in our own light.

"What?" she asks.

I lean over and kiss her. Just once.

"That," I say.

• • •

She is my first and only love. Most people know that their first love will not be their only love. But for me, she is both. This will be the only chance I give myself. This will never happen again.

There are no clocks in here, but I am aware of the minutes, aware of the hours. Even the candles conspire, getting shorter as time grows shorter. Reminding me and reminding me and reminding me.

I want this to be the first time we've met. I want this to be two teenagers on a first date. I want to already be planning the second date in my head. And the third.

But there are other things I have to say, other things I have to do.

When we're finished, she pushes the trays aside. She closes the distance between us. I think she's going to kiss me, but instead she reaches into her pocket. She pulls out one of Alexander's pads of Post-it notes. She pulls out a pen. Then she draws a heart on the top Post-it, peels it off, and places it on my heart.

"There," she says.

I look down at it. I look up at her.

"I have to tell you something," I say.

I mean I have to tell her everything.

• • •

I tell her about Nathan. I tell her about Poole. I tell her I might not be the only one. I tell her there might be a way to stay in a body longer. There might be a way not to leave.

The candles are burning down. I am taking too much time. It's almost eleven when I'm done.

"So you can stay?" she asks when I'm finished. "Are you saying you can stay?"

"Yes," I answer. "And no."

When first love ends, most people eventually know there will be more to come. They are not through with love. Love is not through with them. It will never be the same as the first, but it will be better in different ways.

I have no such consolation. This is why I cling so hard. This is why this is so hard.

"There might be a way to stay," I tell her. "But I can't. I'll never be able to stay."

Murder. When it all comes down to it, it would be murder to stay. No love can outbalance that.

Rhiannon pulls away from me. Stands up. Turns on me.

"You can't do this!" she yells. "You can't swoop in, bring me here, give me all this—and then say it can't work. That's cruel, A. Cruel."

"I know," I say. "That's why this is a first date. That's why this is the first time we've ever met."

317

"How can you say that? How can you erase everything else?"

I stand up. Walk over. Wrap my arms around her. At first she resists, wants to pull away. But then she gives in.

"He's a good guy," I say, my voice a broken whisper. I don't want to do this, but I have to do this. "He might even be a great guy. And today's the day you first met. Today's your first date. He's going to remember being in the bookstore. He's going to remember the first time he saw you, and how he was drawn to you, not just because you're beautiful, but because he could see your strength. He could see how much you want to be a part of the world. He'll remember talking with you, how easy it was, how engaging. He'll remember not wanting it to end, and asking you if you wanted to do something else. He'll remember you asking him his favorite place, and he'll remember thinking about here, and wanting to show it to you. The grocery store, the stories in the aisles, the first time you saw his room—that will all be there, and I won't have to change a single thing. His pulse is my heartbeat. The pulse is the same. I know he will understand you. You have the same kind of heart."

"But what about you?" Rhiannon asks, her voice breaking, too.

"You'll find the things in him that you find in me," I tell her. "Without the complications."

"I can't just switch like that."

"I know. He'll have to prove it to you. Every day, he'll have to prove he's worthy of you. And if he doesn't, that's it. But I think he will."

"Why are you doing this?"

"Because I have to go, Rhiannon. For real this time. I have

to go far away. There are things I need to find out. And I can't keep stepping into your life. You need something more than that."

"So this is goodbye?"

"It's goodbye to some things. And hello to others."

I want him to remember how it feels to hold her. I want him to remember how it feels to share the world with her. I want him, somewhere inside, to remember how much I love her. And I want him to learn to love her in his own way, having nothing to do with me.

I had to ask Poole if it was really possible. I had to ask him if he could really teach me.

He promised he could. He told me we could work together.

There was no hesitation. No warning. No acknowledgment of the lives we'd be destroying.

That's when I knew for sure I had to run away.

She holds me. She holds me so hard there's no thought in it of letting go.

"I love you," I tell her. "Like I've never loved anyone before."

"You always say that," she says. "But don't you realize it's the same for me? I've never loved anyone like this, either."

"But you will," I say. "You will again."

If you stare at the center of the universe, there is a coldness there. A blankness. Ultimately, the universe doesn't care about us. Time doesn't care about us.

That's why we have to care about each other.

The minutes are passing. Midnight is approaching.

"I want to fall asleep next to you," I whisper.

This is my last wish.

She nods, agrees.

We leave the tree house, run quickly through the night to get back to the light of the house, the music we've left behind. 11:13. 11:14. We go to the bedroom and take off our shoes. 11:15. 11:16. She gets in the bed and I turn off the lights. I join her there.

I lie on my back and she curls into me. I am reminded of a beach, an ocean.

There is so much to say, but there's no point in saying it. We already know.

She reaches up to my cheek, turns my head. Kisses me. Minute after minute after minute, we kiss.

"I want you to remember that tomorrow," she says.

Then we return to breathing. We return to lying there. Sleep approaches.

"I'll remember everything," I tell her.

"So will I," she promises.

• • •

I will never have a photograph of her to carry around in my pocket. I will never have a letter in her handwriting, or a scrapbook of everything we've done. I will never share an apartment with her in the city. I will never know if we are listening to the same song at the same time. We will not grow old together. I will not be the person she calls when she's in trouble. She will not be the person I call when I have stories to tell. I will never be able to keep anything she's given to me.

I watch her as she falls asleep next to me. I watch her as she breathes. I watch her as the dreams take hold.

This memory.

I will only have this.

I will always have this.

He will remember this, too. He will feel this. He will know it's been a perfect afternoon, a perfect evening.

He will wake up next to her, and he will feel lucky.

Times moves on. The universe stretches out. I take a Post-it of a heart and move it from my body to hers. I see it sitting there.

I close my eyes. I say goodbye. I fall asleep.

Day 6034

I wake up two hours away, in the body of a girl named Katie.

Katie doesn't know it, but today she's going far away from here. It will be a total disruption to her routine, a complete twist in the way her life is supposed to go. But she has the luxury of time to smooth it out. Over the course of her life, this day will be a slight, barely noticeable aberration.

But for me, it is the change of the tide. For me, it is the start of a present that has both a past and a future.

For the first time in my life, I run.

ACKNOWLEDGMENTS

For most of the novels I've written, there's been a definite starting point—the spark of an idea that turned into the story. Usually I remember it. But for this book, I must admit I don't. But I do remember three pivotal moments that pushed me into writing it. The first was a conversation with John Green while we were on tour. The second was a conversation with Suzanne Collins while *she* was on tour. And the third was an afternoon at Billy Merrell's apartment, where I read him the first chapter (all that had been written at that point) and paid very careful attention to his reaction. I'd like to thank all three of them for giving me fuel for the fire. And I'd like to thank the man who was driving me and John, for keeping his promise not to steal the idea and publish it first.

As always, I must thank my family and my friends. My parents. Adam, Jen, Paige, Matthew, and Hailey. My aunts, uncles, cousins, and grandparents. My author friends. My Scholastic friends. My school friends. My librarian friends. My Facebook friends. My best friends. And the friends who sat across from me writing their own books while I was working on this one (Eliot, Chris, Daniel, Marie, Donna, Natalie). And the one friend who was painting while I wrote (Nathan).

Huge thanks to my intrepid agent, Bill Clegg, as well as

the fantastic team at WMEE, including Alicia Gordon, Shaun Dolan, and Lauren Bonner. Thanks to my fantastic home base at Random House, across all the sales, marketing, editorial, and art departments. (I would like to give a special shout-out to Adrienne Waintraub, Tracy Lerner, and Lisa Nadel, for almost a decade's worth of dinners and booth signings, and to the watchful eye of Jeremy Medina and the careful planning of Elizabeth Zajac.) Thanks, too, to my champions at Egmont in the UK, Text in Australia, and the other international publishers of this book.

Finally, I give thanks every day to have Nancy Hinkel as my editor. I love it when I've got wheels and you want to go for a ride.

ABOUT THE AUTHOR

David Levithan is the author of many acclaimed novels, some of them solo works, some of them collaborations. His solo novels include *Boy Meets Boy*, *The Realm of Possibility*, *Are We There Yet?*, *Wide Awake*, *Love Is the Higher Law*, and *The Lover's Dictionary*. His collaborations include *Will Grayson, Will Grayson* (written with John Green), *Marly's Ghost* (illustrated by Brian Selznick), and *Every You, Every Me* (with photographs by Jonathan Farmer), as well as three novels written with Rachel Cohn: *Nick & Norah's Infinite Playlist*, *Naomi and Ely's No Kiss List*, and *Dash & Lily's Book of Dares*. He lives in Hoboken, New Jersey, and spends his days in New York City, editing and publishing other people's books.